णाणं पयासयं

वीर नि.सं. 2470

भारतीय ज्ञानपीठ

ई.सन् 1944

Āchārya Amitagati's

YOGASĀRA - PRĀBHṚTA

(Gift of the Essence of Yoga)

Āchārya Amitagati's

YOGASĀRA - PRĀBHṚTA

(Gift of the Essence of Yoga)

Translation and Annotation

by

Dr. S. C. Jain

BHARATIYA JNANPITH

ISBN 81 - 263 - 0893 - 1

Moortidevi Granthamala : English Grantha No. 14

YOGASĀRA - PRĀBHṚTA of Āchārya Amitagati
(Jaina Phylosophy)

Translation and Annotation by
Dr. S.C. Jain

Published by
Bharatiya Jnanpith
18, Institutional Area, Lodi Road
New Delhi-110 003

Printed at
R.K. Offset, Delhi-110 032

First Edition : 2003
Price : Rs. 150

Introduction

स्वयम्भुवा भूतहितेन भूतले समञ्जसज्ञानविभूतिचक्षुषा।
विराजितं येन विधुन्वता तमः, क्षपाकरेणेव गुणोत्करैः करैः ॥1॥
प्रजापतिर्यः प्रथमं जिजीविषुः शशास कृष्यादिषु कर्मसु प्रजाः।
प्रबुद्धतत्त्वः पुनरद्भुतोदयो ममत्वतो निर्विविदे विदांवरः ॥2॥
विहाय यः सागरवारिवाससं वधूमिवेमां वसुधावधूं सतीम्।
मुमुक्षुरिक्ष्वाकुकुलादिरात्मवान् प्रभुः प्रवव्राज सहिष्णुरच्युतः ॥3॥

Svayaṁbhū Stotra, 1.1.3.

(The self-born Ṛṣabha, appeared on earth for the welfare of the living beings, possessing the knowledge, righteousness, and was majestic. He possessed the eyes through which he could remove the darkness like the moon rays. Prajāpati, at the start of the earth, getting desirous of the survival, initiated into it farming and several other vocations among the people. Realising the truth of the substances and objects, he again infused astonisting splendour in it. He was not involved in worldly attachments, was quite detached, the wisest and the noblest of all. Lord Ṛṣabha, who had full control of all the senses, and was fully competent and indepedent, tolerant to all impediments, infallibe in the Ikṣāvaku dynasty, desirous of attaining *mokṣa*, renounced his vast kindom, extending upto the ocean and his family and himself turned into a recluse and achieved sainthood).

The Jaina doctrines may be broadly divided into two schools viz. philosophical and practical. These schools of philosophy contain ontology, metaphysics and psychology.

The practical doctrines are covered under ethics and ascetism, monasticism and the life of laity.

(a) Philosophy

The Āraṇyakas and Upaniṣadas had maintained, or even believed to maintain that being is one, permanent, without beginning, change or end. In opposition to this void, the Jainas declare that the being is not of a persistent and unalterable nature. Being, according to Jaina thought, is joined to production, continuation and destruction. This theory is interpreted by them as the theory of indefiniteness of being (or Anekāntavāda). It comes to this that the existing things are permanent, only as regards their substances but they with their qualities, originate and perish. To explain : anything material (substantial), for Jina, continues for ever to exist as matter and this matter may assume any shape and change of quality. Thus the clay as substance may be regarded as permanent but the form of the jar of clay, or its colour may come into existence and perish. Thus the Brahmanical concept is concerned with transcendental Being, while the Jaina views deal with the being as given in common experience.

(b) Metaphysics

In Jainism, all things or substances (*dravyas*) are divided into lifeless things (*ajīvas*) and lives or souls (*jīvas*). The former are again divident into (i) space (*ākāśa*), (ii) and two other substances called *dharma* and *adharma*, and matter (*pudgala*). Space, *dharma,* and *adharma* are the necessary conditions for the substances of all other things, viz. soul and matter, space affords them room to subsist; *dharma* makes it possible for them to move or to be moved, and *adharma* to rest.

(c) *Ethics*

Jaina Ethics has for its end, the realization of Nirvāṇa or *mokṣa*. The necessary condition for reaching this end is the acquisition of right faith, right knowledge and right conduct. These three excellences are metaphorically named jewels (*triratna*)—an expression also used by the Buddhists but in a different sense. They are manifested on the romoval of obstructing or osbcuring species of *karma*. To affect this, the rules of conduct must be observed and the corresponding virtues may be acquired. Of the first importance are the five vows, the first four of which are also acknowledged by the Hindus and the Buddhists. The five vows of the Jainas are (a) not to kill, (b) not to lie, (c) not to steal, (d) to abstain from sexual association, and (e) to renounce all interest in the worldly things. These vows are to be strictly followed by monks, who have to take them on entering the order, or as it is commonly expressed on the eve of receiving *dīkṣā*.

The *Ṣaṭkhaṇḍāgama* of Puṣpadanta and Bhūtabali, is the earliest and most authorative work on Jaina philosophy. Its six sections deal with *Jīvasthāna, Kṣudrakbandha, Bandhasvāmitva, Vedanā, Vargaṇā* and *Mahābandha*. The last of these is almost an independent work and is popularly known as *Mahādhavala*. It is composed in *sūtras*, the language of which is Śaurasenī Prākrit strongly influenced on the one hanḍ by *Ardha-Māgadhī*, particularly in is technical phraseology, and on the other by Mahārāṣṭrī Prākrit. It gives a very systematic and thorough exposition of the doctrine of *karma* association and the results of action which form the most essential part of Jaina philosophy. The *Kaṣāyapāhuḍa* of Guṇadharācārya is also devoted to particular aspects of *karma* doctrine. It is composed in 233 *gāthā-sūtras* which have been elaborated by the *chūrṇī-sūtras* of Yativṛṣabha. Many commentaries are said to have been written on these works but the only one now available to us is the *Dhavalā* of Vīrasena on the *Ṣaṭkhaṇḍāgama* and the *Jayadhavalā* of Vīrasena and Jinasena on the *Kaṣāya-pāhuḍa* written during the ninth century in Śauraseni Prākrit. They are very voluminous and masterly. During the tenth century, their subject-matter was compressed by Nemicandra Siddhāntacakravartin in his *Gommaṭasāra (Jīvakāṇḍa* and *Karmakāṇḍa)*, the *Labdhisāra* and the *Kṣapaṇasāra* in about 2,400 *gathā* verses. These works now form the basis of studies in Jaina philiosophy, particularly amongst and Digambaras.

The Śvetāmbara literature on the *karma* doctrine, besides the canonical works, consists of the six *Karmagranthas,* separately called *Karmavipāka, Karmastava, Bandhasvāmitva, Ṣaḍaśīti, Śaṭaka* and *Śaptaṭikā* of uncertain authorship and date and also *Kammapayaḍi of Śiva-śarman* and the *Pañcasaṁgraha* of Candrarṣi all composed in *gathāsūtras* and covering the same ground in subject-matter as the works of Nemicandra.

Next to the *Karma* doctrine in religious importance are the duties and practices of monks and householders. The earliest works on this subject amongs the Digambaras is the *Mulārādhanā* of Śivārya which contains 2,166 Prākrit verses giving an exposition of the four devotions, namely, faith, knowledge, conduct, and austerities, but at the same time also dealing practically with all aspects of Jainism. Narrative and descriptive elements are also not wanting in the work. At places the poet in the author gets the better of the religious teacher, and he flashes forth in beautiful fancies and figures of speech. The *Mūlāchāra* of Vaṭṭakera prescribes, in a thoroughly systematic manner, in about 1,250 Prākrit verses, the duties, practices, and observances of ascetics. The work has close affinities with the *Mūlārādhanā* of Śivārya as well as with the Āgama texts of the Śvetāmbaras dealing with similar topics. The *Kārttikeyānuprekṣā* of Kumāra contains

500 Prākrit verses, a beautiful exposition of the twelve reflections recommented for the promotion of the feeling of renunciation.

But the author who exercised the greatest and the most dominant influence on Jaina literature and gave form and shape to the Digambara creed as it exists today is Kundakundāchārya. He flourished in the early centuries of the Christian era and was the most celebrated of the Jaina authors and who belonged to *Kondakundā*–a place in South. His original name was Padmanandi, but he was called Kundakunda after the name of the place where he lived. His other traditonal names are Elāchārya, Vakragrīva etc. He is believed to be the pupil of Bhadrabāhu but this claim is contested by scholars. His *Pānchāśatikāya* and *Pravachana-sāra* are the systematic compositions of the Jaina ontology and epistemology. His *Samayasāra* is full of spiritural fervour and deals with the quintessence of the Jaina doctrines. Tradition ascribes to him a large number of works, of which more than a dozen text called *pāhuḍas* (*prābhṛtas*) are now available. They are on the subjects of *Darśana* (36 verses), *Caritra* (44), *Sūtra* (27), *Bodha* (62), *Bhāva* (163), *Mokṣa* (106), *Liṅga* (22), *Śīla* (40), *Ratna* (162), *Dvādaśānuprekṣā* (91), *Niyamasāra* (187), *Pañchāśtikāya* (180), *Pravachanasāra*, and *Samayasāra* (415). The last three works are particularly popular and the *Samayasāra* is regarded as the author's best and most sacred production on spiritual topics. The works of Kundakundācārya may be regarded as the earliest models of that ascetic poetry and philosophy which became so popular through a long line of Jaina, Buddhist, and Hindu saints, cutting across all communal barriers. Yativṛṣabha's *Tiloyapaṇṇatti* covers a wide range of topics and has served the purpose of a source-book. The compilation or composition of all these works, based on traditional material, might be assigned to the early centuries of the Christian era.

A good deal of Prākrit literature has grown round the canon itself by way of explanation, detailed exposition, illustration through tales, and topical systematization. On some canonical texts, there are *niryuktis*. A *niryukti* is a kind of metrical commentary which explains the topics by instituting various inquires. The *niryuktis* are attributed to Bhadrabāhu and are undoubtedly anterior to Devarddhi's Council. Some of them, in turn, on account of their systematic exposition, accuracy of details, and solidity of argument, became the objects of learned endeavour of great scholars. For instance, Jinabhadra Kṣamāśramaṇa (A.D. 609) wrote a highly elaborate *bhāṣya* (commentary) in Prākrit on the *Āvaśyaka-niryukti* round which has grown almost a world of literature. On some works both *bhāṣya* and *chūrṇi* commentaries are found. A *bhāsya* is an elaborate exposition of the text in Prākrit at times incorporating and supplementing the *niryukti* verses; while *chūrni* is a prose gloss written in an admixture of Prākrit and Sanskrit. Jinadāsa Mahattara wrote his *Nandi-chūrni* in A.D. 676.

The language of Jaina Literature was primarily the Prakrits which were prevalent amongst the people at one time or the other in different parts of the country. But Sanskrit was not altogether discarded. Amongst the Jainas, the earliest work in Sanskrit, devoted to religious writing, is the *Tattvārthādhigama-sūtra* of Umāsvāmin which epitomizes the whole Jaina creed in about 375 *sūtras* arranged in ten chapters. The work occupies a unique position in Jaina literature as it is recongnized as authorative equally by the Digambaras and the Śvetāmbaras with a few variations in its readings, and is very widely studied by both. It has been commented upon by the most eminent authors of both the sects. There is an old *bhāṣya* on it which the Śvetāmbaras claim to have been written by the author of the *sūtras* himself. But this claim is not admitted by the Digambaras who regard the

Sarvārthasiddhi-vṛtti of Pūjyapāda (sixth century) as the earliest commentary. Pūjyapāda has made full use of *Ṣaṭkhaṇḍāgama-sūtra* in explaining some sūtras of this work.

The next commentary on it is *Tattvārtha-rāja-vārttikā* of Akalaṅka (eighth century) which offers more detailed explanations of the sūtras, as well as of the important statements of Pūjyapāda. *Tattvārtha-ślokas-vārttika* of Vidyānandin (ninth century) gives expositions in verse and also in prose and makes valuable clarifications. For yogic practices, the *Jñānārṇava* of Śubhacandra and the *Yogaśāstra* of Hemachandra are valuable guides, while the *Ratnakaraṇḍa-śrāvakācāra* is more popular amongst the laity. Jaina Sanskrit literature is considerably enriched by a series of works on *Nyāya* (logic) initiated by Sāmantabhadra and Siddhasena Divākara and followed up by Akalaṅka, Vidyānandin, Prabhācandra, Māṇikyanandin. Hemacandra, and many others.

For the present age, after the *nirvāṇa* of Mahāvīra, a ranaissance of Jaina spiritualism took place with Kundakundācārya. He is adored with great reverence by the Jainas. His triology of the *prābhṛatas* of *Samayasāra, Pravachanasāra* and *Pañchāstikāyasāra* is very well known to the scholars of Jainism. His *Niyamasāra* and *Rayaṇasāra* may also be usefully added to his triology. The language adopted by Kundakundācārya is Prākrit.

After an interval of several centuries there appeared Ācārya Amṛtachandra Sūri and Ācārya Jayasena with their commentaries of Āchārya Kumdakunda's works specially of *Samayasāra-Prābhrta* with these two āchāryas a revival of Jaina spiritualism took place, and it continues till now. It was with Āchārya Amṛtachandra that a scheme of chapters was devised for *Samayasāra-prābhṛta* of Kundakundāchārya. The language adopted by these commentators is Sanskrit.

Āchārya Amitagati has followed almost the same scheme of division of subject-matter as of *Samayasāra Prābhṛta* along with change of language from Prakrit to Sanskrit. Hence the *Yogasāra Prābhṛta* of Āchārya Amitagati may very suitably be called as Sanskritised *Samayasāra.* Āchārya Amitagati paid special attention to present the essence of the works of Kundakundāchārya at one place in one volume. His work is based on a thorough survey and study of the literature of Jaina sipirtualism available to him. The Āchārya was himself a Yogin, hence his writing reflects the richness of his experience in the field of the practice of Yoga. For these reasons his *Yogasāra Prābhṛta* is more exhaustive in contents, logical in treatment and lucid in expression. Āchārya Amitagati's *Yogasāra Prābhṛta* is an immeasurably valuable gift of the Essence of Yoga.

The *Yogasāra Prābhṛta* is the title of this work, which comprises of the three words viz : *Yoga + Sāra + Prābhṛta.* According to the Āgamas, the performance of the body, speech and the mind, is known as yoga, the deeds emanate from the same and are known by the technical term of *āsrava.* The word *yoga* also stands for combining or to unite one element or thing with the other. The physicians interpret the word *yoga* for the combination of various medicines into one, making a combination of the same. In the religious treatises, *yoga* means the performing of meditation with the concentration of mind. Āchārya Kundakunda, has, however, divided the yogic practices into two distinct categories viz : *Praśasta* and *Apraśasta.* The yogis have, however, described *yoga* to be the one, by which one concentrates in his mind, getting free from all the worldly attractions and devotes himself to the spotless *Ātma-tattva*, as a result of which one achieves the self-realisation. Such a state of mind is called the *Yoga* by the *Yogis.*

Yogasāra on the other hand stands for the factual position of the yogic practices which are devoid of the undesirable elements. In other words the *Yogasāra* means the discussion on the gist of the yogic practices or the best part of it. *Prābhṛta* on the other hand stands for the gift or a present, which one makes to the deity or to the monarch. Similarly the *Yogasāra Prābhṛta* stands for a precious gift which the great Āchārya Amitagati has presented to the world for the self-realisation of the Supreme soul or the Brahman.

There had been two Āchāryas in Jainism, named Amitagati, one of whom was the disciple of Mādhavasena sūri and the grand disciple of Nemiṣeṇāchārya and the other was the preceptor of Nemiṣenācārya and the disciple of Devasena Sūri. Both of them were associated with the Amitagati Mathura Saṅgha. The *Yogasāra Prābhṛta* was possibly composed by Amitagati-I, whose qualities have been lavishly praised by Amitagati-II. Anitagait-I has not mentioned the date of the composition of his work, but Amitagati-II has immensely praised Amitagati-I, in his work, *Śubhāṣita-Ratna-Sandoha,* which was composed by the latter in the tenth century A.D. when Muñja was in throne.

The *Yogasāra Prābhṛta* has been divided into nine chapters as follows :

(i) Jīvādhikāra
(ii) Ajīvādhikāra
(iii) Āsravādhikāra
(iv) Baṅdhādhikāra
(v) Saṁvarādhikāra
(vi) Nirjarādhikāra
(vii) Mokṣādhkāra
(viii) Charitrādhikāra
(ix) Chūlikādhikāra

These nine chapters contain 550 Sanskrit verses, and the broad outlines of the subject discussed in each one of these chapters are given hereunder :

Chapter-1 : According to this chapter, a yogi is the one who aims at lifting his soul to its original supreme position or to establish a sort of unity and affinity with the Supreme spirit. Accordingly a yogi is required to ceaselessly endeavour to overcome all the passions, and delusions, which are the greatest hinderances on his way. The ideal for his meditation is the pure soul, with its natural intrinsic qualities, chiselled out of all the impurities. Even the deviation, for a moment, from such thoughts and ideals is not permissible for him. The ultimate goal of all his endeavours would be the attainment of *mokṣa*—the highest stage, which is free form the cycle of birth, death, and oldage, besides the pleasure or pain.

Chapter-2 : In this chapter, the five substances of *Dharma, Adharma, Ākāśa* (space), *Kāla* and *Pudgala* have been described to be *ajīvas* or unconcues ones, because they are devoid of any important use to the *jīvas*. These elements do not change their respective nature though they, in one way or the other, are related to each other. All of them come in contact with one another but they do not discard their natural property. Out of these, except the *pudgalas* (atoms) all other elements are formsless and inactive. These *pudgalas* (atoms) are said to be pervading the entire universe. Two priciples of *jīva* and *ajīva* have been in very close relationship with each other, temporarily or even functionally in the universe from the time immemorial. This state of affairs leads to a very deep and fatal confusion between two. The discriminatory knowledge of the two is the only means to carve out a way to the final destination, i.e. the achievement or the redemption of the soul from the wandering in the universe. It is only this light which can lead us to the self-enlightened divine status of the supreme soul.

Chapter-3 : According to this chapter, the most formidable enemy of the soul is the group of eight *karmas* along with the malignant manifestations, caused to the soul, Such malignant manifestations are solely responsible for the loss of the soul's power of discrimination between what is its own and the 'other'. This keeps the soul moving into the mire of the worldly existence. The one, who aspires for the spiritual difference, renouncing all connections with such *karmas* and then the ever widening of its results, can realize the soul in its purest form. It is like the return of the soul to its own home, which was so far lost, due to its association with the *karmas.* Besides an advice is rendered for those who choose to advance on the path of freedom or *mokṣamārga.*

Chapter-4 : In this chapter, the āchārya, besides highlighting the relationship between the *jīva* and the *karmas*, points out towards the path leading to the final emancipation of the *jīvas*. The first step is the abandonment of the objects of sensuous pleasures, which makes the *jīvas* constantly conscious and attentive to their spotless identity. They are required to get rid of their understanding or rather misunderstanding which has so far kept them deluded by love of merit and aversion of demerit. They are to be aware of the fact that such manifestations on their part, are bound to keep them whirling in the ocean of the universe. They must realize it well that the world is through and through, a place of tear and fear. The final result of such endeavours and steps is the release of the *jīvas* from the bondage of *karmas* and the realization of their purity. This state is termed as *nirvāṇa* or *nirvṛtti*, where nothing else remains to be achieved.

Chapter-5 : The chapter deals with *Saṁvara* (the safeguarding of the soul), which means obstructing completely, the inflow of the *karmas.* According to the Jaina philosophy, the *karmas* are conceived as material conglomerations which stick to the souls in order to fructify the various distortions and limitations of their natural powers. The *jīvas* are the substantial counter-parts of the material *karmas.* Thus the process of *Saṁvara* is taken to be of two types i.e. subjective and objective. The association of *karmas* with *jīvas* is due to passions, which are there due to the *karmas.* The one who is bereft of the passions, and all the worldly performances, the one who distinguishes between the soul and the other substance, has no desires for merit or demerit, the one who has no inclination towards the universe, and meditates upon the effulgent soul, destroys the element of passion. The conscious soul established in itself is always to be resorted to or repeatedly pondered over by one who is desirous of *Saṁvara,* which is the sure protection of the soul. The chapter indicates the path for attaining *mokṣa* through *Saṁvara* and for this purpose a novice has to make a choice between the conscious and the unconscious by resorting to the former and completely abstaining from the latter.

Chapter-6 : The chapter deals with *Nirjarā* - the process of the explusion of *karmas,* which is defined as the partial destruction of the *karmas* accumulated in the past and the present lives. These *karmas* are of two kinds—those being operative on maturity and those lying immature. The chapter deals with the principle and practice of the gradual separation and the fall of the *karmas* from the soul, highlighting the means to do so.

Chapter-7 : This chapter deals with *Mokṣa* or liberation which is seventh principle of the Jaina philosophy. It is the culmination of the process for the salvation of *jīva* suffering in the whirlpool of the universe. It is attained by a jīva, because of its having been emerged in the universe suffering the inflow of the *karmas* on the one hand and on the other hand it has also been able to continue the process of *Nirjarā* for the expulsion of the *karmas* already accumulated by the *jīva.* As a necessary consequence, its association with the *karmas* must come to an end. This is the state of *mokṣa* or liberation, after which, in the absence of the causes, for further entry into the universe, there is no further birth in the world.

Chapter-8 : This chapter deals with the conduct of the truth seeker, which has to be essentially observed by him. After realising the truth about the seven principles of the world, a spotless urge emerges in the mind of the truth seeker. When such a consciousness dawns upon the truth seeker, he should disown his entire household and be free from the family bondage. He is then ordained to receive initiation from a perceptor. The names of twenty eight *essentials* have been spelt out, which are to be strictly followed by a yogi. The saint who is bereft of attachment, aversion, confusion, pride, sex, anger, and greed, who has practical intellect, and has lost all interest in the world, following the noble conduct, attains the abode of the sacred ones, which is all blissful. Having meditated upon the pure soul itself it has been freed from the *karmas*.

Chapter-9 : In the ninth chapter, the blissful position of the liberated soul has been explained by the *āchārya*, highlighting the fact that inspite of the liberation of the soul, its consciousness never vanishes, nor does it become superfluous. Thereafter describing the symptoms of *yoga*, the insignificant symptoms of the pleasure and the pain, the merits earned by those symptoms, and the pains emanating from the worldly pleasrues, have been highlighted. The forms of pleasures have been indicated. The universe has been described as the vale of great ailment and getting relieved of that ailment, and after getting free from that ailment, the situation like the liberated soul is achieved. Such a liberated soul never enters the world again. Thus having realised all other than the pure soul as delusive, like the city of clouds in the sky, or like a dream or a false appearance, Āchārya Amitagati composed the *Yogasāra Prābhṛta* with the primary aim of realising Brahman–the purified soul.

The words Amitagati and *Yogasāra* are indicative of the names of the writer and his most valuable work. These could be interpreted as having unlimited knowledge and the essence of *yoga* respectively.

The translation work has been carried out by Dr. S.C. Jain, an eminent scholar of Jainism. The main difficulty with a translater from Sanskrit is its terminology, and to express those terms in a foreign language is in itself a great problem. Because of this, long phrases fo Sanskrit terms have to be used in Roman and italics, in order to minimise the loss of understanding of the context by the readers. Besides, faithfulness of the original text and ideology has been the guiding light-post for the translation and the commentary over the verses. I am confident that the English rendering of the *Yogasāra* by Dr. Jain will surely interest the readers and will create the same effect on them as the original verses of Āchārya Amitagati's highly esteemed work does. Dr. Jain therefore deserves all praise for the excellent work he has done for the benefit of the people in the country as well as those abroad.

New Delhi. *–Shanti Lal Nagar*
Dated the 10th February, 2003

CONTENTS

Chapter 1

Jīvādhikāra

विविक्तमव्ययं सिद्धं स्व-स्वभावोपलब्धये।
स्व-स्वभावमयं बुद्धं ध्रुवं स्तौमि विकल्मषम् ॥1॥

To realize my own (pure) nature I eulogise the perfect one, who is completely shorn off (from all 'other'), who is above decay, who has identified himself with his (unruffled) nature, who is enlightened, who has become permanently stable (with no fear of fall) and who does not suffer from any distortion.

It has been been almost a disciplinary practice with the writers from ancient times that they remember and extol their deity (*deva*) in the first verse of their work. They do so paying their obeisance to the deity, his perfect knowledge, his word and also by making a mention of the characteristics attained by him. This practice serves a number of purposes. It accounts for the humility of the writer on one hand and his sense of reverence to the deity on the other. There is also a strong belief that this practice will help the writer to achieve success against all obstructions. Very often by means of this auspicious verse the writer also expresses the main objective of the work he is going to undertake. This aspect of the work is very well brought to light by *Āchārya* Amitagati in his *Yogasāra.* The appellations mentioned in the verse directly suggest that he is very seriously attempting to give and explain a way to the readers, by following which they will free themselve from the anguish of wroldly life and will attain a pure and stable state for themselves. The use of the singular number for the deity is only a collective expression for the plurality of the liberated souls. It should not be taken to suggest oneness of God as expounded in monistic philosophies. Jainism upholds the plurality of souls both in mundane existence and liberation.It will be made very clear as we advance with the text of the book.

जीवाजीवं द्वयं त्यक्त्वा नापरं विद्यते यतः।
तल्लक्षणं ततो ज्ञेयं स्वस्वभावबुभुत्सया ॥2॥

As there exists nothing except the two, (principles of) consciousness (*jīva*) and its antithesis (*ajīva*) (in the universe); hence, being impelled by the strong desisre to understand one's own (pure) nature, the differentia of the two becomes an object of our knowledge.

Lord Ṛiṣbhadeva, the first exponent of the present aeon, taught us the dualism of *jīva* and *ajīva.* The contents of the universe are exausted under these two categeries, though each category covers an infinity of individuals. Our worldly existence is a result of the action and interaction between these two categories. To realize our true nature we have to select the category of jīva and reject the other. For achieving this discrimination we are required to acquaint ourselves with either of them, though in practice we shall be inclined to the former. In the absence of the discriminatory knowledge of the two the practice, by confusing one with the other, will not be at all possible. Hence the *Āchārya* has truly emphasised the need of such a discriminatory knowledge at the very outset of the programme to attain libration.

यो जीवाजीवयोर्वेत्ति स्वरूपं परमार्थतः।
सोऽजीवपरिहारेण जीवतत्त्वे निलीयते ॥3॥
जीवतत्त्वं निलीनस्य रागद्वेषपरिक्षयः।
ततः कर्माश्रयच्छेदस्ततो निर्वाणसंगमः ॥4॥

He, who knows the (differential) identity of the soul (*jīva*) and the non-soul (*ajīva*) from the view point of ethically ultimate reality, absorbs in the principle of the soul by abandoning the non-soul.

The total elimination of attachment and aversion is actualized for one who is absorbed in the soul as comprehended from the view point of ethical ultimacy. Then follows the dissociation of the soul's dependence on *karmas,* which in turn, culminates in the attainment of liberation (*nirvāṇa.*)

In the worldly existence the soul and the non-soul come into so close a relationship that they are so confused that their distinction becomes a knotty problem. The practice of self-realization starts with discriminatory knowledge of the soul and the non-soul. Gradually advancing on the path the novice discards eveything which is of the nature of the non-soul, resulting in his inclination towards absorption in thc principles of the soul. This stage leads to the extinction of attachment and aversion which necessarily implies the dissociation of *karma*-matter from the soul. The final release of the soul from *karma*-mattar is what we call complete self-realization, the state of liberation. The individuality of the soul is maintained even in liberation.

परद्रव्य बहिर्भूतं स्वस्वभावमवैति यः।
परद्रव्ये स कुत्रापि न च द्वेष्टि न रज्यति ॥5॥

He who knows his own (pure) nuture as (totally) excluded from all other substances, does not entertain aversion to and attachment with the 'other' substances anywhere.

The pure natrue of soul does not admit anything of the non-soul into itself. When it is so realized, the question of falling a victim of attachment and aversion towards the non-soul does not arise.

उपयोगो विनिर्दिष्टस्तत्र लक्षणमात्मनः।
द्विविधो दर्शनज्ञानप्रभेदेन जिनाधिपैः ॥6॥

There, conscious manifestation (*upayoga*) which is of two kinds by its diversion into conation and knowledge has been affirmed as the differentia of the soul by the Conquerer-Lords.

The substance of the soul is well identified by the manifestation of its essentional attribute of consciousness. The term *'upayoga'* is taken to imply the function of the attribute of consciousness. *Upayoga* is consciousness in action, while consciousness is the soul's potency for such function. This manifestation of consciousness follows two channels, one of conation and the other of knowledge. This philosophical tradition has originated with the Great Tīrthanikaras of Jainism who were perfect souls with perfect knowledge. This establishes the authentcity of the tradition under the term *Āgama* which literally means what has come to us in fullness through the chain of *Āchāryas.*

चतुर्धा दर्शन तत्र चक्षुषोऽचक्षुषोऽवधेः।
केवलस्य च विज्ञेयं वस्तु सामान्यवेदकम् ॥7॥

There the types of conation are four–the ocular, the non-ocular, the clairvoyant and the perfect (*kevala*). This conation is the prehension of reality in its generality.

Conation (*darśana*) is the essential precondition of knowlege. Conation and knowledge both are conscious but by that conation cannot be covered under knowledge. Conation is no part of knowledge, however elementery knowledge may be. The soul is said to possess two different faculties to determine the modes of conation and knowledge. These faculties continue even in the soul's pure condition in liberation. Moreover, the two types of *karmas* - the conation-obscuring (*darśanāvarṇīya*) and the knowledge - obscuring (*jñānāvararṃīya*) are conscieved to distort these two faculties of the soul. The four types of conations are determined by the instrumentality of senses and the capacity of the soul resulting from the destruction–subsidence and the destruction of the concerned *karma* forces.

मतिःश्रुतावधी ज्ञाने मनःपर्यय-केवले।
सज्ज्ञानं पञ्चधावाचि विशेषाकार-वेदनम् ॥8॥
मत्यज्ञानश्रुताज्ञानं विभङ्गज्ञान-भेदतः।
मिथ्याज्ञानं त्रिधेत्येवमष्टधाज्ञानमुच्यते ॥9॥

Knowledge is a detailed comprehsion of objects. Sensuous knowledge, scriptural or extended knowledge clairvoyance, telepathy and perfect knowledge are its five kinds : the vitiated sensuous knowledge vitiated scriptural knowledge and vitiated clairvoyance are the three types of wrong knowledge. Thus knowledge (in general) is said to be of eight kinds. 8,9.

Knolwdge, as distinguished from conation, is comprehension of objects with their details; while conation is only a grasp of objects in their generality. The knowledge-faculty of a soul manifests in five ways because of the instrumentality of senses and the varying capacity for comprehension of objects determined by its association with *karma* forces. The perfect knowledge results from the complete destruction of the knowledge-abscuring *karma*. Out of these five types of knowledge, only the three types i.e. the sensuous, the scriptural and the clairvoyant types are liable to be vitiated on account of the opration of faith deluding (*darśana mohanīya) karma*. The right types of knowledge funcition with a flavour of the good of the soul turned soulward, while the wrong types of knowledge are so directed that the soul continues its wandering in the world (*saṃsāra*). The former types leads the soul in the direction of gradual redemption;

while the latter are responsible for detaining the soul in the world with no possibility of its redemption.

उदेति केवलज्ञानं तथा केवलदर्शनम्।
कर्मणः क्षयतः सर्वं क्षयोपशमतः परम् ॥10॥

Perfect knowledge and perfect conation emerge on the destruction of the (corresponding) *karmas*; all of the others manifest, on account of the destruction-subsidence (of the necessary *karmas*).

Five types of the manifestations of the soul's power for knowledge in its varied conditions of existence, are enumerated clearly in the Jaina works on the subject. They are : the destructive, the substential (*aupaśamika*) the destructive-subsitential, the operative (*audayika*) and the natural ones (*pārṇāmika*). Perfect knowledge and perfect conation are the destructive ones. other types of knowledge and conation require what is called the destruction-subsidence of the *karmas*. The destruction here means the non-operative condition of the *karma*, which is accompanied by the subsidence of other necessary *karmas*. Thus, the ground for emergence of partial and limited functions of the faculties of the soul is made possible. These two types of manifestations are mentioned in this verse, and these cover all the types of manifestations of knowledge and conation.

यौगपद्येन जायेते केवल-ज्ञान-दर्शने।
क्रमेण दर्शनं ज्ञानं पहं निःशेषमात्मनः ॥11॥

Perfect knowledge and perfect conation appear in the soul simultaneously, all other types of conation and knowledge (of the soul) appear in succession.

In the total absence of the corresponding warring forees of the *karmas* the full and simltaneous appearence of conation and knowledge in a soul is a necessarily logical conclusion.

This accounts for the actual existance of omniscience attained by a soul. Such a soul is called the Adorable Perfect one (*Arhat Kevalī*). In case of the other forms of manifestations of conation and knowledge, the partial, limited and successive function is due to the association of the necessary *karmas* with the soul. It may be noted that no conation is required in case of scriptural and telepathic knowledge as no such type of conation is enumarated in the list.

मिथ्याज्ञानं मतं तत्र मिथ्यात्व-समवायतः।
सम्यग्ज्ञानं पुनर्जैनैः सम्यक्त्वसमवायतः ॥12॥

The Jainas accept that the wrong knowledge results from its association with the wrong type of faith, while the right knolwedge results from its association with the right faith.

Herein the causes of knowledge becoming wrong or right are explained. Knowledge is a distinct faculty of the soul, and it works in its own right. When it combines with the faculty of faith appearing as right or wrong, it is influenced by it and appears as right or wrong. This distinction among manifestations of knowledge becomes necessary as the one guides the soul on the path to liberation, while the other keeps it confined to conditions of mundane existance.

वस्त्वन्यथा परिच्छेदो ज्ञाने संपद्यते यतः।
तन्मिथ्यात्वं मतं सद्भिः कर्मारामोदयोदकम् ॥13॥

What causes the comprehension of reality otherwise is said to be the wrong faith by the noble ones. This wrong faith works like water in the growth of the garden of *karmas*.

The distorted and the otherwise manifestation of knowledge is caused by the accompaniment of wrong faith with knowledge. The maintenance, expansion and duration of such a knowledge are also due to the same factor of wrong faith.

उदये दृष्टिमोहस्य गृहीतमगृहीतकम्।
जातं सांशयिकं चेति मिथ्यात्वं तत्त्रिधा विदुः ॥14॥

When the faith deluding *karma* attains an operative stage, its gives birth to the earned, the unearned and the dubious forms of wrong faith. Thus wrong faith is said to be of three kinds.

Wrong faith pollutes knowledge, but, in itself, it takes three forms. A soul gathers some such conditions as cause of the emergence of wrong faith in its present life, it is the earned type of wrong faith. The unearned type of wrong faith accompanies the soul from its past lives. The third form of wrong faith deprives the soul from having right atttitude towards reality and wraps it in a condition of dubiety. Wrong faith, whatever type it may assume, is, by nature, deterimental and harmful the soul's well-being.

अतत्त्वं मन्यते तत्त्वं जीवो मिथ्यात्वभावितः।
अस्वर्णमीक्षते स्वर्णं न किं कनकमोहितः ॥15॥

A soul that has been repeatedly impressed by wrong faith takes in right (ethically helpful in its ascent towards liberation) view of reality as a wrong one. Does one under delusion by swallowing the herb called '*dhattura*' not perceive what is not gold as gold?

How does wrong faith work with the soul? This question is answered by means of an example. A person who has taken *dhatturā* (thorn apple) suffers from a destortion of his ocular perception. He sees every thing as yellow like gold. So also a soul suffering from wrong faith takes all things ethically useful as harmful to it.

यथा वस्तु तथा ज्ञानं संभवत्यात्मनो यतः।
जिनैरभाणि सम्यक्त्वं तत्क्षमं सिद्धिसाधने ॥16॥

That, by which it is made possible for a soul to know

things as they exist, is said to be right faith by the (Lord) *Jinas* (the cenquerors); it has the potency to achieve the final objective.

As against the wrong faith, the right faith is said to enable the soul to know things as they exist in themselves with no attachment or aversion to them from the side of the soul. Such a pure faith can lead and help the soul on the path to libertion – the final goal for all the beings in the world.

मिथ्यात्व-मिश्र-सम्यक्त्व-संयोजनचतुष्टये ।
क्षयं शमं द्वयं प्राप्ते सप्तधा मोहकर्मणि ॥17॥
क्षायिकं शामिकं ज्ञेयं क्षायोपशमिकं त्रिधा ।
तत्रापि क्षायिकं साध्यं साधनं द्वितयं परम् ॥18॥

When the seven types (*prakritis*) of faith-deluding *karma* named as the wrong faith (*mithyātva*), the right-wrong faith (*samyak-mithyātva*), the right (*samyāktva*) and the four passions-anger, pride, deceit and greed- of the strongest type (potent to keep a soul wandering in the whirlpool of infinite mundane (*anantānu bandhī*) attains the state of destruction, subsidence, and destruction-subsidence, there arisese the three types of right faith knwon as the destructive (resulting from the first state) the subsidencial (resulting from the second state) and the destructive-subsidencial (resulting from the third state). Among these three, the destructive one is the final object of our achievement, the remaing two are instrumental to the attainment of the first.

Herein technical terms of Jaina philosophy are made use of to explain the causes that obstruct the apperance of various types of right faith. These very obstructive causes have been enumerated above. The liquidation of these conditions takes three forms as given in the verse. These three forms of liquidation of the faith deluding *karma* cause the emergence of three types of right faith. Among these the destructive type is the pure right faith and it is not liable to be vitiated. The other two types of right faith are not so; but to attain the first one the passage runs through the remaing two types, which have been taken to be helpful in the attainment of the first. This fight between the soul and the *karma*-forces goes on till the soul is totally freed from the grip of the *karmas.*

ज्ञानप्रमाणमात्मानं ज्ञानं ज्ञेयप्रमं विदुः।
लोकालोकं यतोज्ञेयं ज्ञानं सर्वगतं ततः ॥19॥

They (*Jinas*) say that the soul has the same magnitude as knowledge and the knowlege has the same magnitude as the knowables (the system of reality). The cosmos and the acosmos constitute the knowables, hence knowledge is all pervasive with them.

The writer herein reitarates on the subject of knowledge after dealing with the topic of faith. He attempts to establish a sort of commensurability among the three constituents of the process of knowledge i.e. the soul, the knowledge and the knowables. The soul is the substance wherein knowledge basically resides and evolves to attain its final and complete form. The relation between knowledge and the knowables is nature-born. As such knowledge cannot refuse to know a knowable; on the other hand no knowable can refuse to enter this relationship with knowledge. Hence knowledge and the knowables are said to have the same dimension. It reaches the entire universe i.e. the cosmos and the acosmos to comprehend the contents found therein.

In Jaina cosmology the entire infinite expansion of the substence of space is divided into two parts–the cosmos and the acosmos. Cosmos is that part of space-extension where all the six substances i.e. *jiva* (consciousness), matter (*padgula*), space (*ākāśa*), medium of motion (*dharma*), medium of rest (*adharma*) and time (*kāla*) exist. The remaining part of space-extension where the substance of space alone exists, is called the acosmos. We cannot conceive of trans-space area, for it is an impossibility.

यद्यात्मनोऽधिकं ज्ञानं ज्ञेयं वापि प्रजायते।
लक्ष्यलक्षणभावोऽस्ति तदानीं कथमेतयोः ॥20॥

If knowledge is more than the soul or the knowable is more than the soul, then how to maintain the relation of the defined and the definition between the two?

If knowledge exists beyond the soul, its part lying beyond the soul will be without its necessary substance. If the knowable is more than the soul, then the extraneous part of the knowable must become unknowable to the soul. Both the cases are inconsistent and also contradictory to the basic position implied by the relation between the soul and knowledge and also between knowledge and the knowable. The right position and conclusion thus is that the soul is characterized by its essential attribute of knowledge, and the knowledge and the knowable have equal extension and magnitude.

क्षीरक्षिप्तं यथाक्षीरं मिन्द्र नीलं स्वतेजसा।
क्षेयक्षिप्तं तथा ज्ञानं ज्ञेयं व्याप्नोति सर्वतः ॥21॥

Just as the blue jewel (*Indranīla*) when merged in milk imparts its own blue lustre (to milk), so also the knowledge, when applied to the knowable pervades them through and through.

The way of the function of knowledge with respect to the knowable is explained here by means of an illustration. The soul when characterized by knowledge remains at its own place but it emanates its brilliance so as to cover the entire range of the knowables. This relationship between the soul and its knowledge on one hand and between knowladge and the knowable, on the other, is nature-born. On the assumption of this situation reasoning may be advanced in favour of or against the situation, to test the alternative; but the basic situation stands as beyond reasoning, being nature-born.

चक्षुर्गृह्णद्यथारूपं रूपरूपं न जायते।
ज्ञानं जानन् तथा ज्ञेयं ज्ञेयरूपं न जायते ॥22॥

Just as an eye catches the shape and colour (of a thing) but also not get transformed into the shape and colour (of the thing); in the same way knowledge knows the knowable but is not transformed into the identity of the knowable.

The relation between knowledge and the knowable is further explained by means of the above example. This relation is governed by a necessary; restriction in the form of mutual non-transformation. It is certain that this relation is very close and necessary; but the bar of non-transformation between the two is also equally strong and it is granted by nature. It is like a pre-established harmony limited by the impossibility of mutual transformation.

दवीयांसमपि ज्ञानमर्थं वेत्ति निसर्गतः।
अयस्कान्तः स्थितं दूरे नाकर्षति किमायसम् ॥23॥

Knowledge, by nature, knows even the distant things. Does a magnet not attract the iron even when it is placed at distance?

It is emphasized here that for knowledge distance is no obstruction (to its function). This part is again explained by the example of a magnet where attraction is seen effective with a piece of iron seprated by a distance between them. If you try to enter into the physics of a magnet attracting a piece of iron, the question of the magnetic field intervenes. This field is also a physical creation to facilitate the working between the two. Moreover, beyond the magnetic field the relationship between them breaks down. So we are led to think whether any such medium between knowledge and the knowable can be searched out. This is an extension of the example which is not acceptable to the Jaina thinkers. The implication of the example should be taken only to the extent it serves our purpose in view. Actually speaking, Jaina philosophy is not prepared to accept the existance of any medium between knowledge and the knowable. It is also a speciality of knowledge that it can comprehend things at distance without any medium.

ज्ञानमात्मानमर्थं च परिच्छित्ते स्वभावतः।
दीप उद्योतयत्यर्थं स्वस्मिन्नान्यमपेक्षते ॥24॥

Knowledge knows itself and the objects by nature. A lamp enlightens an object and in itself needs no other (entity).

The above statement stands upon the sound ground that therse can be nothing which is unknowable to knowledge. As such not only the objects are comprehended by knowledge but even the knowledge is known by itself. A lamp is seen by us along with the things it enlightens. This is only an exmaple which illustrates the theme under consideration, it cannot take the place of an argument to prove its truth. A counter-example is very aften quoted in this context. Just as an acrobat cannot climb his own shoulders, so also knowledge cannot know itself. Thus we are kept moving from one example to another coming to no conclusion. Again the problem is solved by putting a question as to how one would not like to hold knowledge to be known by itself when one holds the objects of knowledge as known by knowledge. It is just like re-establishing the propriety of the first example. Knowledge must also know itself. If it is excluded from the span of its of knowing, it well looses even the title as knowledge.

क्षायोपशमिकं ज्ञानं कर्मापाये निवर्तते।
प्रादुर्भवति जीवस्य नित्यं क्षायिकमुज्ज्वलम् ॥25॥

Knowledge determined by the destruction-subsidence of (necessary) *karmas* comes to an end in the absence of such (a state of) *karmas*. Fully effulgent knowledge determined by the (total) destruction of the (knowledge-obscuring) *karma* emerges in a soul to last for ever.

Destruction subsidence is a stage in the process of the working of *karmas*. It helps only the partial and limited emergence of knowledge. In the absence of such a help from the side of the *karmas* it must disappear. But when perfect and full knowledge dawns in a soul as a result of the total eradication of the *karmas*, there remains no chance of its being-defiled by them. Hence such knowledge must continue to shine endlessly enlightening the contents of the universe, including the knower with its knowledge.

सन्तमर्थमसन्तं च काल-त्रितयगोचरम्।
अवैति युगपज्ज्ञानमव्याघातमनुत्तमम् ॥26॥

(*Ksāyika*) Knowledge (emerging on the total destruction of the *karma*) comprehends the existing and non-existing objects simultaneously and hence knows objects of present, past and future. It knows no obstruction, and it is par-excellence.

Some of the characteristics of perfect knowledge are enumerated in this verse. It knows all thing present or hidden in the past or in the future. It is able to know all things or events belonging to the present, past and future. In this pure state of knowledge it does not suffer from successive manifestation of knowledge. Besides its simultaneous function being above all obstructions and its being par-excellent, is the other characteristic of perfect knowledge.

असन्तस्ते मता दक्षैरतीता भाविनश्च ये।
वर्तमानाः पुनः सन्तस्त्रैलोक्योदरवर्तिनः ॥27॥

The noble ones hold these (things and events) that have passed into the past and those that are to come into existence (in future) as non-existent (with respect to the present); while the present ones are those taking place at present. All those are lying in the womb of the three worlds.

Cosmos has been divided into three great parts known as the nether world (*adholoka*), the middle world (*madhya loka*) and the upper world (*ūrdhva loka*). This cosmos is the locus for all the things and events belonging to the three times; past, present and the future. Perfect knowledge has thus immensely vast scope of the knowledge to cover. Actually speaking there is nothing in the vastness of space and times and the subtlity of the elements of the universe which can escape the grip of perfect knowledge.

अतीता भाविनश्चार्थाः स्वे स्वे काले यथाखिलाः।
वर्तमानास्ततस्तद्वद्वेत्ति तानपि केवलम् ॥28॥

All the objects of the past and the future exist in their own times. Omniscience therefore knows them also according to their existence.

We know the past things and events by memory, and those of the future, by imagination. Now does the omniscient Lord (*Kevalin*) know them without the help of memory or imagination or any other aid? It is admitted that Omniscient Lord knows all things and events directly and simultaneously. All the entities of the universe exist in their times–the present, past, and future; and these are their existence-forms. These existent-forms are directly and simultaneously comprehended by omniscience. The time adjuncts present no difficulty in the way of omniscience; the past and the future need not transform into present for omniscience.

सर्वेषु यदि न ज्ञानं यौगपद्येन वर्तते।
तदैकमपि जानाति पदार्थं न कदाचन ॥29॥
एकत्रापि यतोऽनन्ताः पर्यायाः सन्ति वस्तुनि।
क्रमेण जानता सर्वे ज्ञायन्ते कथ्यताम् कदा ॥30॥

If the (perfect) knowledge does not cover all the objects (of the universe) simultaneously, then it can never know even one object (completely).

As the infinite modes of the objects exist even at one place, then tell me when can they all be known if comprehended successively?.

An infinity of objects with their infinite attributes exists in the unvierse. If perfect knowledge proceeds to comprehend them successively, one after the other, then the infinite series of objects can never be exausted by it. Then, it can never become perfect. Hence the only alternative for it, to be true to its title, is the simultaneous comprehension of all the objects. Moreover, perfect knowledge or ominiscience emerges in a soul only on the total destruction of obstructive karmic forces. As such we can think of no obstructions like time, distacne, subtlity and an infinity of objects in the way. An intervention by auxiliary conditions and causes is out of place in our discussion on the subject of omniscience.

घातिकर्मक्षयोत्पन्नं यद्रूपं परमात्मानः।
श्रद्धत्ते भक्तितो भव्यो नाभव्यो भववर्धकः ॥31॥

The liberable one cherishes faith with devotion in the (ethically) highest identity of the soul, which emerages on the (complete) eradication of the destrcutive types of *karmas*. The non-liberable one does not do so, (cherish such a faith) and (thus) he elongates (the chain of) his mundane existance.

The tradition of the division of souls into two classes i.e the liberable (*bhāvya*) and the non-liberable (*abhāvya*) is as old as Jainism itself. The liberable ones are those that possess the capacity of liberating themselves by menas of developing such faculties of the soul as right faith, right knowledge etc. The souls that have attained liberations so far were certainly liberable ones, the rest of the liberable ones will attain liberation, however long a time they may take in future. On the other hand the non-liberable souls are so fated that they will never make the necessary efforts required for liberation. We know well that the souls that are leading a mundane life at present had been in such a state for the infinite past time. So also many of the present mundane souls will not be able to attain liberation, in spite of the fact that some of these will be able to achieve the final objective of liberation at a suitable point of time in future. This distinction among souls is drawn on the basis of the possibility of directing their lives on the right path. The non-liberable ones will never choose the right path and will wander in the labyrinths of mundane life for all time to come. The question of cheristing faith and devotion in the pure and perfect souls does not arise in the case of the non-liberable ones (*jīvas*).

यत्सर्वार्थवरिष्ठं यत्क्रमातीतमतीन्द्रियम् ।
श्रद्दधात्यात्मनो रूपं स याति पदमव्ययम् ॥32॥

He, who has faith in the (pure) identity of the soul, which is the highest (among all entities of the universe) and which has gone beyond the successive and the sensuous (consiousness), attains the imperishable status (of the liberated ones).

The object of faith for the liberable souls necessarily is divinity characterized by the special attributes as enumerated in this verse. By dint of this faith liberable souls will certainly step on the road leading to liberation, hence they will be certainly blessed with the grant of the highest status of liberation with no possibility of fall.

निर्व्यापारीकृताक्षस्य यत्क्षणं भाति पश्यतः।
तद्रूपमात्मनो ज्ञेयं शुद्धं संवेदनात्मकम् ॥33॥

That should be known as pure and conscious identity of the soul, which is felt for a moment by one who is attentive to it and has completely suspended the activity of his senses.

A glimpse of the spiritual ideal of the pure soul though lasting only for a moment can be expected to be experienced by a devotee, when he is attentive towards it and who reduces the action of his senses to nullity. Such a short lived glimpse of the ideal can be experienced by a novice in the course of his efforts in the direction of self realization. This short lived vision can be enlarged mentally to gain some acquaintance with the ideal. It will enable us to intensify our efforts to mitigate the difference between the ideal and the actual.

आत्मा स्वात्मविचारज्ञैर्नीरागी भूतचैतनैः।
निरवद्यश्रुतेनापि केवलेनेव बुध्यते ॥34॥

The (ideal) soul, free from attachment and aversion, is also known by unblemished scriptural knowledge (*śrutajñāna*), as (known) by perfect knowledge, by those who possess such conciousness (inclination) and also cognitive copacity to think about their souls.

A perfect soul comprehends itself with its perfect knowledge. But the soul that has not yet attained perfect knowledge and is still on the path, making all possible efforts to attain it, can also get the knowledge of the pure soul with the help of scriptural knowledge (which is) free from all blemishes. The necessary conditions for such an attainment are firstly, the inclinnation towards the pure soul and secondly, sufficient knowledge of scriptures to enable the devotee to extend his thought processes in the same direction. This means that the comprehension of the ideal is effected both by the perfect knowledge and the scriptural knowledge. The difference between the two comprehensions is that the former is direct and completely vivid, while the latter is indirect and vivid only partially. Again, the former stands in no need of the instrumentality of senses or any other type of knowledge; while the latter, assuming a highly rarified form, is able to drop the instrumentality of the senses and other forms of knowledge. It is said, that it is the highest form of scriptural knowledge in its subjective form, which gets transformed in to the perfect knowledge on the eradication of the remaining obstructive conditions. There is a basic difference, as Jaina epistemology admits, between perfect knowledge and the above mentioned scriptural knowledge regarding the clarity of knowledge and the span of their knowleables. While making a comparision between the two types of knowledge, the stress is mainly laid on the experience of the identity of the pure soul.

रागद्वेषापराधीनं यदा ज्ञानं प्रवर्तते।
तदाभ्यधायि चारित्रमात्मनो मलसूदनम् ॥35॥

When knowledge functions without dependence on (being vitiated by) attachment and aversion, then it is said to be the soul's conduct, the destroyer of the filth (of *karma*).

The association of attachment and aversion with knowledge vitiates the quality of knowledge, hence it cannot function in a pure way agreeing with the pure nature of the soul. This state of knowledge directly affects the quality of conduct; then the faculty of conduct also gets vitiatcd. Hence to attain the purity of conduct in the soul, knowledge must not be contaminated with attachment and averison and also delusion which is manifest in the form of passion like anger, pride, deciet and greed and also in the form of quasi-passions like laughter, grief, sex etc.

अहिंसा सत्यमस्तेयं ब्रह्म सङ्गविवर्जनम्।
कषाय-विकले ज्ञाने समस्तं नैव तिष्ठति ॥36॥
हिंसत्वं वितथं स्तेयं मैथुनं सङ्गसंग्रहः।
आत्मरूपगते ज्ञाने निःशेषं प्रपलायते ॥37॥

Non-violence, truthfulness, non-stealing, chastity and renunciation of possession all necessarily find no lodgement in knowledge (which is) disturbed by passion.

Violence, falsehood, theft, unchastity and possession flee away, without leaving even a trace behind, from knowledge which has attained the form of the pure soul.

The five vows or virtues of Jaina Ethics are accomplished only when knowledge is not allowed to be contaminated by different types of passions. Passions are very highly fatal to the pure function of knowledge. Hence elimination of passions from knowledge is the basic necessity for the pure functioning of knowledge, which, in turn, grants one the purity of the soul.

Conversely, the five sinful activities, are the antitheses of the five vows or virtues which cannot cling to the soul, and pollute the purity of its knowledge, if the soul has been sucessful in attaining its pure identity.

चारित्रं दर्शनं ज्ञानमात्मरूपं निरञ्जनम्।
कर्मभिर्मुच्यते योगी ध्यायमानो न संशयः ॥38॥

Unvitiated conduct, faith and knowledge are the (pure) identity of the soul. (Hence) a Yogi (novice) attains freedom from (the clutches of) *karmas*. It is an undoubted fact.

One who aims at realizing his pure soul by observing the necessary course prescribed by the great seers is called a yogi. Such a yogi must keep himself fully engaged in meditating about his pure soul. Then alone will he be able to shrug off the dust of the *karmas* which had been clinging to it and polluting its identity from beginningless times. Meditation of the pure soul is the only certain and unfailing means to achieve the highest aim of human life. Life in other forms in not sufficiently evolved to achieve the aim of self-realization.

यः करोति पर-द्रव्ये रागमात्म-पराङ्मुखः।
रत्नत्रयमयो नासौ न चारित्रचरो यतिः ॥39॥

One who, turning away from his (pure) soul, entertains attachment for the 'other' (non-soul) substance has not identified himself with the three jewels, nor is he a saint observing (the rules of) conduct.

Right faith, right knowledge and right conduct constitute the way leading to the emancipation of the soul; and for this reason they are more known as the three jewels, the most precious possession of the soul on the path to liberation. The gravest mistake of the worldly soul lies in the fact that it loses all interest in the spiritual purity and is entangled and allured by all that is the 'other' of the soul. Thus such a person is driven away and away from the right path, he is no more a practioner of the conduct potent to carry him nearer and nearer to the goal of his life.

अभिन्नमात्मनः शुद्धं ज्ञानदृष्टिमयं स्फुटम्।
चारित्रं चर्यते शश्वच्चारुचारित्रवेदिभिः ॥40॥

(Right) conduct of the soul is very clearly permeated by (right) knowledge and (right) faith and is non-distinct from the (pure) soul. Such a conduct (of the soul) is always (continously) practised by the knowers of the graceful conduct.

To be right, conduct is not only accompanied by right knowledge and right faith, but all the three form one unity and, further all of them are identical with the (pure) soul. At this level of existence and experience, better known as the pure point of view, a level of *Niścaysnaya*; the three jewels of right faith, right knowledge and right conduct become indistinguishable among themselves and also indistinguishable from the (pure) soul itself. Such a situation is certified as a fact by the experience of the saint who has risen so high.

आचारवेदनं ज्ञानं सम्यक्त्वं तत्त्वरोचनम्।
चारित्रं च तपश्चर्या व्यवहारेण गद्यते ॥41॥

To experience conduct is knowledge, interest directed towards the (seven) principles is right faith and the practice of the courses of penance is the conduct. It is said (so) from the practical point of view.

In the previous verse the three jewels of the path of liberation were explained from the real or pure point of view (*niścayanaya*). Now they are explained from the practical point of view (*vyavahāranaya*). To facilitate their understanding at the lower level a resort is made to the practical point of view. The pictures of the three jewels drawn under the two *nayas* are not only different but also contradictory. This contradiction is overcome by an adoption of the logic of view points (*naya vāda*). Then it would appear that the practical point of view leads to the heights of the real point of view, the latter helps one to lift itself to the former. But one's true aim is always to reach the higher level, without which the final aim of life will not be achieved. The author also makes a mention of the seven principles involved in the journey of the soul from the worldly existence to its emancipated state.They are the *jīva, the ajiva,* the influx (*āsrava*), the bondage (*bandha*), the check of influx (*saṁvara*), the liquidation of *karmas* (*nirjarā*) and the final freedom from *karmas* (*mokṣa*). This enumeration of the principles of Jainism presents to us a dramatic scene of the journey. The first two principles, i.e. the *jīva* and the *ajīva* (specially karmas) are the two actors on the stage. The next four principles represent the various activities taking place between the first two. The seventh and the last principle represents the destination of the journey where the association between the soul and *karmas* is finally broken leaving the soul in its own and pure state with no possibility of a fall therefrom.

सम्यक्त्व-ज्ञान-चारित्रस्वभावः परमार्थतः ।
आत्मा राग-विनिर्मुक्तो मुक्तिमार्गो विनिर्मलः ॥42॥

From the highest point of view the right faith, the right knowledge and the right conduct are the (very) nature of the soul. (From the same point of view) the soul (itself), completely free from attachment (etc.), constitutes the way to liberation, which is perfectly free from all blemish.

From the highest point of view the unity of the soul and the unity of the way to liberation are again emphasized by the āchārya in this verse by way of a conclusion of what has been said so far.

यश्चरत्यात्मनात्मानमात्मा जानाति पश्यति ।
निश्चयेन स चारित्रं ज्ञानं दर्शनमुच्यते ॥43॥

Because the soul sees (believes), knows and behaves itself by itself, so from the real point of view the soul (itself) is said to be faith, knowledge and conduct.

The soul, in its pure state, is a self determined principle or entity, then it (itself) becomes the subject, the object and the instrument of its functions like believing, knowing and behaving. In this stage all the three functions shrink to one reality of the soul perfectly undistinguishable in the form of its attributes and their functions. It is again an attempt at the perfect unity of the soul, where no form of dualism is experienced.

तस्मात्सेव्यः परिज्ञाय श्रद्धयात्मा मुमुक्षुभिः ।
लब्ध्युपायः परो नास्ति यस्मान्निर्वाणशर्मणः ॥44॥

Therefore the (pure) soul is worth attempting for

realization with devotion (faith) after knowing it fully, for there is no other way of realizing it by those who are desirous of attaining the bliss of *nirvāna.*

The realization of the pure soul is sought for the sake of bliss which is found only in the state of *mokṣa*. All our energies and powers like faith, knowledge and conduct are to be harnessed to the attainment of this unforseen realization. One should clarily understand that there is no other way to achieve this aim of life.

निषिध्य स्वार्थतोऽक्षाणि विकल्पातीतचेतसः ।
तद्रूपं स्पष्टमाभाति कृताभ्यासस्य तत्त्वतः ॥45॥

Really speaking, the identity (of the pure soul) is experienced by one who has refused (disallowed) the function of the senses with their objects, whose mind is free from mental vicissitudes and who has undergone (sufficient) practice.

The experience of the identity of the pure soul is possible only when one is well able to control his senses against sensuous perceptions and pleasures. He has also to control his mind against mental ramblings and thoughts. These conditions cannot be fulfilled unless one has resorted to a prolonged practice to attain stability in maintaining them. Such a practice will enable him to conquer the senses and the mind; and as a result, he will be blessed with the experience of his pure soul.

स्व-संविदितमत्यक्षमव्यभिचारि केवलम् ।
नास्ति ज्ञानं परित्यज्य रूपं चेतयितुः परम् ॥46॥

The highest identity of the conscious soul lies nowhere except in perfect knowledge (*kevala jñāna*) which is self conscious, direct and free from (all the) blemish (of knowledge).

The experience of the pure soul is now equated with the attainment of perfect knowledge which involves the knowledge of the entire universe along with the knowledge of the soul. The emphasis on the knowledge of the soul is meant to refute the views of some thinkers who admit the possibility of the former but hold that being the knower, the soul cannot be known by itself. Perfect knowledge does not require the instrumentality of the senses and the mind as we notice in case of the worldly souls. In perfect knowledge there is perfect correspondence between it and the objects of knowledge, it comprehends all the objects vividly in form and substance.

यस्य रागोऽणुमात्रेण विद्यतेऽन्यत्र वस्तुनि।
आत्मतत्त्व-परिज्ञानी बध्यते कलिलैरपि ॥47॥

One, who entertains even the slightest attachement with any entity except one's soul, may know well the principle of the soul, but still gets bound with the demerit (of *karmas*).

The experience of one's soul cannot exist even with a tinge of attachment, aversion and delusion. So long as the deluding *karma* is clinging to the soul, the emergence of spiritual experience is impossible. Perfect knowledge manifests in a soul only on the complete destruction of the deluding *karma*. However learned one may be, one will not attain experience of his soul in the presence of the effects of the deluding *karma*; on the contrary such a soul will continue to bind *karma*, a permanent hinderance in the way of the experience and realization of one's soul.

यो विहायात्मनो रूपं सेवते परमेष्ठिनः।
स बध्नाति परं पुण्यं न कर्मक्षयमश्नुते ॥48॥
नागच्छच्छक्यते कर्म रोद्धुं केनापि निश्चितम्।
निराकृत्य परद्रव्याण्यात्मतत्त्वरतिं विना ॥49॥

ये मूढा लिप्सवो मोक्षं परद्रव्यमुपासते।
ते यान्ति सागरं मन्ये हिमवन्तं यियासवः ॥50॥

One who, deviating from the identity of his soul, resorts to serve the five Great ones binds the highly meritorious *karmas*, but does not gain the destruction of *karmas*.

It is certain that the *karmas* flowing to a soul cannot be checked (kept off) by anyone without removing the entities other than one's soul (from the way) and without resorting to devotions to one's soul.

The ignorant persons, desirous of (attaining) mokṣa (release from worldly existence), resort to serve the substance other than (their own) souls, are, I hold, moving towards the sea, though being desirous of reaching the *Himavāna* (mountain).

For a true seaker of the experience and realization of his soul it is absolutely necessary that he should confine himself to his (pure) soul alone and nothing else.Love and devotion for self-realization is no form of attachment, as it cannot result from the working of *karmas*. Even the attachment retained for the service of the *Siddhas* (liberated souls), *Arihantas* (souls on the verge of liberation but still in body), the *Ācaryās* (the heads of the organization of *munis*), the *Upādhyayas* (professors–*munis* in the organization) and the *Sādhus* (saints ordained in the organization) is an obstruction in the way of the realization of one's soul. It only grants a bondage of meritorious *karmas* and can lift the soul to highly pleasurable regions in the world, but cannot lead to the destruction of *karmas*. The real objective before a soul desirous to advance on the path of liberation is the check of the *karmas* from entering the soul and the complete freedom from the shackles of *karmas*. It is possible only when one keeps the ideal of his pure soul constantly in view. Even the slightest contamination of the idea by an attention on any thing other than this ideal is highly injurious for the aspirant, for it is bound to result in its most alluring and deluding entanglements caused by the meritorious *karmas*. The *āchārya* goes to the extent of asserting that such a diversion on the path of liberation will lead the soul just against the true ideal and keep it confined in the worldly existance for incalculably long times.

परद्रव्यीभवत्यात्मा परद्रव्य-विचिन्तकः ।
क्षिप्रमात्मत्वमायाति विविक्तात्म-विचिन्तकः ॥51॥

A soul, meditating on entities other than itself, becomes absorbed in other entities. A soul, meditating on itself as chiselled (from all 'other' than itself), very soon attains its identity (absorption in itself).

A soul becomes identical with what it meditates upon. So when meditating upon entities other than itself, it forgetting itself, becomes identical with other entities. It is a clear loss on the path of liberation. When the soul meditates upon itself and is confined within itself with a complete exclusion of the 'other' entities, it, with no loss of time, becomes identical with itself. It is like a return to the soul's original and pure home and marks a clear gain on the path of liberation.

कर्म-नोकर्म-निर्मुक्तममूर्त्तमजरामरम् ।
निर्विशेषमसंबद्धमात्मानं योगिनो विदुः ॥52॥

The *yogis* describe the (pure) soul as free from *karmas* and quasi-*karmas*, non-corporeal, beyond dotage (old age) and death, with nothing particular and completely dissociated.

Some special quatlites that can be analysed in a pure soul are enumerated in this verse. The purity of the soul is attained only when the *karmas* bound with it are completely destroyed; the pure soul is then free from *karmas*. the quasi-*karmas* constitute the material for making the garb in the form the body for a soul. This matter and its products must be naturally dropped in the absence of the *karmas*. Death and dotage are related with the body, which being dropped, the pure soul will not suffer from these worldly limitations and frailities. The pure soul is left now to itself, it cannot share any quality of matter. It is then non-corporeal. Now no qualities, and faculties even those of faith, knowledge and conduct can be perceived as distinct from the substance of the soul, it has become completely free from all particularities. Finally it has attained purity by breaking all its associations with all that is other than itself and thus it has become perfectly non-relational.

वर्ण-गन्ध-रस-स्पर्श-शब्द-देहेन्द्रियादयः ।
चेतनस्य न विद्यन्ते निसर्गेण कदाचन ॥53॥

By nature (intrinsically) colour, smell, taste, touch, word, body, senses etc. are never found in a (pure) soul.

शरीरयोगतः सन्ति वर्ण-गन्ध-रसादयः ।
स्फटिकस्येव शुद्धस्य रक्तपुष्पादियोगतः ॥54॥

Colour, smell, taste etc. are admitted of the soul on account of its association with the body, just as colour is seen in the pure quartz crystal on account of its association with red flowers etc.

Colour, smell, taste, touch, word, body and senses all intrisically belong to matter; they are the qualities and modes of matter. The soul, being a different substance, does not possess them by its very nature. But our perception certifies that an embodied soul is possessed of these qualities. It is so because of the soul's association with the body.Even attachment, aversion and similar psychological phenomena are seen as belonging to the embodied soul. It is so only due to the soul's confinement in the body. If we fix our eyes on the pure soul alone, we can very well appreciate the situation.

The basic truth of Jaina ontology is that a substance is inconvertible into another substance; still the truth of our perception is admitted in a practical or concessional sense which stands on the ground of the Jaina theory of auxiliary or *nimitta* causation. A mere proximity between the conscious soul and the unconscious substance of matter or *karma* becomes an occasion for such vitiated manifestations. It is the Jaina Occasionalism which saves the Jaina position from absolute Inter actionism as well as from absolute Parallelism. The truth of both the theories of Interactionism and Parallelism is admissible in Jaina system but only when a proper and suitable setting and reference-system is provided. If taken in an absolute form, the contradiction betwen them can never be wiped out.

राग-द्वेष-मद-क्रोध-लोभ-मोह-पुरस्सराः ।
भवन्त्यौदयिका दोषाः सर्वे संसारिणः सतः ॥55॥
यदि चेतयितुः सन्ति स्वभावेन क्रुधादयः ।
भवन्तस्ते विमुक्तस्य निवार्यन्ते तदा कथम् ॥56॥

All the operative malicious manifestations of *karmas* like attachment, aversion, pride, anger, greed, delusion etc. are found in a worldly soul which is (also) existent.

If anger etc. are admitted as existent in the conscious soul by nature, then how can they be got rid of in a liberated (soul)?

All the psychological states and modes as enumerated above in the verse are seen as really existent in a worldly soul, because the worldly existence of the soul is also a reality. The *āchārya* reiterates that they are never the modes and function of the pure faculties of a pure soul, their emergence in worldly life is, in no way, in agreement with the pure state of the soul. From a pure substance flows its pure modification. If the impure states, and modifications of the soul are held to flow from a pure soul, it will become impossible and also unintelligible to check their emergence in the state of liberation. Impure modification of a soul and its liberated state are contractory by their very nature. The states of liberation and worldliness are contradictory, one cannot go with the other.

गुणजीवादयः सन्ति विंशतिर्याः प्ररूपणाः ।
कर्मसम्बन्ध-निष्पन्नास्ता जीवस्य न लक्षणम् ॥57॥

The stages of spiritual evolution, the classification of the *jīvas* and the twenty (*prarūpaṇas*) ways (of dealing with the soul) are all accomplished by the association of *karmas* (with the soul). They are not the differentia of the *jīva*.

In Jaina philosophy twenty ways and heads have been devised to deal with the subject of the *jīva*. They are the stage of evolution of the (*guṇasthāna*), the classification of the *jīvas* (*jīva samāsa*), developableness (paryāpti), the vitalities (*prāṇa*), the instincts (saṁjñā), the soul quests (*mārgaṇā*), conscious function (*upayoga*), condition of existence (*gati*), senses (*indrīya*), body (*kāya*), vitratiofus of soul-units (yoga), sex (*veda*), passions (*kaṣāya*), knowledge (*jñāns*), restraint (*saṁyāma*), conation (*darśana*), thought-paint (*leśyā*), librability (*bhavyatva*), right faith (*samyaktva*), rationality (*saṅjñitva*), intake for formation of body (*āhāra*) and conscious function (*upayoga*). Besides these twenty ways divised for the study of the principle of *jīva* some other ways lying between them are also mentioned under the title inter-*prarūpaṇas*. It is to be noted that all these ways are meant to study *jīva* existing in association with *karmas*; the pure *jīva* is not approachable through these ways of study. These ways cannot take us to the pure soul, they can only enable us to guard ourselves against confusing the *non-jīva* with the *jīva*. This discriminatory knowledge helps us throughout our journey to reach the ideal, and thus provides a check against any deviation from the path.

क्षायोपशमिकाः सन्ति भावा ज्ञानादयोऽपि ये।
स्वरूपं तेऽपि जीवस्य विशुद्धस्य न तत्त्वतः ॥58॥

These knowledge etc. are destructive-cum-subsidential modifications of the *jīva*. They too, from the real point of view, do not constitute the identity of the pure *jīva*.

The workings of the *karmas* play an important part in determining the modifications of the soul. Such modifications are classified into five groups. The destructive (*kṣāyika*) modification emerge in a soul on the destruction of *karmas*, the subsidential (*aupaśamika*) ones appear on the subsidence of *karmas*, the destructive-cum-subsidential (*kṣāyopaśamika*) ones (mentioned in this verse) appear in a soul on the destruction-subsidence of some *karmas* acted upon by the opreation by some other *karmas*, the operative (*audayika*) ones are caused by the operation of *karmas* and lastly the natural (*pāraṇāmika*) ones appear by themselves without the intervention of the *karmas*. Amongst from the five types of the above mentioned manifestations, the āchārya singles out the third category which covers the phenomena like knowledge, conation etc. and stresses that they too cannot be said to belong to the pure soul. When our ideal is the pure soul, when we aim to understand the soul from the pure point of view, any phinomenon contaminated by the *karmas* in any way cannot be said to belong to it. We shall have to rise above this category of spiritual manifestations and reach a stage which is marked by freedom of the soul from the *karma*-effects.

गलित-निखिल-राग-द्वेष-मोहादि-दोषः,
सततमिति विभक्तं चिन्तयन्नात्म-तत्त्वम्।
गतमलमविकारं ज्ञान-दृष्टि-स्वभावं,
जनन-मरण-मुक्तं मुक्तिमाप्नोति योगी ॥59॥

A yogī, who has liquidated all attachements, aversion, delusion, etc. who continuously meditates upon the principle of soul as free from all blemishes (of *karmas*), not suffering from any melicious manifastation and as having pure knowledge and conation as its nature, attains liberation - a stage above birth and death.

A yogī is the one who aims at lifting up his soul to its original Godhood, i.e. to establish a sort of unity and affinity with God. The basic qualification of a yogi is that he should strenuously try to overcome all passions and delusions which are the greatest obstacles on his way. For him the ideal for meditation is the pure soul with its natural and intrinsic qualities chiselled of all contamination of everything that is 'other' than the soul. Even a moment of deviation from such thoughts and ideals will not be tolerated by him. The final result of all his endeavours will be the attainment of liberation (*mokṣa*), a stage where there is no birth, no death, no pain or pleasure and no fear of fall or return to the worldly existence.

Here ends Chapter-1, Jīvādhikāra of Yogasāra-prābhṛta by Āchārya Amitagati.

Chapter 2

Ajīvādhikāra

धर्माधर्मनभःकाल-पुद्गलाः परिकीर्तिताः।
अजीवा जीवतत्त्वज्ञैर्जीवलक्षणवर्जिताः ॥1॥

Medium of motion (*dharma*), medium of rest(*adharma*), space, time and matter (*pudgala*) are said to be non-soul (substances) by the knowers of the principle of soul (*jīva*). They are bereft of the differentia of *jīva.*

Jaina Ontology divides the entire scope of reality into two classes of the conscious (*jīva*) and the unconcious (*ajīva*). The *āchārya* has dealt with the former in the first chapter of this work *Yogasāra* under the title *jīvadhikāra.* In the second or the present chapter he takes up the discussion of the unconscious (*ajīva*) under the title *ajivādhikāra*: the principle of the non-soul or *ājīva* includes the above-mentioned five substances. Thus Jaina ontology pronounces the truth of six substances which are mutually ireeducible and self-contained. Among them the *jīva*, the matter and the time substances cover many individuals mutually irreducible and self-contained; while the remaining three substances are *dharma*, *adhrma* and space each one of which is a single substance. The substance of space is self-accommodating and fulfils the function of accommodating all other substances. The substance of time determines its own dynamism and continuance and provides a medium for the same fuctions for all the other substances. The substance of *dharma* is required to work as medium of motion for the souls and the atoms and molecules of matter. The souls and matter alone can change their states of rest to that of motion and vice-versa. Similarly the substance of *adharma* is required to provide a medium of rest for all other substances. These functions so assigned to different substances are performed by them only in a passive manner, and do not help active causation.

Yogasāra mainly aims at providing way of emancipation for everyone who is at least inclined to choose it. For this, as already mentioned, he must be well acquainted with what is other than his soul to avoid all types of misunderstanding, confusion and astray attempts. It is for this reason that the *āchārya* attempts an exposition of the substances other than the souls.

अवकाशं प्रयच्छन्तः प्रविशन्तः परस्परम् ।
मिलन्तश्च न मुञ्चन्ति स्व-स्वभावं कदाचन ॥2॥

(These substances), mutually accommodating, interpenetrating and contacting, never relinquish their nature.

The extension of space, according to Jaina Ontology, is infinite, but it is conceived into its two divisions; the cosmos (*lokākāśa*) and the acosmos (*alokākāśa*). The former is full with the six substances, while space extends also in the latter. Naturally all the six substances exist in the same space. They are co-spatial. But by that we should not understand that their co-existence results in an integrated unity of the various substances. Inspite of their mutual accommodation, affinity etc. they are essntially different in their substantial bases and attributes and modal expansions.

अमूर्ता निष्क्रियाः सर्वे मूर्तिमन्तोऽत्र पुद्गलाः ।
रूप-गन्ध-रस-स्पर्श-व्यवस्था मूर्तिरुच्यते ॥3॥

All (of them) are non-corporeal; only matter or *pudgala*

is corporeal. A determination (in existence) by colour, smell, taste and touch is corporeality.

All the susbtance except matter are described as non-corporeal; only matter, in all its forms, is corporeal in the above sense. They are also free from moving or vibrating activity. The above list of substances includes the liberated souls only; while the worldly souls, being in association with *karmic* matter, physical body and environment are only concessionally held to be corporeal, because in their pure state, they are perfectly non-corporeal and without activity or motion. In case of gross matter its determination by colour, smell, taste and touch are quite understandable, but this peculiarity of matter is also extended to its finer and subtler forms. So an atom is also held to the coroporeal in the above sense, though its characteristics are no object of sensuous perception. Matter even in its finer molecular form is so held for the same reason. Sound is very clearly generated by and related with matter, but is held to be no property of matter. It is only a mode of matter–an accidental emanation from the impact of the material bodies.

जीवेन सह पञ्चापि द्रव्याण्येते निवेदिताः।
गुणपर्ययवद्द्रव्यमिति लक्षणयोगतः ॥4॥
द्रूयते गुणपर्यायैर्यद्यद् द्रवति तानथ।
तद्रव्यं भण्यते षोढा सत्तामयमनवश्रम् ॥5॥

Along with the *jīva* all these five are said to be the substances, because of the application of the definition of substance as possessed of attributes and modes.

That which liquefies by attributes and modes or that which causes liquefaction to those (attributes and modes) is said to be a substance. (it is) of six kinds, (it is) identical with existance, and (it is) non-destructible.

There goes well known dictum that a substance is defined

by its identical relation with and possession of its attributes and modes. The six mutually irreducible entities of Jaina ontology, as already enumerated, are all characterized by this specialliy, so they have been called the six substances of the Jaina system of thought. This is one way of dealing with the concept of substances. The other way of dealing with same subject is etyomological. In Sanskrit, the term '*dravya*' is derived from the root '*dru*' which implies liquefaction or flow. so a substance (*dravya*) is defined as that which liquefies or flows into its attributes and modes to continue in terms of its attribute and modes. This speciality is also seen in every substance, and thus it can also work as a definition of substance. Actually speaking the kernel of reality is substance, and it exists and continues in terms of its attributes and modes. We can never think of a substance without its attributes and modes. A substance is not a distinct entity running under its attributes and modes, nor are attributes and modes distinct entities covering their substance under them. A substance is identified with and also analysed into attributes which originate and determine the flow of the substance into varied channels. We cognize a substance in terms of its attributes and modes. It may also be held that the generality of modes (dependent on an attribute) is an attribute and the generality of the attributes of substance can be understood as a substance.

ध्रौव्योत्पादलयालीढा सत्ता सर्वपदार्थगा।
एकशोऽनन्तपर्याया प्रतिपक्षसमन्विता ॥6॥

Imbued with permanence, origination and decay existence permeates all the reals. It can have one to infinite modes and is (also) coeval with its antithesis.

A real must be characterized by existence and existence means a compendium of permanence, origination and decay-all the three put into one. Origination and decay refer to the modal aspect of the real, what implies origination and decay is an attribute and the variety of attributes implies the unity of substance. Thus goes the existence of reality. This unity of substance is analysable into a variety of attributes or rather an infinity of attributes. These attributes have their individual flows, and thus each of them is responsible for generating an infinity of modes.

The above trio is covered under two groups, one covering permanence and the other covering origination and decay. Hence reality is described as permanent-cum-impermanent. A number of such dyads are assigned to reality under the Jaina non-absolutism. The apparent contradiction is dispelled by the logic of view points (*nayas*) in Jaina philosophy. By assigning proper reference-systems the truth of the thesis and the antithesis is maintained consistently. Reality, by its vey nature, admits of such nature; and hence its cognition, explanation and communication must be accordingly maintained.

नश्यत्युत्पद्यते भावः पर्यायापेक्षयाखिलः ।
नश्यत्युद्यते कश्चिन्न द्रव्यापेक्षया पुनः ॥7॥

The totality of existance decays and originates from the modal point of view. Again, from the point of view of substance, no existence decays and originates.

The position is further explained and made concrete. The application of the point of view of modes makes reality decaying and originating. If the point of view of substance is adopted, reality does not suffer from origination and decay. Change is determined by the adoption of the modal point of view and permanence is determined by the substance point of view. Such a situation emanates from the very nature of reality.

किंचित् सम्भवति द्रव्यं न विना गुण-पर्ययैः ।
सम्भवन्ति विना द्रव्यं न गुणा न च पर्ययाः ॥8॥

No substance is possible with attributes and modes; neither attributes nor modes are possible without substance.

The relation; between a substance and its attributes into which it is only analysed and its modes which result from the flow of attributes, is that of identity. Hence a substance exists in terms of its attributes and endures in terms of modes of its attributes. Conversely, we cannot get a substance without its attributes and modes, and no attributes and modes can be obtained without a substance.

धर्माधर्मैकजीवानां प्रदेशानामसंख्यया।
अवष्टब्धो नभोदेशः प्रदेशः परमाणुना ॥9॥

A part of space i,e the universe is occupied by an innumerable units of *dharma, adharma* and one *jīva;* and the unit of space (called *pradeśa*) is occupied by an atom.

The substance of *dharma, adharma* and one *jīva* exists in the cosmos - a part of the universe. The magnitude of these substances is measured in terms of their units, each unit conceived as coeval with the unit of matter. The number of souls is infinite, and what is said of one soul applies to all the souls taken individually. The substances of *dharma, adharma* and *jīvas* are seen in the cosmos, which when, measured in the above manner possess innumerable units each. The susbtance of soul or *jīva which*, as will be explained later, possesses the capacity of contraction and expansion, does not occupy the whole of cosmos; but the number of its units remains the same whatever size it may assume. If a soul happens to attain its maximum expansion, it will also occupy the whole of the cosmos like *dharma* and *adharma.* The substance of space extends beyond the cosmos. As all the substances are real; the way of their existance and measurement as explained above is a necessary implication of the Jaina theory of existence.

द्रव्यमात्मादिमध्यान्तमविभागमतीन्द्रियम् ।
अविनाश्यमग्निशस्त्राद्यैः परमाणुरुदाहृतम् ॥10॥

An atom is said to a substance, without beginning, middle and end, indivisible, beyond sense perception, and without destruction by fire or (any other) weapon.

An atom is taken to be the unit of measurement for all the susbtances both in respect of substanliality and expansion. An atom is an indivisble part of matter; it is a distinct substance like other substances. It is obtained by an ultimate division of matter, hence it is so small that the beginning, the middle and the end are indistinguishable in it. For the same reason it cannot be further divided, and cannot be percieved with the help of the senses. The existence of the atom cannot be wiped out by any means possible in nature or made with human efforts. It may also be noted that the number of units of the substances as mentioned above does not give us a vague or a rough measurement. The Jaina theory of number gives us mainly three classes of numeration. They are the numerable (*saṁkhyāta*), the innumerable (*asaṁkhyāta*) and the infinite (*ananta*). All these numbers are definite, though not all comprehensible and expressible by us; only a part of the numberable is amenable to human undertstanding. Just as a substantial basis is necessary to definitise the substanes, so also numerical basis must be there to further strengthen the reality of the substances.

प्रदेशा नभसोऽनन्ता अनन्तानन्तमानकाः ।
पुद्गलानां जिनैरुक्ताः परमाणुरसंशकः ॥11॥

It has been said by Jina that the units of space are infinite, those of matter are 'infinite times infinite' and an atom has no (such) units.

The measurement of the substances in terms of units devised in the aforesaid manner is now extended to space and matter. We should not feel bewildered to see the definiteness of the number 'infinite' which represents the extension of space. Again, we see that the number infinite is multiplied by infinite to get another number which represents the magnitude of the substance of matter. The manner by which all the substances exist has also been explained above by the *āchārya.* Coming to the existence of an atom, no type of number of such units has been affirmed of it. It means that an atom does not possess all the three types of numbers. The reason for such a treatment in case of an atom may be traced in the Jaina theory of numbers, where categorization starts with the number 2, not with 1. The number 1 falls under no category of number, hence the negation of numeration in case of an atom is admitted. If an atom is denied its existence (not extension) in one unit of space, it will lose its existance. Moreover, an atom has been taken as a unit to determine the numeration of units in various substances.

असंख्या भुवनाकाशे कालस्य परमाणवः।
एकैका व्यतिरिक्तास्ते रत्नानामिव राशयः ॥12॥

The units of the substance of time (*kāla*) are innumerable (and exist) in the cosmos. They are separate (mutually) as one from the other like the heaps of jewels.

For some speciality the substance of time (*kāla*) is now taken up separately by the *āchārya.* This substance exists in time atoms, each time atom holding the status of a substance. They exist in the whole of the cosmos which extends over innumerable space-atoms. Hence the number of time-atoms, mutually substantially distinguishable, is held to be innumerable. Just as in a heap of jewels or grains of oil seed, the jewels and the oild seeds exist separately, so the time-atoms exist in the cosmos separately from each other. Thus the innumerable time-atoms collectively constitute the substance of time.

धर्माधर्मौ स्थितौ व्याप्य लोकाकाशमशेषकम् ।
व्योमैकांशादिषु ज्ञेयाः पुद्गलानामवस्थितिः ॥13॥

The substances of *dharma* and *adharma* exist permeating the entirety of the cosmos; the existemce of (atoms and particles of) matter should be known to be on the parts of space (beginning) from one part etc. (to so many parts).

The extension of the substances of *dharma*, *adharma* and matter are described in this verse. *Dharma* and *Adharma* (not merit and demerit), occupy the whole of space in the cosmos, or they extend over the innumerable space-units of the cosmos. Hence they are measured as each having innumerable such units. The position of existence in case of material atoms and their conglomerations is different. They occupy space-points or units beginning from one to many; an atom always occupies only one space-unit.

लोकासंख्येयभागादाववस्थानं शरीरिणाम् ।
अंशा विसर्प-संहारौ दीपानामिव कुर्वते ॥14॥

The existence of the embodied (souls) is on the innumerable parts of the cosmos. The soul-units (of the embodied souls) undergo extension and contraction like (the light of) the lamps.

The extension of the substance of a soul is now taken up for exposition. We have been already informed of the fact that the souls are infinite in number, each holding the status of a substance.So what is said of one soul or souls in general applies to all the souls individually. Regarding the extension of the substance of the soul, it should be noted that it is variable, and it is so only under the pressure of the *karmas*. Hence when the *karma* shackles are completely dropped, it is but natural that the soul should be free from contraction and expansion. Thus in liberation the soul will have only one extension i.e. of its last embodiment. The processes of extension of a soul take place by the interpenetration and the reverse of it i.e. extirpation of the soul-units, there is no loss or gain of soul-units under these processes and there is no change in the magnitude of a substance anywhere.

जीवानां पुद्‌गलानां च धर्माधर्मौ गति-स्थिती।
अवकाशं नभः कालो वर्तनां कुरुते सदा ॥15॥

Dharma and *adharma* perform the functions of motion and rest for the *jīvas* and the (atoms and molecules of) matter, space performs the function of accommodation and (the substance of) time performs the function of continuance.

The function as motion, rest, accommodation and continuance are performed by the substances as given in the verse. The way of performing these functions is not direct or active, but it is indirect or passive. It means that the proximity and presence of these substances is potent to cause these functions. It should never be taken to mean the superfluity of their existence, for in their absence occurence of the corresponding function will become impossible.

The auxiliary, indirect and passive functions of the substances of *dharma, adharma,* space and time are illustrated by water helping the fish in their movement, by shade stopping a tired traveller for rest, by milk absorbing the little particles of powdered sugar, and by the base under the potter's wheel in the continuance of the motion of the wheel respectively. These illustrations may not explain the nature of passive causation fully but they certainly give us an idea of the passive (*nimitta*) causation.

संसार'वर्तनोऽन्योन्यमुपकारं वितन्वते।
मुक्तास्तद्‌व्यतिरेकेण न कस्याप्युपकुर्वते ॥16॥

Jivas wandering in the world do (some) secondary or

virtual work to eaeh other; to distinguish it from *'kāra'* which must involve the transformation of the cause into effect. As regards the modes of the same substance which itself undergoes a transformation from one mode to another, the term *'kāra'* is very justly applied. Where such transformation is not seen and the process is carried on after the manner of auxiliary or *nimitta* causation, we need another term to express and explain the position. Such a term is wisely coined as *'upakāra'* or secondary, virtual, auxiliary or *nimitta* work. This restriction results from the very nature of a substance as an entity which does not give anything of itself or does not absorb anything from others. The conception is comparable with Leibnitz's monadology which holds its monads to be perfectly closed. Under the circumstances the mutual *'upakāra'* of *jivas* must be subserveint to the Jaina theory of substance. Actually speaking what is said to be the *upakāra* of one *jīva* to another is the acceptance by one *jīva* of the work done by another. The capcity to accept such work lies with the *jīva* itself, and hence the process becomes possible. In case of the liberated *jīvas*, who have completely freed themselves from the *karmas*, the capacity required for the process of *upakāra* has also been finished for ever, so they are said to be performing no *upakāra* to any other entity the possibility of *'kāra'* being out of question. Under this auxiliary or *nimitta* theory of causation our devotional worshipful and eulogical attitudes and actions can be consistently explained. The worldly souls themselves accept the auxilary causation of the liberated souls to help themselves on the path of spiritual evolution, while the liberated ones do not project themselves as causing or helping the cause of such events. Factually the auxiliary or *nimitta* theory comes out to be the true theory of causation in case of various substances.

जीवितं मरणं सौख्यं दुःखं कुर्वन्ति पुद्गलाः।
उपकारेण जीवानां भ्रमतां भवकानने ॥17॥

The plurality of matter (*karmas* of various types) do (cause) animation, death, pleasure and pain to the *jīvas* wandering in the forest of the world after the manner of *upakāra* (as explained above).

The wandering souls undergo the states of living, dying, pleasure and pain on account of their association with matter, specially the material *karmas*. This association of *karma*-matter works upon the souls after the manner of the aforesaid auxiliary causation; so also the matter transforms itself into *karma* matter in the same manner and causes various states to the soul. In liberation the situation undergoes a change which keeps the souls free from such variations, hence they constitute no party in the above relationship and thus are free from such states as take place in case of worldly souls.

पदार्थानां निमग्नानां स्वरूपं परमार्थतः।
करोति कोऽपि कस्यापि न किंचन कदाचन ॥18॥

From the real point of view, all entities being absorbed in their own identity, no one ever does anything to any other entity.

If we fix our attention on the entities themselves as free from the auxiliary causation prevalent among them, we perceive that all entities are self-determined and need no assistance, even in the form of auxiliary or *nimitta* causation, for their continuance and for the flow of their self-determined modes. This sort of self-determination is very essential for the existence of all the substance. This sort of manifestation and transformation exists in case of the liberated souls, and the substances of *dharma*, *adharma*, space and time; and it is designated as natural (*svabhāvika*) manifestation. The changes and manifestations which take place between the worldly souls and matter and are mutually vitiated and contaminated, are designated as vitiated (*vibhāva*) manifestations. They may be concessionally held to give us a form of interactionism as upheld in Jaina philosophy, but it does not suffer at all from the mutual transformations of substances between the souls and matter (karma).

स्कन्धो देशः प्रदेशोऽणुश्चतुर्धा पुद्गलो मतः।
समस्तमर्धमर्धार्धममिविभागमिमं विदुः ॥19॥

Matter has been conceived in its four varieties i.e. (full) molecule, part molecule, part of the part-molecule and the indivisible atom. They (great seers) describe it (so).

We just come across big or small moelcules of matter in our perception. It has been called a moelcule (*skandha*). The half of it is called the part-molecule (*deśa skandha*). Again, the half of it is called the part of a part-skandha (*pradeśa skandha*). Lastly when it its further divided to a stage where further division is not possible, such an indivisible part of a molecule is called the atom (*parmānu*). This scheme is drawn to understand the magnitude of matter in its varied forms.

सूक्ष्मैः सूक्ष्मतरैर्लोकः स्थूलैः स्थूलतरैश्चितः।
अनन्तैः पुद्गलैश्चित्रैः कुम्भो धूमैरिवाभितः ॥20॥

The cosmos is all full with various subtle, subtler and gross, grosser infinite molecules of matter like a pot (filled) with smoke.

No part of the cosmos is without the presence of matter found in a varicty of nature, form and magnitude. Infinitely huge amount of matter occupies the entire extension of the cosmos in a compact way. We may see matter existing in a dispersed form only in case of gross matter, but fine matter leaves no space-points vacant. Nay, matter finds accommodation in the cosmos not only in a compact way but by mutual interpretation also. This is the only way by which infinite matter can be accommoded in the innumerable (not infinite) space-points of the cosmos.

मूर्तामूर्तं द्विधा द्रव्यं मूर्तामूर्तैर्गुणैर्युतम्।
अक्षग्राह्या गुणा मूर्ता अमूर्ता सन्त्यतीन्द्रियाः ॥21॥

Being with their corporeal and incorporeal attributes the substances are said to be corporeal and incorporeal. The attributes comprehensible by the senses are corporeal and (those) beyond comprehensibility by the senses are incorporeal.

All the six substances along with an infinity of *jīvas* and infinite times infinite matter are grouped under two classes, the corporeal and the incorporeal. The attributes of these substances are also grouped into the same classes of the coroporeal and the incorporeal ones; the definition of these attributes is ascertanied on the basis of their comprehension, which must imply such nature behind the definitions. We are favoured with five senses and mind. In general the corporeality is defined by their comprehensibility by the senses. The senses too are seen varying in their power of comprehension. Moreover, with the help of the newly devised instruments the power of sensuous comprehension can be enhanced very considerably. So for fixing a standard of this power a very feeble mention and discussion has been given. This unhesitatingly leads to the acceptance of sense-comprehensibility in all its details as a defining characterestic for the concept of corperporeality. But in case of an atom of matter, it has been very clearly mentioned that it is totally beyond sense comprehension. Similar is the case with fine matter, known by the term *'vargaṇā'*, meaning a conglomeration of fine particles and atoms of matter. The difficulty is noted out and dissolved by holding that the statement is not very exact but only concessional and practical.

Behind the whole scene so represented the true secret, seems to lurking below these situations and statements. We may well see that there is something in the substances and their attributes that disenables the senses to comprehend them in the general and tangible ways of our comprehension. Gradually deviating from this kernel of reality by stages the formation and enunciation of varying and modifiable definitions is made possible.

कर्मवेदयमानस्य भावाः सन्ति शुभाशुभाः ।
कर्मभावं प्रपद्यन्ते संसक्तास्तेषु पुद्गलाः ॥22॥

The meritorious and the demeritorious (conscious) modifications are seen in one (self) under the experience of the *karma* (effect). Fine material particles attendent on such modifications gain the nature of *karmas*.

Now the *āchārya* begins a study of matter, specially fine matter, with reference to the conscious *jīvas*. The matter in its entirety is not the subject of our study. There exists a very fine matter which can be so associated with our consious activities. On account of the special capacity of matter, the fine matter, under consideration at present, actualizes its capacity into *karmas* and gets associated with the worldly souls to contaminate them in various ways.

योगेन ये समायान्ति शस्ताशस्तेन पुद्गलाः ।
तेऽष्टकर्मत्वमिच्छन्ति कषाय-परिणामतः ॥23॥

(Such fine particles of) matter enter (thc soul) through the meritorious and demeritorious vibrations (*yoga*) on the part of the soul. They (then) transform (themselves) into eight kinds of *karma* on account of the manifestation of passions (of various kinds).

We have already seen that a soul must occupy a part of space to make its existence possible. The worldly souls find lodgement in physical bodies of varying magnitude, their capacity for expansion and contraction becomes a necessary conclusion. Besides, one more capacity in the substance of the soul for vibrating activity is supposed to reside in the soul, though due to its association with the various types of *karmas*; nay, Jaina philosophy is very sure about it. This vibrating activity of a soul takes place and is explained in terms of the soul-units. This very activity of the soul is held responsible for the entrance of the particles of *karma*-matter into its constitution. Then the process is helped and furthered by the generation of the various passions in the soul to effect a division of the *karma*-matter into eight basic kinds of *karma*.

ज्ञान-दृष्टयावृती वेद्यं मोहनीयायुषी विदुः।
नाम-गोत्रान्तरायौ च कर्माण्यष्टेति सूरयः ॥24॥

The *āchārya* enumerate the eight *karmas* as knowledge-obscuring, conation-obscuring, feeling, deluding, age-determining, body-making, status-determining and the obstructing ones.

The eight primary types of *karmas*, as mentioned in the previous verse, are enumerated herein. Though further divided into one hundred and forty eight secondary types, they are so devised as to cover the various functions of the worldly souls. These *karmas* nullify, obstruct and distort the various powers of the soul, which flourish fully and freely in the state of liberation.

कल्मषोदयतो भावो यो जीवस्य प्रजायते।
स कर्ता तस्य भावस्य कर्मणो न कदाचन ॥25॥

Whatever manifestation of a *jīva* is generated on account of the operation of the (filth) *karmas*, the *jiva* is the doer of that manifestation (alone), (it is) never (the doer) of the (material) *karma*.

The underlying truth of the relationship between a conscious soul and the unconscious *karma*-matter is that the soul is responsible for the generation of its conscious manifestations, and the material *karmas* follow their own ways for their different manifestations. This position is an outcome from the basic theory of mutual non-reduction and non-transformation among the various susbtances. Still the close relationship between the two is admitted and explained by the theory of auxiliary or *nimitta*-causation in Jaina philosophy.

विविधाः पुद्गलाः स्कन्धाः सम्पद्यन्ते यथा स्वयम्।
कर्मणामपि निष्पत्तिरपरैरकृता तथा ॥26॥

Just as various types of matter and their molecules come into existence by themselves, so also the accomplishment of *karma* (into its various forms) is not determined by anything else.

We have seen in the previous verse that the *jīva* does not require anything other than itself to genarate its manifestations. In the present verse the same independence is said to be granted to matter and *karmas*.

कर्मभावं प्रपद्यन्ते न कदाचन चेतनाः।
कर्म चैतन्यभावं वा स्वस्वभावव्यवस्थितेः ॥27॥

The conscious substances can never gain the nature of *karma*, the *karma*-matter (can never gain) the nature of consciousness. Such is the order (of the world) in terms of the individual nature (of the various susbstances and entities).

Nature has placed the contents of the cosmos, the various substances and entities, in such a way that they are determinable only in terms of their individual potentialities. In view of the limitations imposed on the various substances by nature their mutual transformation is out of question. This is also necessary to save the cosmic arrangement from falling into a chaos. We may not advance our reasoning against this natural order and arrangement.

जीवः करोति कर्माणि यद्युपादानभावतः।
चेतनत्वं तदा नूनं कर्मणो वार्यते कथम् ॥28॥

If a *jīva* does the *karmas* by transforming itself into *karmas,* how then the transformation of *karma* into conscious (entity) can be warded off?

यद्युपादानभावेन विधत्ते कर्म चेतनम्।
अचेतनत्वमेतस्य तदा केन निषिध्यते ॥29॥

(Similarly) if *karma* does the conscious (*jīva*) by transforming itself into *jīva*, how can then uncosciousness be denied of it (*jīva*).

एवं सम्पद्यते दोषः सर्वथापि दुरुत्तरः।
चेतनाचेतनद्रव्यविशेषाभावलक्षणः ॥30॥

Thus there occurs the absolutely unsolvable fallacy defined as the absence of differentia between the conscious and unconscious (entities).

If the contentions that the *jīva* does the *karmas* or the *karma* does the *jīva* by mutual transformation of their substances, a very serious type of inconsistency of annihilating the differentiating characteristics of the two, occurs there. This situation is bound to contradict the basic conception that the various substances are distinct and mutually irreducible, and it will also turn the cosmos into a chaos.

सरागं जीवमाश्रित्य कर्मत्वं यान्ति पुद्गलाः।
कर्माण्याश्रित्य जीवोऽपि सरागत्वं प्रपद्यते ॥31॥

Material particles, on account of their association with a *jīva* with attachment, gain the capacity of being *karmas;* a *jīva* on account of its association with (such) *karmas* gains the capacity of being with attachment.

The theory of relationship between *jīva* and *karmas* comes out to be a form of occasionalism, one is only an occasion for change in the other. This theory saves the situation from falling into the inconsistent and hence absolutely unanswerable positions upheld by interactionims and parallelism. This theory saves the situation form the annihilation of boundaries supplied to every susbtance to manitain its individuality, without which the cosmos will be totally deprived of its natural order. This very theory has been designated as the theory of auxiliary or *nimitta* causation.

कर्म चेत् कुरुते भावो जीवः कर्ता तदा कथम्।
न किंचित् कुरुते जीवो हित्वा भावं निजं परम् ॥32॥

If *karma* does the manifestations (of *jīva*), then how can *jīva* be held to be the doer (of those manifestations). (Actually speaking) the *jīva* does nothing else except its own manifestations.

If we do not take the theory of auxiliary causation into our purview, the *jīva* is left alone to generate its manifestation completely unaffected by the associations of *karmas, thus* disturbing their mutual auxiliary causation.

कर्मतो जायते भावो भावतः कर्म सर्वदा।
इत्थं कर्तृत्वमन्योन्यं द्रष्टव्यं भाव-कर्मणोः ॥33॥

(With the acceptance of the theory of auxiliary causation) the manifcstations (of *jīva*) are always generated by *karma* and (those of *karma*) are generated by *jīva*. Thus the mutual doership of the (manifestations of) jīva and *karma* should be seen (understood).

It is the theory of auxiliary causation that holds the mutual doership between the *jīva* and the *karma* possible. In ultimacy this theory itself does not hold good, hence such a relationship between *jīva* and *karma* (i.e. matter) will not yeild a true explanation of the position.

कोपादिभिः कृतं कर्म जीवेन कृतमुच्यते।
पदातिभिर्जितं युद्धं जितं भूपतिना यथा ॥34॥

(From the practical point of view) actions done with anger etc. are said to be done by the *jīva*, just as a battle conquered by the (fighting) infantrymen is said to be conquered by the king.

देह-संहति-संस्थान-गति-जाति-पुरोगमाः।
विकाराः कर्मजा सर्वे चैतन्येन विवर्जिताः ॥35॥

Body, bony structure, form of body, conditions of life, generality of bodily structure etc. (associated with the *jīva*) are all the *karma*-generated malignant manifestations (of the *jīva*), all of them being bereft of consciousness.

मिथ्यादृक् सासनो मिश्रोऽसंयतो देश-संयतः।
प्रमत्त इतरोऽपूर्वस्तत्त्वज्ञैरनिवृत्तकः ॥36॥
सूक्ष्मः शान्तः परः क्षीणो योगी चेति त्रयोदश।
गुणाः पौद्गलिकाः प्रोक्ताः कर्म प्रकृतिनिर्मिताः ॥37॥

The thirteen stages of the spiritual evolution i.e. the stages of wrong faith (*mithyātva*), downfall (*sāsādana*), mixed (*samyak-mithyātva*), *unrestraint* (*asaṁyata*), part restraint (*deśa saṁyata*), with indolence (*pramatta*), without indolence (*apramatta*), unforeseen thought-activity (*apūrva*), advanced thought-activity (*anivṛtti karaṇa*), slight delusion (*sūkṣma moha*), subsided delusion (*upaśanta moha*), destructed delusion (*ksīṇa moha*) and with vibration of soul-units (*sayogī*) are (all) material and determined by the varieties of *karmas*.

The above two verses contain the names of the thirteen stages of spiritual evolution. The English translation of these technical and defining terms can give only a faint idea about the stages. A detailed descripiton of the same may be seen in works written mainly on these stages. It will be seen that these stagtes emerge mainly on the different states of the faith-duluding and the conduct-deluding *karmas*, alongwith vibratory activity in the soul-units being their necessary accompaniment. Keeping in view the pure state of the soul none of these stages are intrinsic to the nature of the soul, hence in themselves they are all material and anti-spiritual. There is one more and last stage on the path, which is marked by the total cessation of the vibrations of soul-units. Its duration is very short. After this stage the pure soul flies to the top of the universe to live there in full effulgence of spiritual powers with no fear of fall into worldly existence. The true seekers of the spiritual relization must not get entangled with these stages, this will amount to his attachment with what is anti-spiritual in the true sense.

देह-चेतनयोरैक्यं मन्यमानैर्विमोहितैः।
एते जीवा निगद्यन्ते न विवेक-विशारदैः ॥38॥

By the deluded (persons) who believes in the oneness of the body and consciousness (such souls) are said to be *jīvas,* (they) are not described (so) by those well-versed in discriminatory knowledge.

The conclusion of this discussion carried on in the previous verses is now pronounced by the *āchārya* in this verse. It is some type of delusion that keeps the *jīvas* confined and identified with these stages of spiritual evolution. Those who have risen in their realization of the pure soul never fall a victim of such delusion.

प्रमत्तादिगुणस्थानवन्दना या विधीयते।
न तया वन्दिता सन्ति मुनयश्चेतनात्मकाः ॥39॥

Whatever salutation is done to the saints of the spiritual stages beginning from one with indolence (*paramatta*) (to the *sayoga kevalī*), by that the saints identified by consciousness are not saluted.

In all the stages of spiritual evolution the souls are found with physical bodies. The homage paid to them is performed in terms of the physical body; hence it does not touch the saints (their souls) because they are conscious; while their bodies are material and unconscious. If such is the situation, the reason for our current religious practices must be traced out.

परं शुभोपयोगाय जायमाना शरीरिणाम् ।
ददाति विविधं पुण्यं संसार-सुखकारणम् ॥40॥

But the (act of) salutation done to the embodied (saints) goes as the meritorious conscious action. It grants a variety of merit which is the cause of the worldly peace (and pleasure).

The question regarding the salutation done to the embodied saints is being answered in the present verse. It is true that the bodies of the saints cannot be a substitute for their pious souls, but these bodies alone are perceievable by us. So our actions like salutatation done to them are limited to their bodies. Such actions can also be held desirable and useful as they grant us easy and comfortable conditions of life which are very likely to take us nearer and nearer to our goal. Very few persons are able to rise above the bodily conditions and attend to and meditate on the pure spiritual conditions in which the rising souls are placed.

नाचेतने स्तुते देहे स्तुतोऽस्ति ज्ञानलक्षणः ।
न कोशे वर्णिते नूनं सायकस्यास्ति वर्णना ॥41॥

On the unconscious body being eulogised the one (*jīva*)

distinguished by knowledge is not eulogised. Verily, on the sheath being described, it cannot be a description of the sword.

The truth that the soul and its embodiment are very different from each other is again asserted and illustrated by an example of the sword and its cover, well known for their separate identities.

यत्र प्रतीयमानेऽपि न यो जातु प्रतीयते।
स ततः सर्वथा भिन्नो रसाद् रूपमिव स्फुटम् ॥42॥
काये प्रतीयमानेऽपि चेतनो न प्रतीयते।
यतस्ततस्ततो भिन्नो न भिन्नो ज्ञानलक्षणात् ॥43॥

One which is never perceived on the perception of something (other than the one) is quite clearly distinct from that something like shape and colour (rūpa) from taste (of a thing).

The body even being perceived, the conscious (soul) is not perceived. Because of this the conscious soul is different (and distinct from the body), but it is not different from (its) differentia of knowledge.

Now an argument is advanced to establish the distinction between the conscious soul and the unconsious body. Some thing that is not perceived in the presence of some other thing, must be held distinict from it, the two things cannot be identical. Some thing, which is necessarily perceived in the presence of some thing else may be held identical with it. The concepts of identity and distinction are introduced after the manner which is adopted in applying the joint method of Agreement Enunciated by Mill in the list of his five methods of Inductive Logic and difference to determine causality. Thus our convictions about the position get confirmed.

दृश्यते ज्ञायते किंचिद् यदक्षैरनुभूयते।
तत् सर्वमात्मनो बाह्यं विनश्वरमचेतनम् ॥44॥

Whatever is perceived, known and experienced with the (help of) senses, is entirely external to (different from) the soul, (is) subject to destruction and (is) unconscious.

न निर्वृतिं गतस्यास्ति तद्रूपं किंचितदात्मनः ।
अचेतनमिदं प्रोक्तं सर्वं पौद्गलिकं जिनैः ॥45॥

No (such) characteristic belongs to a liberated soul. (Lord) *Jinas* have described all that as material and unconscious.

After describing some essential charateristics of what is material, it is emphasized that none of them belong to the pure souls in liberation. No identity (oneness) is possible between the conscious *jīva* and unconscious matter.

विकाराः सन्ति ये केचिद्रागद्वेषमदादयः ।
कर्मजास्तेऽखिला ज्ञेयास्तिग्मांशोरिव मेघजाः ॥46॥

Whatever malignant manifestation like attachment, aversion, pride etc. are there, they are all to be known as born of *karma* like the sun's part-brilliance generated by the (covering) born of clouds.

The psychological phenomena like attachment, averion, pride etc. present a difficulty. On the psychological level they cannot be called purely material and unconscious. Pure souls and pure matter both are unable to generate them. As some of *āchāryas* have described them, they are the joint products of conscious souls and unconcious matter, partly sharing the properties of the two. An example is often quoted to explain the situation. Just as the birth of a son is due to the joint efforts of the father and the mother and none of them taken singly can bring about such a result; in the same way the occurance of the psychological phenomena can be made explainable and understandable. The entire process goes on after the fashion of auxiliary or *nimitta* causation, and is held true under the practical point of view. From the pure point of view the *jīva* and matter are quite different and distinct, and no iota of the substance of one is transerable into that of the other. This point of view does not admit even the existence of such joint products. So all the psychological phenomena are declared material under the pure point of view.

अनादावपि सम्बन्धे जीवस्य सह कर्मणा।
न जीवो याति कर्मत्वं जीवत्वं कर्म वा स्फुटम् ॥47॥

Inspite of the beginningless relationship of the *jīva* with the *karma*, clearly neither the *jīva* gains the nature of the *karma*; nor the *karma*, that of the *jīva*.

The *jīva* and the *karma* have been together in their worldly existence which, too, has no beginning. It again causes some tantalization. If we hold that this relationship has a beginning, then the *jīva* must be pure before that point of time. If so, we again are unable to find out a cause of fall of the *jīva* into the labyrinths of the world. So both logically and existentially the beginningless relation between the two is the only consistent position. Inspite of the fact that the two have been so close to each other both in time and space, they have not been able to become one substantially.

आत्मना कुरुते कर्म यद्यात्मा निश्चितं तदा।
कथं तस्य फलं भुङ्क्ते स दत्ते कर्म वा कथम् ॥48॥

If it is certain that the soul does the *karma* by the soul (itself), then how does (the soul) enjoy the fruit of it (the *karma*) or how the *karma* gives it (the fruit) to the soul.

From the pure and real point of view the soul is held doing pure acts by itself, the intervention of material *karma* does not arise between the soul and its acts. This means that the soul is alone in its continuance along with its pure modes. In such a situation the distinction between the soul's acts and fruits thereof vanishes; and there remains only the continuance of the soul without doing anything or enjoying anything.

कर्मणामुदयसंभवा गुणाः शामिकाः क्षयशमोद्भवाश्च ये।
चित्रशास्त्रनिवहेन वर्णितास्ते भवन्ति निखिला विचेतनाः ॥49॥

Whatever specialities (manifestations) like the operative generated by the operation of *karma*, the subsidential (emerging on the subsidence of *karmas*), destructive (emerging on the destruction of *karmas*) and destructive-cum-subsidential (emerging on the subsidence equated with destruction of *karmas*) are there, all of them have been described by the group of various scriptures as unconscious (material).

From the real point of view the five types of manifestations (generally held to be belonging to the soul from the practical point of view) have been isolated from the continuance of the pure soul, and are declared unconscious and material for being generated by one or the other state of the material *karmas*. It is only under the theory of auxiliary causation the truth of such psychological phenomena becomes acceptable from the practical point of view. The underlying and essential truth is that not even an iota of the substance of the soul can be transformed into matter of *karma* and vice-versa. As has already been shown, this rigid state of the contents of the cosmos is very essential to save it from becoming a chaos.

अजीवतत्त्वं न विदन्ति सम्यग् ये जीवतत्त्वाद्विधिना विभक्तम्।
चारित्रवन्तोऽपि न ते लभन्ते विविक्तमात्मानमपास्तदोषम् ॥50॥

Those who do not know well the principle of *ajīva* (covered under the category called *ajīva*), as distinct from the principle of *jīva* (the conscious soul), rationally (logically and by experience), will not realize the soul as chiselled and bereft of (all) blemishes, inspite of their attainment of (good) conduct by them.

This is the concluding verse of the chapter. It emphasizes the necessity of deep knowledge of the principle of *ajīva* also to safeguard the knowledge of the principle of *jīva* in its pure form. The two principles i.e. the *jīva* and the *ajīva*, have been in a very close relationship with each other spatially, temporarily and even functionally in the world from times immemorial and begnningless. This state leads to a very deep and fatal confusion between the two. Discriminatory knowledge of the two is the only means to carve out a way to our destination the redemption of the soul from the wanderings and sufferings of the world. It is the only light that can lead us to the self-enlightened divine status of Godhood.

Here ends Chapter-2, Ajīvādhikāra of Yogasāra-prābhṛta by Āchārya Amitagati.

Chapter 3

Āsravādhikāra

शुभाशुभोपयोगेन वासिता योगवृत्तयः।
सामान्येन प्रजायन्ते दुरितास्रव-हेतवः ॥1॥

The activities (of mind, speech and body), when perfumed (after the manner of auxiliary causation) by meritorius and demeritorious manifestations (of the soul), become, in general, the causes of the inflow of *karmas* (into the soul).

The souls perform various activities through the media of mind, speech and body. These activities have a counterpart in the substance of the souls in the form of vibrations of the soul-units. This counterpart has been technically called the '*yoga*'. It accepts the auxiliary causality of three types of fine matter of mind, speech and body designated as *mano varganā*, *bhāṣā vargaṇā* and *kāya vargaṇā.* This vibratory activity on the part of the souls gets associated with their conscious manifestations and thus it is able to cause the inflow of karmic matter into the souls. This process taking place between the souls and the fine molecules of *karma*-matter has been termed as the principle of inflow (*āsravatattva*).

मिथ्या-दृक्त्वमचारित्रं कषायो योग इत्यमी।
चत्वारः प्रत्ययाः सन्ति विशेषेणाघ-संग्रहे ॥2॥

Specially wrong faith, non-restraint, passion and activity (vibratory activity), are the four causes (in the process) of attracting *karma*-matter.

Wrong faith, non-restraint and passions are the meritorious and demeritorious manifestations of the worldly souls. They go to assist the vibratory activity of the soul to enable it to attract the karma-matter. So in finality it is the vibratory activity of the souls, which can be directly held to be responsible for the inflow of karma-matter. It is why the vibratory activity has been described as the inflow (*āsrava*) itself. Very often the vibrating activities dependent on mind, speech and body are called the three channels by which the karma-matter flows into the souls. It means that if these three channels are somehow closed the entry of the karma-matter into the soul will be stopped.

सचित्ताचित्तयोर्यावद्द्रव्ययोः परयोरयम्।
आत्मीयत्त्व-मतिं धत्ते तावन्मोहो विवर्धते ॥3॥

So long as this *jīva* identifies itself with other animate and inanimate substances, to that extent delusion (wrong faith and wrong conduct) goes on increasingly.

तेषु प्रवर्तमानस्य कर्मणामास्रवः परः।
कर्मास्रव-निमग्नस्य नोत्तारो जायते ततः ॥4॥

For one, indulged in (such) activities and completely drowned in the inflow of *karmas,* there is a heavy inflow and therefore there is no (possibility of) redemption.

मयीदं कार्मणं द्रव्यं कारणेऽत्र भवाम्यहम्।
यावदेषा मतिस्तावन् मिथ्यात्वं न निवर्तते ॥5॥

This karma-matter (or products thereof) is in me and I am there as a cause of it (karma matter). So long as (such an) understanding is there, wrong faith is not diverted (away.)

आसमस्मि भविष्यामि स्वामी देहादि-वस्तुनः।
मिथ्यादृष्टेरियं बुद्धिः कर्मागमन-कारिणी ॥6॥

'I was, I am and I shall be the owner of things like the body.' Such understanding belongs to a wrong believer, and it creates the inflow of *karma*.

चेतनेऽचेतने द्रव्ये यावदन्यत्र वर्तते।
स्वकीय-बुद्धितस्तावत्कर्मागच्छन् न वार्यते ॥7॥

So long as one indulges with other conscious and unconscious substance understanding it as self, to that extent the inflowing karma-matter cannot be diverted (away).

In the foregoing five verses the *āchārya* attempts to enumerate the various forms of wrong faith, which, with the medium of the vibrating activity of the souls, marks a beginning of the entrance of the karma-matter into the souls. The common characteristic of all these forms of wrong faith is the soul's confusion, doubt and prevision about the distinguishing features of the souls on one hand and the entirety of what is other than the souls on the other. The 'other' includes the animate and the inanimate objects like the other souls, the bodies, the possession, the karmic matter and even the perverted psychological conditions resulting from such associations. Such an understanding and inclination have been continuing with the worldly souls since the hoariest past, and, through the present, it is considered to be continuing in the long extending future. The wrong believer has not tasted at all the bliss of the discriminatory knowledge, for which reason he undergoes long spans of sufferings, wanderings in the world and the attendent restlessness - a total absence of tranquilitity and spiritual peace.

शुभाशुभस्य भावस्य कर्तात्मीयस्य वस्तुतः।
कर्तात्मा पुनरन्यस्य भावस्य व्यवहारतः ॥8॥

Really speaking, the *jīva* is the doer of its own meritorious and demeritorious manifestation; in a practical sense it is the doer of the manifestations of the 'other'.

From the existential point of view or from the psychological point of view, merit and demerit belong to the worldly souls, hence the *jīva* undergoes such manifestations in its contaminated substance. Thus the meritorious and the demeritorious perversions of the souls are accommodated only under the existential and psychological conditions, but never from the pure point of view. What is other than the *jīva*, our usage allows its manifestations to belong to the *jīva*; but it is a very common point of view.

श्रित्वा जीवपरिणामं कर्मास्त्रवति दारुणम्।
श्रित्वोदेति परीणामो दारुणः कर्मदारुणम् ॥9॥
कार्यकारणभावोऽयं परिणामस्य कर्मणा।
कर्म-चेतनयोरेष विद्यते न कदाचन ॥10॥

With the assistance of the manifestation of the *jīva* extremely painful *karma* flows into the soul. With the assistance of extremely painful *karma* the manifestation of the *jīva* emerges.

This (so called) causal relationship of the manifestation of the jīva exits with *karma*, in no case it (this relationship) exists between *karma* and conscious soul.

The theory of auxiliary causation between the *jīva* and *karma*-matter has now been given a little definite form by holding that one so continues with the assistance of the other. This is a form of Jaina Occasionalism. One member in this relationship assists the other without the least of the transformation of the substance of the one into that of the other. We have already seen that this restriction is very necessary for saving the cosmos from chaos. It is also mentioned herein that this relation of mutual assistance does not exist between the pure souls and the *karma*-matter. Hence the liability of this mutual assistance lies with the worldly souls alone, the other associate is the *karma*-matter equally present with the worldly souls and the liberated souls. Mere presence of the two members is not sufficient to effect the occasionalism of the type under consideration. Along with their presence both the relata must possess the necessary capacity for effecting the required relationship.

आत्मानं कुरुते कर्म यदि, कर्म तथा कथम्।
चेतनाय फलं दत्ते? भुङ्क्ते वा चेतनः कथम ॥11॥
परेण विहितं कर्म परेण यदि भुज्यते।
न कोऽपि सुखदुःखेभ्यस्तदानीं मुच्यते कथम् ॥12॥

If *karma*-matter does (generates) the soul (substantially), then how does *karma* awards the fruit to the soul or how does the soul suffer (or enjoy) it?

If the action done by the other (i.e. the karma) is enjoyed by the other (i.e. the soul), then how either can be freed from the pleasure and pain (so caused).

If the soul and *karma* generate each other susbtantially, it becomes exteremely difficult to determine the accountability of a bad or good action along with their pleasant or unpleasant fruits. The same fact is stated in a general form in the above verse. It is certified by our reason and practice that the award of an action should go to the one who has performed it. If the *jīva* is held to do (generate) the matter and *vice versa* substantially, the question of accountability cannot be decided constently. Moreover, if such a situation really exists between the *jīva* and its 'other', the infinite prolongation of the situation cannot be checked and stopped, leading to the impossibility of liberation which otherwise has been firmly established in *Jaina* philosophy.

जीवस्याच्छादकं कर्म निर्मलस्य मलीमसम्।
जायते भास्करस्येव शुद्धस्य घनमण्डलम् ॥13॥

The filthy *karma* obsures the pure soul, as the group of clouds covers the pure (bright) sun.

So distinct and different from *karma*, the *jīva* suffers obscuration of its faculties by it by way of covering on it generated by the *karma*. The example of the sun and covering caused by the clouds is purposed to lead us near the situation. This is another way of explaining the Jaina occasionalism between the *jīva* and *karma*. It may suggest that the *jīva* continues in its full purity and and effulgence behind the cover of the *karmas*. Then in reality no harm is done to the *jīva* by the *karmas*, and hence the need of any ethics to redeem it from its worldly state is totally nullified. There are some schools of philosophy which uphold the theory of absolute purity of the *jīva*. The Jaina may not accept the position as such absolutely, he must find out a context in which the contamination of the *jīva* also becomes real to make room for an ethics for the redemption and purification of the *jīva* itself.

कषायस्रोतसाऽगत्य जीवे कर्माऽवतिष्ठते।
आगमेनेव पानीयं जाड्यकारं सरोवरे ॥14॥

Coming in by the spring of passion the *karma* finds lodgement in the *jīva*. as frozen (solid) water stays in a pond, flowing into it through some channels.

Here by means of an example an attempt is made to bring the *karma* close to the *jīva* to coexist with it. The *jīva* is responsible to create the channels for the *karma* to flow into it in the form of its passionate manifestations. With the assistance and auxiliary causation of these possionate manifestations the *karma*-matter is attracted to be coexistent and coextensive with the substance the soul. The example of the water and the pond is meant to give us an idea of the situation and position in which the *jīva* and the *karma* are now placed.

जीवस्य निष्कषायस्य यद्यागच्छति कल्मषम्।
तदा सम्पद्यते मुक्तिर्न कस्याऽपि कदाचन ॥15॥

If filth (of *karma*) flows into a passionless *jīva*, then liberation will never be possible even to any one (soul).

Passions in the form of anger, pride, deceit and greed are the main causes of the confinement of the *jīvas* into the world. In their absence such a state of the *jīvas* must come to an end, and then the continuance of the worldly state is impossible.

नान्यद्रव्य-परीणाममन्य-द्रव्यं प्रपद्यते।
स्वान्यद्रव्य-व्यवस्थेयं परस्य(था) घटते कथम् ॥16॥

The manifestation belonging to one substance cannot be obtâined by another substance. This is the order between one susbtance and the other. How (then) can this order be possible in case of other (substance)?

A universal law regarding the relation between the manifestation of one substance and that of the other substance is enunciated herein in support of the freedom of the *jīva* from the manifestations of the *non-jīva*, specially the *karma*. The pure *jīva* will undergo its own manifestations and never those of the *karma*.

परेभ्यः सुखदुःखानि द्रव्येभ्यो यावदिच्छति।
तावदास्रव-विच्छेदो न मनागपि जायते ॥17॥

So long as one holds the (generation of) sufferings and pleasures (for one self) from (the agency of) other substances, the discontinuance of the inflow cannot take place even in the least.

It is our long imbibed tendency that we always hold other agents and conditions responsible for our sufferings and pleasures, while the truth is that we ourselves are responsible for our painful and pleasant states. This misunderstanding causes the constant inflow of *karma*-matter into the structure of our souls, and it will thus make our journey in the whirlpool of the world endless.

अचेतनत्वमज्ञात्वा स्वदेह-परदेहयोः ।
स्वकीय-परकीयात्मबुद्धिस्तत्र वर्तते ॥18॥

Being ignorant about the unconscious nature of one's (own) and other's embodiments the (perverse) understanding about one's and others' bodies as the *jīva* persists there.

Whether it is our own body and it is the consideration of other's bodies, these must be very clearly believed in and understood as utterly unconscious, while the souls, in their pure nature are conscious. In the absence of such a realization the perversion of taking the bodies as souls will go on unchecked.

यदात्मीयमनात्मीयं विनश्वरमनश्वरम् ।
सुखदं दुःखदं वेत्ति न चेतनमचेतनम् ॥19॥
पुत्र-दारादिके द्रव्ये तदात्मीयत्व-शेमुषीम् ।
कर्मास्त्रवमजानानो विधत्ते मूढमानसः ॥20॥

So long as the foolish minded *jīva* does not discriminate between its own and its 'other', between the mortal and the immortal, between pleasure-bearing and pain-bearing (entities) and between the conscious and the unconscious (entities), to that extent, not knowing the (perverse) understanding regarding his sons and wives as itself, creates the inflow of *karma*-matter (for himself).

The above described forms of misunderstanding on the part of a *jīva* are what make it ignorant about the style of life necessary for its true welfare and keep the incessant flow of *karma*-matter always active and forceful against the good of the poor and helpless *jīva*.

कषायानोपयोगेभ्यो नोपयोगाः कषायतः।
न मूर्तामूर्तयोरस्ति सम्भवो हि परस्परम् ॥21॥

Mutual generation between what in corporeal and what is non-corporeal is not possible. (Hence) passions from conscious manifestations or conscious manifestations from passions do not emanate.

Substantial irreducibility between the substances of the *jīva* and matter, specially *karma* matter is very firmly affirmed in Jaina Ontology and the same has been very expressively reaffirmed herein.

कषाय परिणामोऽस्ति जीदस्य परिणामिनः।
कषायिणोऽकषायस्य सिद्धस्येव न सर्वथा ॥22॥
न संसारो न मोक्षोऽस्ति यतोऽस्यापरिणामिनः।
निरस्त-कर्म-सङ्गश्चाऽपरिणामी ततो मतः ॥23॥

Passionate manifestation is there in a *jīva* with passion changing its modes, such a state can, in no case be possible in the passionless liberated souls.

As neither the worldly nor the liberated states are there for the non-manifesttaing (permanent) this (liberated) *jīva*, therefore the pure *jīva*, being the destroyer of *karma* associations, is accepted as non-manifesting (or non-changing).

In these verses the *jīva* is seen in its two positions i.e. the pure and the impure. We well understand that the two positions arise on account of its association with the *karmas*. The worldly changes are seen to occur in the *jīva* on account of its association with *karma*, which in turn are seen to be related with the *jīva* on account of passions. But in the present context and also form the pure point of view passions and *karmas* both are held to be material. A state of the *jīva* is envisaged where these external and substantially distinguished accompaniments of the *jīva* are completely separated and dropped down. Then what remains there is the pure *jīva* with nothing that is its 'other'. Then there is no fear and possibility of its fall into the whirling world, hence it is held to be above all these worldly manifestations coloured with passions. One, under these circumstances, should not feel disturbed in his conviction, cognition and conduct, if such *jīvas* are held above manifestations and hence permanent in their state of purity.

नान्योन्य-गुण-कर्तृत्वं विद्यते जीव-कर्मणोः ।
अन्योन्यापेक्षयोत्पत्तिः परिणामस्य केवलम् ॥24॥
स्वकीय-गुण-कर्तृत्वं तत्त्वतो जीव-कर्मणोः ।
क्रियते हि गुणस्ताभ्यां व्यवहारेण गद्यते ॥25॥

The mutual doership of attributes between *jīva* and *karma* does not exist; with mutual reference of one to the other, only the manifestation (mode) is generated (not the substance).

From the real point of view the doership (ownership) of their own individual attributes is admitted. The mutual doership of attributes by the two is admitted from the practical or concessional point of view.

The law of mutual irreducibility among the substances prohibits the generation of the attributes of one substance from those of the others. Thus the individuality of substances is maintained through the irreducibility of the attributes of one substance to those of any other. This saves the Jaina concept of the cosmos i.e. an orderly universe from being reduced to a chaos. Still we, in common parlance, are seen to say that one substance causes the attributes of the other substance. For example in case of the worldly soul wc speak of the *jīva* causing consciousness in material bodies in the form of passions and limited knowledge of various types. For making such statements we have to make a resort to the practical point of view which only takes the surface view of the facts and is not able to penetrate deep as to the reach the kernel of reality.

उत्पद्यन्ते यथा भावाः पुद्गलापेक्षयात्मनः ।
तथैवौदयिका भावाः विद्यन्ते तदपेक्षया ॥26॥

Just as the manifestations of the soul are generated with reference (auxiliary causation) to matter; so also the operative manifestations (of the soul) are found (in the soul).

So many manifestations cannot be consistently held to belong to the soul alone, because they are not pure and self-determined. The worldly or the impure souls fall a victim to the contamination caused in them by their association with matter or *karma*. This association of *karmas* just generates a vitiated capacity in the souls to accept the auxiliary causation of the *karmas*. The result is the perversion of the path of emancipation of the souls and the unfortunate and painful continuance of their journey in the *saṁsāra*. Only the pure and free manifestations of the souls are desirable on the path of liberation.

कुर्वाणः परमात्मानं सदात्मानं पुनः परम् ।
मिथ्यात्व-मोहित-स्वान्तो रजोग्राही निरन्तरम् ॥27॥

One with a deluded mind by the delusive (type of) *karma* taking (understanding) the soul as the 'other' and the 'other' as the soul, incessantly gathers the dust (of *karmas*).

राग-मत्सर-विद्वेष-लोभमोह-मदादिषु ।
हृषीक-कर्म-नोकर्म-रूप-स्पर्श-रसादिषु ॥28॥
एतेऽहमहमेतेषामिति तादात्म्यमात्मनः ।
विमूढः कल्पयन्नात्मा स्व-परत्वं न बुध्यते ॥29॥

By the perverted soul (*jīva*) that thinks about its identity (with) attachment, jealousy, enmity, greed, delusion, pride etc. and about senses, *karma*, material for embodiment, shape (colour), touch, taste etc. as itself and as it is for them, never understands the discrimination between itself and the other.

The direct effect of the operation of the deluding *karma* on the soul or *jīva* is a perversion of its faculties of faith and understanding, which is very clearly reflected in the manifestations of its faculty of conduct. Forgetting the true and pure functions of its essential faculties, it identifies itself with such manifestations. This becomes the root cause of its entanglement in a close network of the *karmas.* Such manifestations are by the *jīva* seen to be connected with the resulting psychoses and the attendent material elements and associations by a relation of identity or also by a relation of possession. Both these forms of relations and the implied ralata are highly injurious for the welfare of the *jīva.* The *jīva* is so entangled in them that it becomes almost impossible to break the trap. This fact is responsible for the *jīva's* journery in the *saṁsāra* from beginningless times, only a few of the *jīvas* have been able to get rid of it in the past.

हिंसने वितथे स्तेये मैथुने च परिग्रहे।
मनोवृत्तिरचारित्रं कारणं कर्मसन्ततेः ॥30॥

The activity of mind in (the fields of) violence, untruth, theft, coition and possession is the antithesis of (right) conduct, and is the cause of continuance of *karma.*

The *āchārya* now concludes that a *jīva's* indulgence in the five type of sins or sinful activities is equivalent to the complete pollution of the faculty of conduct of the *jīva,* and it causes the endless whirlings in the *saṁsāra* for it. The above five channels have been standardized as the main gateways for the inflow of *karmas* towards the *jīva.*

रागतो द्वेषतो भावं परद्रव्ये शुभाशुभम्।
आत्मा कुर्वन्नचारित्रं स्वचारित्र-पराङ्मुखः ॥31॥

A soul gets turned away from its (real) conduct

performing meritorious and demeritorious manifestations on account of attachment and aversion doing (earning) non-conduct (vitiated conduct) for itself.

यतः सम्पद्यते पुण्यं पापं वा परिणामतः।
वर्तमानो यत(तत)स्तत्र भ्रष्टोऽस्ति स्वचरित्रतः ॥32॥

As there are the (soul's) manifestations which result in earning merit or demerit (for it), therefore the *jīva* indulging in them is (certainly) deviated from its (true) conduct.

Meritorious and demeritorious activities or activities leading to such results, should not be considered desirable for the welfare of the *jīvas*, because they are equally implelled by attachment and aversion which do not find any agreement with the pure faculties of the soul. As such they all help the inflow of *karmas* into the soul and prolong its worldly existence.

श्वाभ्र-तिर्यङ्-नर-स्वर्गि-गतिं जाता शरीरिणः।
शारीरं मानसं दुःखं सहन्ते कर्म सम्भवम् ॥33॥

Embodied (souls) attaining hellish, sub-human, human and celetial conditions of life suffer bodily pain and mental anguish generated by *karmas*.

There are four conditions of life as enumerated in this verse. The *karmas* accompany the souls in all these conditions. It is only in the state of liberation, which has also been some times described as the fifth condition of life, that the *karmas* are not able to chase and accompany the souls.

यत्सुखं सुरराजानां जायते विषयोद्भवम्।
ददानं दाहिकां तृष्णां दुःखं तदवबुध्यताम् ॥34॥

Whatever pleasure generated by the sense-objects is enjoyed by the kings (*indras*) of the celetial beings, know it to be pain, being the giver of a burning desire (for sense-pleasures).

In the celetial condition of life the *jīvas* get abundant pleasure arising from the objects of the senses. Such a pleasure does not grant a calm and equanimous living for them. On the contrary the chain of such pleasures gives rise to a chain of unsatiated desires and thus makes the *jīva's* living all the more painful.

अनित्यं पीडकं तृष्णा-वर्धकं कर्मकारणम् ।
शर्माक्षजं पराधीनमशर्मैव विदुर्जिनाः ॥35॥

The *Jinas* call the pleasure, born of the senses, as restlessness, because of its being unstable, pain-generating, augmenting desire (for sense pleasures), causing *karmas* and being dependent (on the other, not the soul itself).

सांसारिकं सुखं सर्वं दुःखतो न विशिष्यते ।
यो नैव बुध्यते मूढः स चारित्री न भण्यते ॥36॥

The worldly pleasure in (its) entirety is not distinguished from pain. The foolish (*jīva*) that does not realize so, is not said to be having conduct (pure and essesntial for the emanipation of the worldly souls).

Nothing short of that which fails to grant us spiritual serenity, peace and freedom, however pleasant it may be, cannot be counted as an element of spiritual conduct potent to lead us on the path of liberation. The reasons for its being so have been enumerated in the previous verse.

यः पुण्यपापयोर्मूढो विशेषं नावबुध्यते ।
स चारित्र-परिभ्रष्टः संसार-परिवर्धकः ॥37॥

One who does not know the difference between merit and demerit is (certainly) deviated (fallen) from conduct and is prolonging his worldly wanderings.

To cherish a like for merit and a dislike for demerit is

not advisable for those who aim at the perfect release of their souls. Both merit and demerit keep the souls strongly confined in and tied with worldly chains. One may be said to be binding the souls with gold chains; while the other, with iron chains. In both the cases the poor souls are kept imprisoned and are deprived of their natural purity and freedom prolonging their duration in the world.

पापारम्भं परित्यज्य शस्तं वृत्तं चरन्नपि।
वर्तमानः कषायेन कल्मेषेभ्यो न मुच्यते ॥38॥

Inspite of renouncing sinful actions and practising meritorious conduct, one is not granted riddance from *karmas*, (if) continuing with passions.

The practice of conduct leading to merit must be based on the presence of passions with the souls. The demeritorious conduct is vitiated by bad passions. Actually speaking, it is the presence of passionate manifestations of the souls, whether meritorious or demeritorious, which leads to the dense bondage of the souls by the *karmas* and sustains the continuance of their association with the souls. So, in a nutshell, the right conduct consists in conquering the passions completely.

जायन्ते मोहलोभाद्या दोषा यद्यपि वस्तुतः।
तथापि दोषतो बन्धो दुरितस्य न वस्तुतः ॥39॥

From the existential point of view blemishes beginning from delusion, greed etc. are generated (in the souls). Still the bondage by *karma* results from the blemishes; in reality, it is not so.

Generation of passions in the *jīvas* is certainly due to the auxiliary causation accepted by the passionate *jīvas*. From the existential point of view the passions are the joint effects of the *jīvas* and the *karmas* mutually working after the manner of auxiliary causation. If such a situation is not admitted, the *saṁsāra* or the worldly existence of the *jīvas* will not be possible and the prescription of any ethies for their redemption will be futile. If we resort to the pure point of view or if we keep the pure souls in the focus of our vision, the *jīvas* are seen as perfectly pure and free from all blemishes whatsoever. From the pure point of view even the existence of the worldly souls cannot be seen, just as we cannot expect the birth of a son singly from the mother or the father. If, for the sake of encouraging and elevating the fallen souls, the pure point of view is adopted, it is justified by its own right. It is just realizing or rather keeping the ideal of spiritual purity in view in all the real conditions and stages of life.

मिथ्याज्ञान-निविष्ट-योगजनिताः संकल्पना भूरिशः,
संसारभ्रमकारिकर्मसमितेरावर्जने या क्षमाः ।
त्यज्यन्ते स्वपरान्तरं गतवता निःशेषतो येन तास्,
स्तेनात्मा विगताष्टकर्म-विकृतिः सम्प्राप्यते तत्त्वतः ॥40॥

By one, comprehending the difference between the self (one's soul) and the 'other', completely renouncing the varied though-activities generated by the (souls') vibrations imbibed with the wrong knowledge, and potent to attract the collocations of *karmas* responsible for creating worldly delusion, in the true sense the soul, with exaustion of the malicious manifestations caused by the eight *karmas*, is realized.

This is the concluding verse of the chapter and it refers to the realization of the final, the highest and the purest state of the soul or *jīva*. The most formidable enemy of the soul is the group of eight *karmas* along with the malignant manifestations caused to the soul. Such undesirable manifestations are solely responsible for the loss of the soul's power of discrimination between what is its own and the 'other'. This keeps the soul rolling into the mire of the worldly existence. He alone who aspires for spiritual deliverance must renounce all the connections with such *karmas* and their ever-widening family of effects, can realize the soul in its purity. It is like a return of the soul to its own home which was, so far lost sight of, due to the association of *karmas*. The verse contains a sobre, true, and spiritually beneficial advice and instruction for those who choose to advance on the path of freedom, well known as the *mokṣamārga* - the way to liberation in Jaina ethics.

Here ends Chapter-3, Āsravādhikāra of Yogasāra-prābhṛta by Āchārya Amitagati.

Chapter 4

Bandhādhikāra

पुद्‌गलानां यदादानं योग्यानां सकषायतः।
योगतः स मतोः बन्धो जीवाऽस्वातन्त्र्य-कारणम् ॥1॥

The accumulation of material particles fit for becoming *karmas* on account of the *jīvas* being with passions and (also) on account of the vibratory activity (of the *jīvas*) is admitted as bondage (of *karmas*); (and) it is the cause of *jīvas*, loss of freedom.

The process of the influx of the *karmas* has been described in the previous chapter on *āsrava*. The *jīva* now has to undergo the next process of accumulating and assimilating the *karmas* with it. This new process is called the principle of bondage in Jaina philosophy. From here the *jīvas*, being dependent on the *karmas* so bound with it, suffer a fatal loss of their natural freedom.

प्रकृतिश्च स्थितिर्ज्ञेयः प्रदेशोऽनुभवः परः।
चतुर्धा कर्मणो बन्धो दुःखोदय-निबन्धनम् ॥2॥

The bondage of *karmas* is to be known in (its) four types i.e. the determination of the nature, duration, mutual co-spatiality (of the units of *karma*-matter and the soul-units), and the other of the fruition. (all these) cause the emergence of anguish (for the *jīvas*).

निसर्गः प्रकृतिस्तत्र स्थितिः कालावधारणम्।
सुसंक्लिप्तिः (क्लृप्तिः) प्रदेशोऽस्ति विपाकोऽनुभवः पुनः ॥3॥

The nature of *karmas* is *prakṛti*, the determination of time (duration) is *sthiti*, the integration (of the soul and *karma*-matter) is *pradeśa* and again the ripening (fruition) of *karmas* is *anubhava*.

The principle of bondage of *karmas* with the *jīvas* takes place in its four dimensions. The determination of the nature of *karmas* so bound is known as the *prakṛti baṅdha*, the determination of the length of the period of bondage with the *jīvas* is known as *sthiti baṅdha*, the co-spatiality of the karmic matter with the soul-units of the *jīvas* is known as the *pradeśa baṅdha* and the determination of the power and intensity of the fruition of *karmas* is known as the *anubhava* or the *anubhāga baṅdha*. It may be observed that the *pradeśa baṅdha* lies at the root, being the substantial basis for bondage. The other types of bondage may be viewed as the dimensions of this basic bondage. This bondage, taken as a whole, is responsible for the generation of pleasure and pain in all the four conditions of life.

रागद्वेषद्वयालीढः कर्म बध्नाति चेतनः।
व्यापारं विदधानोऽपि तदपोढो न सर्वथा ॥4॥

The conscious (soul), imbued with the dyad of attachment and aversion, binds the *karma;* (but) one not imbued, in no case, binds them, inspite of performing the activity (of mind, speech and body).

सचित्ताचित्त-मिश्राणां कुर्वाणोऽपि निषूदनम्।
रजोभिर्लिप्यते रूक्षो न तन्मध्ये चरन् यथा ॥5॥
विदधानो विचित्राणां द्रव्याणां विनितापनम्।
रागद्वेष-द्वयापेतो नैनोभिर्बध्यते तथा ॥6॥

Just as one with a rough (not oily) body is not soiled by the particles of dust, inspite of performing various activities with the animate, inanimate and mixed objects and (in spite of) moving among them; so also one bereft of the dyad of attachment and aversion is not bound with these, though performing activities with various substances.

The root cause of bondage is found in the presence of attachment and aversion with the souls. These make the *jīvas* liable for their bondage by *karmas*, as one besmeared with oil just gathers particles of dust on one's body. If such a person enters a dusty place but with a rough body, he will not gather the dust particles on his body, however busy he may be even with dust found in the area. So also if one is able to save oneself from all kind of passions, one will not be subjected to bondage by *karmas* at all. It also leads to the conclusion that mere activities performed with mind, speech and body cannot cause any such bondage to *jīvas*.

सर्वव्यापारहीनोऽपि कर्ममध्ये व्यवस्थितः।
रेणुभिर्व्याप्यते चित्रैः स्नेहाभ्यक्ततनुर्यथा ॥7॥
समस्तारम्भहीनोऽपि कर्ममध्ये व्यवस्थितः।
कषायाकुलितस्वान्तो व्याप्यते दुरितैस्तथा ॥8॥

One well adjusted in (with) the *karmas* gets soiled with the various particles (of *karmas*) despite being without all kinds of activities like one with a body besmeared with oil.

In the same way one well adjusted in (with) the *karmas* gets defiled by *karmas*, being with a mind rendered restless by passions despite being without initiation of all kinds (of activities).

The secret of bondage by *karmas* lies in the emergence of passions, which arises only in the *jīvas* that are already entangled in the network of *karmas*. Any kind of preparation for various activities of mind, speech and body and actual occurence of such activities on the part of the *jīvas* is not potent to bring about the bondage. The position is supported by a well known illustration. Just as a person with his body besmeared with oil gathers dust particles with his activities and movements. He will not suffer such soiling of his body with dust particles, if his body and skin are not made oily. So also in case of bondage of *jīvas* by *karmas* the presence of passions is wholly responsible for the bondage, all kinds of activities with no passionate coating are impotent to cause the bondage.

मरणं जीवनं दुःखं सौख्यं रक्षा निपीडनम् ।
जातु कर्तुममूर्तस्य चेतनस्य न शक्यते ॥9॥
विदधानः परीणामं मारणादिगतं परम् ।
बध्नाति विविधं कर्म मिथ्यादृष्टिर्निरन्तरम् ॥10॥

Death, life, anguish, pleasure, safety and causing pain are never possible to do for the incorporeal conscious soul.

But the wrong believer causing manifestation (within himself) involved in killing (others) etc. binds various types of *karma* (constantly) with no interval.

A right believer realizes very well that the soul is above all sorts of corporeality and it cannot be made to suffer from anything which is of the worldly nature. Hence no bondage of *karmas* takes place with him. On the contrary, a person with wrong faith not only fails to realize the true position about the soul but also, entertains perverse beliefs about it, becomes a constant subject of bondage by the *karmas* of various types. He is not able to strike at the root of his worldly existence all full of sufferings and misunderstandings.

कर्मणा निर्मितं सर्वं मरणादिकमात्मनः ।
कर्मावितरतान्येन कर्तुं हर्तुं न शक्यते ॥11॥

Death etc. are all created for the soul by the *karma*.

Nothing is made possible to do for or to snatch away from (the soul) by the another one not causing *karmas* (to the soul).

The ultimate and root cause the *jīvas* fall into worldly existence with its sufferings is the operation of the *karmas* bound with them. No other agency in the world is potent enough to grant the bondage of *karmas* to any *jīvas* whatsoever. Then, logically no other agency can be held responsible for what happens to the *jīvas* in the world. Realizing this secret of existence, one can save oneself from the great enemy of wrong faith.

या 'जीवयामि जीव्येऽहं मार्येऽहं मारयाम्यहम्।
निपीडये निपीड्येऽहं' सा बुद्धिर्मोहकल्पिता ॥12॥
कोऽपि कस्याऽपि कर्तास्ति नोपकारापकारयोः।
उपकुर्वेऽपकुर्वेऽहं मिथ्येति क्रियते मतिः ॥13॥
सहकारितया द्रव्यमन्येनान्यद् विधीयते।
क्रियमाणोऽन्यथा सर्वः संकल्पः कर्मबन्धजः ॥14॥

The understanding which proceeds as I grant life (to others) or I am granted life (by other), I kill others or I am killed (by others) and I cause pain (to others) or I am caused pain (by others) is based on delusion.

No one is the agent for doing good or bad to another. I do good (to others) or I am done good (by others). Thinking in this way (our) understanding is made wrong (perverted).

One substance is made (transformed into) the other by way of assistance. Such a perverted fluctuation of mind is, through and through, a generater of bondage by *karmas*.

A number of forms of understanding and thinking are enumerated in the above verses; they generally emerge in case of the *jīvas* deluded by the operation of the faith-deluding *karma*. This *karma* is the greatest and the most formidable enemy of the *jīvas* on the path of liberation. It causes not only a delusion about the way of liberation but also perverts the very direction of spiritual advancement. In the presence of this *karma* the *jīvas* are rendered completely helpless to advance even a step on the right path leading to liberation.

चारित्रं दर्शनं ज्ञानं मिथ्यात्वेन मलीमसम्।
कर्पटं कर्दमेनेव क्रियते निजसंगतः ॥15॥
चारित्रादि त्रयं दोषं स्वीकरोति मलीमसम्।
न पुनर्निर्मलीभूतं सुवर्णमिव तत्त्वतः ॥16॥

Faith, knowledge and conduct are made wrong (filthy) by the wrong faith, just as (a piece of) cloth is made dirty by mud by its association (with it).

A *jīva* accepts the three perversions like wrong faith etc. (on account of the faith-deluding *karma*); but on the purification (of faith, knowledge and conduct); it does not accept them in the real sense like gold.

As already mentioned, the root cause of the loss of pure nature on the part of a *jīva* is the presence of wrong faith resulting from the operation of the faith-deluding *karma*. This most mischievious *karma* first affects and perverts the faculty of faith of the *jīvas*. The pollution and perversion of the faculties of knowledge and conduct are then owned due to the wrong faith so generated as a necessary consequence. It is why the necessity of destroying the faith-deluding *karma* is said to be the first and foremost step on the path of liberation in Jaina Ethics.

नीरागोऽप्रासुकं द्रव्यं भुञ्जानोऽपि न बध्यते।
शङ्खः किं जायते कृष्णः कर्दमादौ चरन्नपि ॥17॥
सरागो बध्यते पापैरभुञ्जानोऽपि निश्चितम्।
अभुञ्जाना न किं मत्स्याः श्वभ्रं यान्ति कषायतः ॥18॥

A *jīva* bereft of attachment is not bound by *karmas*, despite enjoying animate substance (things). Does a (white) conch turn black despite of rolling in mud?

A *jīva* with attachment is certainly bound by sins (*karmas*) despite not enjoying (substance and things). Do the fish, not enter the hell on account of passions, despite not consuming (other creatures)?

The main factors that lead to the freedom from *karmas* and the bondage by *karmas* are the absence of passions and the indulgence in passions on the part of the *jīvas*. If actions are performed without passions, there is no danger of bondage for the *jīva* by karmas. If actions are performed with passions, the bondage of a *karma* is a necessary consequence. The two situations are explained with the help of the examples of a conch and a greedy fish. A conch, which is white by nature, does not turn black though it is found in dark mud. On the other hand a greedy fish entertaining a strong passion to devour other creatures seen moving around it, is bound with *karmas* leading to the hellish condition of life, though it is not able to eat them all.

ज्ञानी विषय-सङ्गेऽपि विषयैर्नैव लिप्यते ।
कनकं मलमध्येऽपि न मलैरुपलिप्यते ॥19॥
आहारादिभिरन्येन कारितैर्मोदितैः कृतैः ।
तदर्थं बध्यते योगी नीरागो न कदाचन ॥20॥

A *jīva* with right knowledge is not painted with sense-pleasures though (it is) in the company of objects of sense pleasures. Gold is not painted with filth though lying in filth.

A yogī (novice) is never bound (with *karmas*) on account of accepting food etc. prepared, got prepared and approved by some other (person) for his sake.

The principle underlying the bondage of the *jīvas* by *karmas* is that the *jīvas* must entertain attachment, desire or fondness for the objects which become auxiliary causes for their resulting bondage by *karmas*. Such conditions being absent, mere accompaniment of various objects with them is not potent to effect the *jīva's* bondage by *karmas.* A novice with right knowledge takes part in activities like taking food etc. prepared, arranged or approved by others is not liable to any bondage only because of utilizing such aids.

परद्रव्यगतैर्दोषै नीरागो यदि बध्यते।
तदानीं जायते शुद्धिः कस्य कुत्र कुतः कदा ॥21॥

If a *jiva* gets bound (with *karmas*) on account of blemishes caused in substance other than its own, then for whom, where, whence and when does (spiritual) purity take place?

One can suffer from bondage only because of one's own anti-spiritual actions, and blemishes, such actions taking place in other susbtances cannot cause bondage in the *jīva.*

नीरागो विषयं योगी बुध्यमानो न बध्यते।
परथा बध्यते किं न केवली विश्ववेदकः ॥22॥

A yogi bereft of attachment is not bound (with *karmas*) though knowing the objects of pleasure. Does the omniscient Lord get bound (with *karmas*) on account of the ways determined by others?

Mere knowledge of objects, including objects of sense-pleasure, is in no way a determinant of the bondage of *karmas* for a *jīva.* The omniscient Lord possesses the knowledge of the whole of the universe, its contents, attributes and modes; but for that reason he suffers no bondage at all. Knowledge is an intrinsic attribute of the soul, and hence it cannot be inimical to the soul by causing bondage of *karmas* to the soul.

ज्ञानिना सकलं द्रव्यं ज्ञायते वेद्यते न च।
अज्ञानिना पुनः सर्वं वेद्यते ज्ञायते न च ॥23॥

A *jīva* with right knowledge knows all the substances

but does not feel (them). Again, a *jīva* with wrong knowledge feels all (substances) but does not know them.

A difference between knowledge and feeling functions of the *jīvas* is drawn here. One may know things, but may or may not get identified with them. Only identification with and indulgence in other things resulting in a feeling of pleasure or pain cause bondage to the *jīvas* on account of the operation of the deluding *karma*. This state of the *jīvas* makes them liable for the orgination and continuance of bondage; while knowledge, not so affected, is only a natural function of the *jīvas.*

यथावस्तु परिज्ञानं ज्ञानं ज्ञानिभिरुच्यते।
रागद्वेष-मद-क्रोधैः सहितं वेदनं पुनः ॥24॥

By the persons with right knowledge, the comprehension of objects as they exist, is called (right) knowledge (or knowledge). Again when vitiated with attachment, aversion, pride and anger it becomes feeling.

नाज्ञाने ज्ञानपर्यायाः ज्ञाने नाज्ञानपर्ययाः।
न लोहे स्वर्ण-पर्याया न स्वर्णे लोह-पर्ययाः ॥25॥

No modes of knowledge are there in wrong knowledge; no modes of wrong knowledge are there in knowledge. The modes of gold are not there in iron, no modes of iron are there in gold.

The differentiation between right and wrong types of knowledge is explained in the forerunning verses. Now the same is illustrated with examples of gold and iron. Souls free from attachment etc. are like gold; those vitiated by similar blemishes are like iron. Hence the series of modes in the first case includes pure manifestations and that in the second case contains impure and anti-spiritual manifestations.

ज्ञानीति ज्ञान-पर्यायी कल्मषानामबन्धकः।
अज्ञश्चाज्ञान-पर्यायी तेषां भवति बन्धकः ॥26॥

A *jīva* with right knowledge, is the master of the modes of right knowledge, (and hence) is the non-binder of *karmas*. A *jīvas* with wrong knowledge is the master of the modes of wrong knowledge, hence is the binder of them (*karmas*).26

दीयमानं सुखं दुःखं कर्मणा पाकमीयुषा।
ज्ञानी वेत्ति परो भुङ्क्ते बन्धकाबन्धकौ ततः ॥27॥

A *jīva* with right knowledge knows the pleasure and pain yeilded by *karmas* on their maturation, the other (*jīva* with wrong knowledge) enjoys (also suffers) them. Therefore, the one is the non-binder of *karmas* and the other is the binder of *karmas*.

कर्म गृह्णाति संसारी कषाय-परिणामतः।
सुगतिं दुर्गतिं याति जीवः कर्म-विपाकतः ॥28॥
सुगतिं दुर्गतिं प्राप्तः स्वीकरोति कलेवरम्।
तत्रेन्द्रियाणि जायन्ते गृह्णाति विषयांस्ततः ॥29॥
ततो भवन्ति रागाद्यास्तेभ्यो दुरितसंग्रहः।
तस्माद् भ्रमति संसारे ततो दुःखमनेकधा ॥30॥
दुःखतो बिभ्यता त्याज्याः कषायाःज्ञानशालिना।
ततो दुरित-विच्छेदस्ततो निर्वृत्ति-सङ्गमः ॥31॥

The *jīvas* whirling in the world gather *karmas* on account of passionate manifestations, it attains good and bad conditions of life on account of the maturity of *karmas*.

The *jīvas* having attained good and bad conditions of life accept the embodiments. There emerge the senses from them. Then it owns the objects of sense pleasure.

From them are generated attachment etc. and from them follows the accumulation of *karmas*. From them emerges the *saṁsara* - the whirling in the world, from if follows pain in many ways.

The passions are to be renounced by a *jīva* with right knowledge fearing the pain or distress. Thence follows the separation of *karmas* (from the *jīva*), thence follows the attainment of liberation.

The course of the whirling journey of a worldly *jīva* has been traced in the above verses. The chain of intervening elements of the journey are also enumerated here. The journey begins with passionate manifestations and through various conditions of life, embodiments, objects of sense-pleasure, generation of attachment, aversion and delusion, accumulation of various *karmas* and then the continuance of the journey finally results in a series of suffering and tribulences. The root cause of such wanderings thus is the presence of passions which must be abandoned, if one with right knowledge become conscious of the sad, painful and unfortunate consequences. In the absence of the passions the possibility of bondage by *karmas* is reduced and ultimately the *jīva*, being completely free from *karmas*, attains its final aim i.e. *nirvāna* or *mokṣa* from where a return or fall also becomes impossible for want of *karmas* and passions.

सन्ति रागादयो यस्य सचित्ताचित्त वस्तुषु।
प्रशस्तोवाऽप्रशस्तो वा परिणामोऽस्य जायते ॥32॥
प्रशस्तो भव्यते तत्र पुण्यं पापं पुनः परः।
द्वयं पौद्गलिकं मूर्तं सुख-दुःख-वितारकम् ॥33॥

One who entertains attachment etc. in (for) animate and inanimate objects gets the emergence of auspicious or inauspicious manifestations.

There the merit is called the auspicious manifestation; and the demerit, (is called) the other. The dyad of both of them is material, corporeal and generaters of pleasure and pain.

Even the slight feeling of attachment and aversion for the objects of the world proves highly injurious for the conscious souls, as it finally results in the accumulation of merit or demerit which are anti-spiritual by its very nature. Hence this accumulation of *karmas* causes pain and pleasure to the *jīvas* which are so disenabled to achieve the complete and final freedom for themselves.

मूर्तो भवति भुञ्जानाः सुख-दुःखफलं तयोः ।
मूर्तकर्म-फलं मूर्तं नाऽमूर्तेन भुज्यते ॥34॥
मूर्तो भवत्यमूर्तोऽपि पुण्य-पापवशीकृतः ।
यदा विमुच्यते ताभ्याममूर्तोऽस्ति तदा पुनः ॥35॥
विकारं नीयमानोऽपि कर्मभिः सविकारिभिः ।
मेघैरिव नभो याति स्व-स्वभावं तदत्यये ॥36॥

A *jīva*, enjoying the pleasureable and painful fruits of the two (the merit and the demerit), becomes corporeal. The fruition of the corporeal *karmas* is corporeal; it cannot be enjoyed by the incorporeal (soul).

The *jīva*, being pressed by merit and demerit, becomes corporeal, though incorporeal (by nature). When it is freed from them, it is again incorporeal.

Though the *jīva* is led to a vitiated state by the vitiated *karmas*, it attains its own (pure) nature on the disappearance of them (the *karmas*); just as the sky, covered with clouds, becomes clear on the fleeing away of them (the clouds).

These verses deal with the mutual relationship between the *jīva* and the *karmas*. In the worldly existence they have been together from the beginningless time. If the beginning of this relationship is presupposed, then a very serious objection as to how a pure soul could at all enter into this relationship arises. The possibility of the breach of this relationship is very clearly admitted in cases where the *jīvas* are able to acquire such conditions as lead to the complete eradication of the *karmas*. After attaining this state of freedom from *karmas*, the fall of the *jīvas* becomes impossible, as it could have been so when a beginning of the relationship between a *jīva* and the soul was presupposed. Still to explain the state of worldliness a very close association between them is felt necessary; and it is very clearly admitted in the above verses.

The *karmas* are corporeal, and their fruition is corporeal. If a *jīva* is to enjoy or suffer the fruits of *karmas*, it somehow assumes corporeality. Hence it is said that a *jīva* becomes corporeal in its worldly existence. But, using the technology of *nayas*, the position is maintained from the *vyavahāra*, practical or concessional point of view. Again resorting to the pure point of view the *jīva* is held to be free from the association of *karmas* even in the state of worldliness; while it becomes factually and actually free from them in the state of liberation. The worldly and the liberated states of the *jīvas* are actual facts of existence, one necessitating the prescription of the ethics for the emancipation of the *jīvas* and the other granting a real status of perfect freedom to the *jīvas*. This introduces full hope for the *jīvas* in Jaina ethics, though they have been so far under the dominance of *karma* and have never breathed at all in the free atmosphere for which they were entitled by nature.

अर्हदादौ परा भक्तिः कारुण्यं सर्वजन्तुषु।
पावने चरणे रागः पुण्यबन्ध-निबन्धनम् ॥37॥

High devotion in Arhats (embodied souls that have destroyed the destructive type of *karmas* and have attained omniscience) etc. benevolence on all living beings and attachment to pure conduct are the causes of bondage of merit.

Practice of devotion covers the high positioned *Arhats*, liberated ones (*siddhas*), the heads of the saints, the professor-saints, and the saints in general - the pentad of the venerable ones. Benevolence is to be extented to all types of living beings. An inclination to love and attachment for the entire course of discipline required for the purification of the worldly *jīvas*, must bring merit (only) to them.

निन्दकत्वं प्रतीक्ष्ये (इ्ये) षु नैर्घृण्यं सर्व जन्तुषु ।
निन्दिते चरणे रागः पाप बन्ध विधायकः ॥38॥

To revile the venerable, lack of benevolence towards the living beings and attachment to unworthy conduct, bring about the bondage of sin (to the *jīvas*).

This verse enumerates actions and practices just in contradiction with those *jīvas* in the previous verse. Naturally these must bring bondage of demeritorious *karmas* to the *jīvas*.

सुखासुख-विधानेन विशेषः पुण्यपापयोः ।
नित्य-सौख्यमपश्यद्भिर्मन्यते मुग्धबुद्धिभिः ॥39॥

The distinction (of desirability) between merit and demerit in their generation of pleasure and pain is held by persons with deluded understanding, not seeing the permanent bliss (the blissful nature of the pure *jīvas*).

Various actions are performed by *jīvas*. Some of them result in bondage of meritorious *karmas* and the consequent pleasures of the body and the senses. Some other actions lead to bondage of demeritorious *karmas* and the consequent suffering and pain of the body and the senses. These have been termed meritorious and demeritorious forms of conduct. Both these forms of conduct are owned as desirable and undesirable by persons lacking right understanding of the true blissful nature of the *jīvas*.

पश्यन्तो जन्मकान्तारे प्रवेशं पुण्य-पापतः ।
विशेषं प्रतिपद्यन्ते न तयोः शुद्धबुद्धयः ॥40॥

Seeing the entry of the *jīvas* into the forest of births (and deaths) due to merit and demerit, the *jīvas* with pure understanding do not make (any) distinction between them.

Both the meritorious and the demeritorious types of conduct prolong the duration of the journey of the *jīvas* in the world, though one for a pleasant one and the other for a painful one. Both of them keep the *jīvas* imprisoned in the world, as if one with gold chains and the other with iron chains. The final and ultimate aim of the *jīvas* on the path of liberation is to break the worldly imprisonment completely. Hence there arises the need of the third kind of conduct quite in consonance with the pure nature of the *jīvas.* This is called the pure conduct, inclined neither to merit nor to demerit. The practice of such a conduct and course of discipline is absolutely necessary to achieve the final aim of perfect bliss and freedom for the *jīvas.* It embodies an ethics of no merit and no demerit but of the purification of the *jīvas* from all that is 'other' to them.

विषय-सुखतो व्यावृत्त्य स्व-स्वरूपमवस्थितस्
त्यजति धिषणां धर्माधर्म-प्रबन्ध-निबन्धिनीम् ।
जनन-गहने दुःखव्याघ्रे प्रवेशपटीयसीं,
कलिल-विकलं लब्ध्वात्मानं सगच्छति निर्वृतिम् ॥41॥

Turning away from the pleasure of the sense-objects and being established in his (pure) identity he who renounces the understanding (itself) that causes entanglement with merit and demerit and is well expert (potent) in granting entrance to the *jīvas* in the forest all full of births (and deaths) and the tigers of sufferings, attains perfect freedom (*or nirvāṇa*), having realized his soul as bereft of (all) filth (of *karmas*).

In this concluding verse the *āchārya* summarises the various steps and stages which are marked on the path leading to the final emancipation of the *jīvas.* The first step is the abandonment of the objects of sense-pleasure. It makes the *jīvas* constanly conscious of and attentive to their pure identity. Then they are required to get rid of their understanding or rather misunderstaing which had so far kept them deluded by the love of merit and aversion for demerit. They are to know well that such manifestations on their part are bound to keep them whirling in the ocean of the world. They must realize it well that the world is, through and through, a place of tear and fear. In their worldly existence they have to face the painful events of births and deaths repeatedly. Besides, the world for them is like a dense forest haunted by tigers and other wild animals just ready to attack and devour them. The final result of such endeavours and steps is the release of the *jīvas* from the shackles of *karmas* and the realization of their purity. This state is termed as *nirvāṇa* or *nirvṛti* where there remains nothing to be achieved further.

Here ends Chapter-4, Bandhādhikāra of Yogasāra-prābhṛta by Āchārya Amitagati.

Chapter 5

Saṁvarādhikāra

कल्मषागमनद्वार-निरोधः संवरो मतः ।
भाव-द्रव्यविभेदेन द्विविधः कृतसंवरैः ॥1॥

Saṁvara (the safeguarding of the soul) is held to be the plugging of the door for the inflow of *karmas* by those who have achieved *saṁvara.* It is of two kinds, the subjective and the objective.

रोधस्तत्र कषायाणां कथ्यते भावसंवरः ।
दुरितास्त्रवविच्छेदस्तद्रोधे द्रव्यसंवरः ॥2॥

There the checking of the passions is said to be the subjective *saṁvara.* It causes the breech of the inflow of *karmas*; in checking it (the inflow of the objective *karmas*) the objective *saṁvara* (takes place).

Having dealt with the process of the bondage of *karmas* in detail, the *āchārya* takes up the next process of safeguarding of the *jīvas* from the inflow of *karmas.* This process is named as *saṁvara* and is distinguished in its two aspects. We must remember that it is in Jaina philosophy alone that the *karmas* are conceived as very fine material conglomerations which stick to the souls to fructify in various distortions and limitations of the souls' natural powers. These material *karmas* have their counterpart in the form of psychological manifestations on the part of the *jīvas.* Thus the process of *saṁvara* is also viewed in its two aspects i.e. the subjective and the objective. The psychological (conscious) manifestations which help the check and stoppage of *karmas* are called the subjective *saṁvara,* while the check and stoppage of the inflow of the material *karmas* is called the objective *saṁvara.* This step and process is very necessary on the path of liberation.

कषायेभ्यो यतः कर्म कषायाः सन्ति कर्मतः।
ततो द्वितयविच्छेदे शुद्धिः सम्पद्यते परा ॥3॥

(The association of) *karmas* are due to passions and the passions are due to *karmas.* Hence on the destruction of the two the higher purity (for the *jīvas*) is achieved.

कषायाकुलितो जीवः परद्रव्ये प्रवर्तते।
परद्रव्यप्रवृत्तस्य स्वात्मबोधः प्रहीयते ॥4॥
प्रहीण-स्वात्मबोधस्य मिथ्यात्वं वर्धते यतः।
कारणं कर्मबन्धस्य कषायस्त्यज्यते ततः ॥5॥

The *jīvas* being highly disturbed by passions, indulge in the 'other' substance. The realization of the self (soul) gets destroyed for one who is indulged in substance other than the soul.

The wrong faith undergoes an increase for one whose self-knowledge gets destroyed. It is a (potent) cause of the bondage of *karmas.* Hence the passion is to be renounced.

The source of mischief of the bondage of the *jīvas* by *karmas* lies in the emergence of passions - a form of malignant manifestion of the *jīvas.* The intervening links between the two are the *jīvas'* indulgence into things that are 'other' of the soul, the consequent loss of knowledge of the self (one's own soul), and the expanding of the wrong faith which in turn, causes bondage of *karmas* resulting in the emergence of passions. The chain begins with passions and ends with passions to make the continuance of worldly life to go unbroken.

Hence an attempt to get rid of passions becomes a primary and necessary step on the path of redemption of the *jīvas.*

निष्कषायो निरारम्भः स्वान्य-द्रव्य-विवेचकः।
धर्माऽधर्म-निराकाङ्क्षो लोकाचार-निरुत्सुकः ॥6॥
विशुद्धदर्शनज्ञानचारित्रमयमुज्ज्वलम्।
यो ध्यायत्यात्मनात्मानं कषायं क्षपयत्यसौ ॥7॥

One who is bereft of passions and (all) worldly actions, who distinguishes between the substance of the soul and other substances, who cherishes no desire for merit and demerit, who entertains no inclination for the behaviour of worldly persons, and who meditates on the effulgent soul, identified with the highly pure faith, knowledge and conduct, by (his own) soul, destroys the (element of) passion.

The conditions and qualifications which are essentially required of the *jīvas* to get rid of the most formidable enemy existing with them in the form of passion, are enumerated in the above verses. Passion, wordly actions, lack of discrimination between the soul and its 'other', presence of desire for good and bad fruitions and their causes, and interest for worldly behaviour of persons are some of the conditions to be abhored. In his mediation the pure soul imbued with the jewels of the path of liberation becomes the sole object, the process of meditation on the soul is carried on by the soul accepting the soul itself as an instrument of meditation.Then alone the *jīvas* will be able to destroy passions.

वर्ण-गन्ध-रस-स्पर्श-शब्दयुक्तैः शुभाशुभैः।
चेतनाचेतनैर्मूतैरमूर्त्तः पुद्गलैरयम् ॥8॥
शक्यो नेतुं सुखं दुःखं सम्बन्धाभावतः कथम्।
रागद्वेषो यतस्तत्र क्रियते मूढमानसैः ॥9॥

How can this incorporeal *(jīvas)* be led to pleasure and pain by the corporeal animate and inanimate, meritorious and demeritorious matter alongwith its colour, smell, taste, touch and sound on account of the absence of relationship (between *jīva* and matter), for which reason attachement (love) and aversion (hatred) are done there by the persons with deluded minds?

Unless the *jīvas* and matter agree with each other in respect of their essential attributes, there can be no relationship between them to effect states of pleasure and pain in the *jīvas.* Only the persons who do not realize this basic difference between the two and hence are suffering from a misunderstanding about the situation think that matter causes the feelings of pleasure and pain in the *jīvas*, for which they fall victim of love and hate towards matter.

निग्रहानिग्रहौ कर्तुं कोऽपि शक्तोऽस्ति नात्मनः।
रोषतोषौ न कुत्रापि कर्तव्याविति तात्त्विकैः ॥10॥

Nothing (other than soul) is potent to cause obstruction and assistance to the soul (in its functioning). Therefore displeasure and satisfaction (both) are worth doing nowhere at all by those with knowledge of reality.

परस्याचेतनं गात्रं दृश्यते न तु चेतनः।
उपकारेऽपकारे क्व रज्यते क्व विरज्यते ॥11॥

Only the unconscious embodiment of the others is seen (but) not their conscious souls (are seen). Hence where to feel the attachment in causing assistance or aversion in causing obstruction?.

शत्रवः पितरौ दाराः स्वजनाः भ्रातरोऽङ्गजाः।
निगृह्णन्त्यनुगृह्णन्ति शरीरं, चेतनं न मे ॥12॥
मत्तश्च तत्त्वतो भिन्नं चेतनात्तदचेतनम्।
द्वेषरागौ ततः कर्तुं युक्तौ तेषु कथं मम ॥13॥

Enemies, parents, women, brother, offesprings and all

my persons, cause obstruction and assistance to the body, not to my conscious (soul). In reality they are (all) unconscious and different from my conscious soul. Then how can it be just to feel attachment and aversion for them on my part?

पश्याभ्यचेतनं गात्रं यतो न पुनरात्मनः।
निग्रहानिग्रहौ तेषां ततोऽहं विदधे कथम् ॥14॥

Because I perceive only the bodies (of others) not their souls, then, how can I cause obstruction and assistance to them (the others - their souls)?.

स्वदेहोऽपि न मे यस्य निग्रहानिग्रहे क्षमः।
निग्रहानिग्रहौ तस्य कुर्वन्त्यन्ये वृथामतिः ॥15॥

Even my body is not potent to cause assistance or obstruction to myself (my soul). Then to hold that others (different from my soul) cause assistance and obstruction to that (my soul) is a vain conception.

There is the principle of soul–one's own soul, the principle of the 'other' covers the entire range of the remaining reality. The unconscious matter with all its properties and forms of existence falls under the category of the 'other'. As a rule no entity, including the soul, can do help or hinderance to any other entity, each one of them is responsible for determining its own forms of existence. The basic difference between *jīva* and matter is that the one is conscious and the other, is unconscious. Our bodies, our relations and so many adjuncts attached with them can never take the place of our souls, they will ever remain extraneous to our souls. Neither our souls can be perceived by others, nor can the souls of others can be perceived by us. This distance and difference being there between the *jīva* and matter, the understanding regarding their mutual help and hinderance is false, deluded, apparent and totally unwholesome. To achieve the process of *saṁvara*–a strong covering or coat for the *jīva's* protection from the attack of the 'other'–the basic condition is the realization of the insoluble duality between the *jīvas* and their 'other'. Hence the question of deriving pleasure and pain from the 'other' does not at all arise, and also should not at all arise for those who care to practise *saṁvara* in the spiritually true sense of the term.

शक्यन्ते न गुणाः कर्तुं हर्तुमन्येन मे यतः।
कर्तुं हर्तुं परस्याऽपि न पार्यन्ते गुणा मया ॥16॥
मयान्यस्य ममान्येन क्रियतेऽक्रियते गुणः।
मिथ्यैषा कल्पना सर्वा क्रियते मोहिभिस्ततः ॥17॥

For, to create or destroy my attributes by others is not possible, as to create and destory the attributes others of by me is (also) not possible.

My attribute is created or not created by the other; or other's attribute, by me. Such a conception (which is) through and through false, is entertained by the deluded persons.

In their deepest reality all the substances with their attributes are mutually irreducible. This sort of limitation is very essential for saving the universe from becoming a chaos. Hence the susbtances of the *jīvas* and matter always remain so distinct that one cannot be created, emanated or transformed by the other. But on the contrary under the influence of wrong faith and wrong knowledge the *jīvas* are rendered unable to take the right view of the world. Thus they are debarred from advancing on the right path.

ज्ञान-दृष्टि-चरित्राणि ह्रियन्ते नाक्षगोचरैः।
क्रियन्ते न च गुर्वाद्यैः सेव्यमानैरनारतम् ॥18॥
उत्पद्यन्ते विनश्यन्ति जीवस्य परिणामिनः।
ततः स्वयं स दाता न, परतो न कदाचन ॥19॥

Knowledge, faith and conduct are not destroyed by the

objects of sense-perception; nor are they created by the preceptors etc. attended constantly (by one). From the view point of modes they are generated and destroyed in a *jīva* undergoing manifestations. Hence (from the substantial point of view) the *jīva* itself (as a substance) is not the giver or creator (of such attributes), nor are they obtained from anything else.

The conception of mutual creation and extinction among the various substances and attributes is now particularly applied to the *jīva* with its attributes. The *Jiva*, like other substances is dynamic by nature; it is ever undergoing manifestations (modes) in terms of its attributes but with an allowance of perfect safety of its substance. So we have to devise two ways to comprehend the reality of the *jīva.* One is the view point of modes which focuses our attention on the ever changing flow of manifestations of the *jīva.* The other is the substantial point of view which focuses our attention on the permanently underlying reality behind the varying manifestations. This is true of the *jīva* and all the other substances. But for achieving *saṁvara* the concentration on the underlying inner reality is essentially required, hence the supremacy and the importance of the substantial and also the purely substantial, view point is established.

शरीरमिन्द्रियं द्रव्यं विषयो विभवो विभुः।
ममेति व्यवहारेण भण्यते न च तत्त्वतः ॥20॥
तत्त्वतो यदि जायन्ते तस्य ते न तदा भिदा।
दृश्यते, दृश्यते चासौ ततस्तस्य न ते मताः ॥21॥

Body, senses, substances, sense objects, prosperity and ownership (all) are said to be mine from the practical point of view, (they are not so) from the real point of view.

If they belong to the *jīva* from the real point of view, they must not be perceived with a distinction (from the *jīva*).

But they are perceived with a distimction (from it); hence they are not held to belong to it.

From the *vyavahāra* or practical point of view the entire group of the 'other' may be said to belong to the *jīva;* but from the *niścaya* or real point of view, there is a distinction between them, they cannot be said to belong to the *jīva.* A resort to the practical point of view always keeps the novice away from the path on account of the loss of the vision of the ideal; while the resort to the real point of view, by keeping the ideal of the pure soul constantly in view, keeps the *jīvas* always on the path.

विज्ञायेति तयोर्द्रव्यं परं स्वं मन्यते सदा।
आत्मतत्त्व-रतोयोगी विदधाति च संवरम् ॥22॥

Thus knowing the reality (contents) covered under the two points of view, the yogi, absorbed in the reality of his soul, always his soul holds (his soul alone) as his and the 'other' as the other (different from his soul) and (thus) achieves *'saṁvara'.*

To recognize well what is his own and what is to the other for him is almost a precondition for stepping on the true path of liberation. With the help of the two points of view i,e the real or the niścaya and the practical or the *vyavahāra* the *jīva* acquires a good knowledge of his own soul and of all that which is the antithesis of his soul. This helps him to concentrate all his energies on what is really beneficial to his soul. Thus he is able to keep his soul safe from and unpurturbed by the inimical elements on the path of his final emancipation.

विदधाति परो जीवः किञ्चित्कर्म शुभाशुभम्।
पर्यायापेक्षया भुङ्क्ते फलं तस्य पुनः परः ॥23॥
य एव कुरुते कर्म किञ्चिज्जीवः शुभाशुभम्।
स एव भजते तस्य द्रव्यार्थापेक्षया फलम् ॥24॥

मनुष्यः कुरुते पुण्यं देवो वेदयते फलम्।
आत्मा वा कुरुते पुण्यमात्मा वेदयते फलम् ॥25॥
नित्यानित्यात्मके जीवे तत्सर्वमुपपद्यते।
न किञ्चिद् घटते तत्र नित्येऽनित्ये च सर्वथा ॥26॥

Whatever action of merit or demerit a *jīva* does, from the modal point of view the other *jīva* enjoys its fruit.

Whatever action of merit and demerit a *jīva* does, from the point of view of susbtance, the same *jīva* enjoys its fruit.

A man (*jīva* in the mode of man) does merit, a celetial being (*jīva* in the mode of a celetial being) enjoys its fruit (from the modal point of view). (From the point of view of substance) the soul does the action of merit, the (same) soul enjoys its fruit.

All this finds consistency only in the permanent-cum-transitory *jīva*. Nothing is held (consistently) in a *jīva* absolutely permanent or absolutely transitory.

Jaina philosophy is very well known for pronouncing the dual nature of reality in general and that of the *jīva* in particular. It means that the *jīva* manitains its permanance through its changing modes and its modes are possible on the permanent ground of its substance. This leads to the two ways of our perception of the *jīva* under the technique of *nayas* which give us the the partial views of the *jīva*. These *nayas* are known as the point of view of substance and the point of view of modes. The above verses contain statements about the *jīva* from these two points of view. Thus the problem of moral accountability is consistently solved. No absolute philosophy is able to give us a consitent solution in the field of moral accountability. Even in the field of metaphysics the truth of the above theory holds good. It is the very nature of reality that it keeps the duality of such characteristics safe in its womb.

चेतनः कुरुते भुङ्क्ते भावैरौदयिकैरयम्।
न विधत्ते न वा भुङ्क्तते किंचित्कर्म तदत्यये ॥27॥

This conscious *jīva* performs (actions) and enjoys (the fruits of such actions) by means of its operative manifestations. In the absence (of operative manifestation), it neither performs any action nor does enjoy any (action).

The worldly souls are always found in association with *karmas* in their various stages and conditions of life. When the *karmas* attain an operative stage, they cause the *jīva* to perform actions and enjoy their fruition. In other words a *jīva* becomes a doer of actions and enjoyer of their fruits by the auxiliary causation of the operative *karmas.* Thus the root cause of the *jīvas'* fall into the states of doing some actions and enjoying their fruition is the underlying presence of the operation of the *karmas.* The process of *saṁvara* is held to be potent to save the *jīvas* from such undesirable states. Then (with *saṁvara*) the *jīvas* can be held performing no actions and enjoying no fruits resulting from them.

पञ्चाक्ष विषयाः किंचिन नास्य कुर्वन्त्यचेतनाः।
मन्यते स विकल्पेन सुखदा दुःखदा मम ॥28॥

The unconscious objects of the five senses do nothing to it (the *jīva*), but it holds them a giver of the pleasure and the pain for it by a delusion (of his mind).

न द्रव्यगुणपर्यायाः सम्प्राप्ता बुद्धिगोचरम्।
इष्टानिष्टाय जायन्ते संकल्पेन विना कृताः ॥29॥

The substances, the attributes and modes subjected to perception, by intellect (and senses), are not potent for (to bring) the desirable and (to avoid) the undesrirable (for the *jīva*) without deluded understanding.

न निन्दा-स्तुति-वाक्यानि श्रूयमाणानि कुर्वते।
सम्बन्धाभावतः किञ्चिद् रुष्यते तुष्यते वृथा ॥30॥

The sentences of depreciation and appreciation being heard (by one) do nothing (to one) because of the absence of relation, hence to feel displeased or pleased (with them) is useless.

आत्मनः सकलं बाह्यं शर्माशर्म-विधायकम्।
क्रियते मोहदोषेणापरथा न कदाचन ॥31॥

All that is extraneous to the soul is held to be the creator of good and bad (for it) on account of (its) defilement by delusion; otherwise (in the absence of delusion) (it is) never (so).

नाञ्जसा वचसा कोऽपि निन्द्यते स्तूयतेऽपि वा।
निन्दितोऽहं स्तुतोऽहं वा मन्यते मोहयोगतः ॥32॥

Really speaking, no one is depreciated or appreciated (merely) by speech. One thinks oneself depreciated or appreciated on account of one's association with delusion.

नानन्दो वा विषादो वा परे संक्रान्त्यभावतः।
परदोष-गुणैर्नूनं कदाचिन् न विधीयते ॥33॥

Certainly, happiness and misery are never caused (to one) by the good and bad qualities of the other because of the absence of transformation (of the latter into the former).

अयं मेऽनिष्टमिष्टं वा ध्यायतीति वृथामतिः।
पीड्यते पाल्यते वापि न परः परचिन्तया ॥34॥

To meditate (think) that this is desirable or undesirable (for me) is a vain (untrue) idea. No other one suffers or is served (merely) by worrying (about it) on the part of the other.

अन्योन्यस्य विकल्पेन वर्द्धते हाप्यते यदि
न सम्पत्तिर्विपत्तिर्वा तदा कस्याऽपि हीयते ॥35॥

It they (prosperity or adversity) get inereased or deereased (merely) by mutual (deluded) thinking of the one by the other, then no one's prosperity and adversity are dcstroyed.

इष्टोऽपि मोहतोऽनिष्टो भावोऽनिष्टस्तथा परः।
न द्रव्यं तत्त्वतः किंचिदिष्टानिष्टं हि विद्यते ॥36)

On account of delusion a desirable (benficial) entity is taken to be undesirable (unbenefical), so also the undesirable is taken to be desirable. Certainly no substance or entity, from the real point of view, is desirable or undesirable in the least.

The greatest obstacle in the way of initiation and progress of the *jīva* is caused by the operation of the deluding *karma*. The function of the deluding *karma* is basically the distortion and perversion of the *jīvaś* pure faculties of faith, knowledge and conduct. As a result the *jīvas* lose sight of the ideal of the pure soul and go astray. They are now entangled with what is 'other' than the pure soul. The foregoing verses explain how this deviation from the right path takes place. The *jīvas* so affected by the operation of the deluding *karma* entertain not only a confusion but also a perversion of their understanding and also of their behaviour with other things like the objects of sense perception, even the entire system of the reals, the words of praise and depreciation, desirability and undesirability of various things and the consequent emotion of pleasure and unrest. They entertain a wrong understanding that these extraneous entities are responsible for their pleasant and painful states for the *jīva.* They are never able to think that these factors can do no harm or good to them. Right understanding sees no relation between these entities and the *jīvas*, hence they cannot be held responsible for such a change in the *jīvas.* When the *jīvas* are suffering from the operation of the deluding *karma*, such misconceived states of understanding arise in them. These states are vitiated not only by a confusion but also by a perversion of the faculties of the pure souls. Hence what is most essential for enabling the *jīvas* for achieving *saṁvara* for themselves, is the riddance from the effects of the deluding *karma*.

रत्नत्रये स्वयं जीवः पावने परिवर्तते।
निसर्गनिर्मलः शङ्खः शुक्लत्वे केन वर्त्यते ॥37॥

A *jīva*, if left to itself, undergoes manifestations in terms of the pure trio by three jewels (i.e. right faith, right knowledge and right conduct). By what reason is a conch, pure by nature, can be caused to continue in a state of whiteness? (It does so by its very nature).

स्वयमात्मा परं द्रव्यं श्रद्धत्ते वेत्ति पश्यति।
शङ्खचूर्णः किमाश्रित्य धवलीकुरुते परम् ॥38॥

The soul itself believes, knows and sees the other substances. With what help, does the conch-powder whiten (any) other? (It does so by virtue of its own whiteness).

मोहेन मलिनो जीवः क्रियते निजसङ्गतः।
स्फटिको रक्तपुष्पेण रक्ततां नीयते न किम् ॥39॥

A *jīva* is defiled by delusion by its own association with it (delusion). Is a quartz crystal gem (white by nature) not led to redness by (its association with) a red flower? (A quartz crystal gem becomes red by its being placed with a red flower, it does not turn so, by nature).

निजरूपं पुनर्याति मोहस्य विगमे सति।
उपाध्यभावतो याति स्फटिकः स्वस्वरूपताम् ॥40॥

On the liquidation of delusion (delusive *karma*), the *jīva* again attains its own (pure) identity. The quartz crystal gem gains its own (white) identity on the non-existence (negation) of the obstruction.

इत्थं विज्ञाय यो मोहं दुःखबीजं विमुञ्चति।
सोऽन्यद्रव्य-परित्यागी कुरुते कर्म-संवरम् ॥41॥

Knowing thus one who gives up delusion, the seed of (all) pain, achieves *saṁvara* (protection) from *karmas* after renouncing the (association of) other substances.

If a *jīva* is left to itself untainted by anything else, specially the *karmas,* it becomes perfectly purified. It then loses all its liability to become impure by the company of anything else and continues with the pure modes of its pure faculties. The status of the *jīvas'* association with anything other than itself is so fickle, weak and apparent, that the moment the other is separeted from it, it immediately comes to and attains its pure nature. This association is also extraneous to the *jīva,* and is not able to pollute its nature completely. Thus it is only accidental to the *jīva.* An understanding of this situation is what is most required for achieving *saṁvara.* On the attainment of such an understanding the riddance from the grip of the 'other' becomes easy, and also necessary, to enable the *jīva* for further advance in the process of achieving *saṁvara.*

शुभाशुभ-परद्रव्य-रागद्वेष-विधायिनः।
न जातु जायते शुद्धिः कुर्वतोऽपि चिरं तपः ॥42॥

For the one who entertains attachment and aversion for meritorious and demeritorious other substances, (spritual) purity never appears, though performing (a course of) penance for a long period.

कुर्वाणः कर्म चात्मायं भुञ्जानः कर्मणां फलम्।
अष्टधा कर्म बध्नाति कारणं दुःखसन्ततेः ॥43॥

And this soul doing *karma* and enjoying the fruition of *karmas* binds eight kinds of *karmas*–the cause of the chain of unrest.

सर्वं पौद्गलिकं वेत्ति कर्मपाकं सदापि यः।
सर्वकर्म-बहिर्भूतमात्मानं सः प्रपद्यते ॥44॥

One who always understands the entire fruition of *karmas* to be material, attains the soul chiselled of all the *karmas*.

ज्ञानवांश्चेतनः शुद्धो न गृह्णाति न मुञ्चति।
गृह्णाति मुञ्चते कर्म मिथ्याज्ञान-मलीमसः ॥45॥

A conscious pure soul with right knowledge neither assimilates nor renounces the *karma*; the soul vitiated by wrong knowledge, assimilates and renounces *karma*.

Observance of austerities is prescribed to be the cause of freedom from *karmas*; but this course of austerities becomes impotent for achieving the aim, if it is accompained with love and hatred for things other than the soul. The chain of bondage of *karmas* is never broken, if there remains attachment for the *karmas* and their fruits. *Karmas* and their fruits are material and hence are 'other' than the soul. So long as one is so entangled in the cobweb of the 'other' does not get blessed with right knowledge; his soul being rendered filthy and impure, he is not fit to follow the path of *saṁvara* at all.

सामायिके स्तवे भक्त्या वन्दनायां प्रतिक्रमे।
प्रत्याख्याने तनूत्सर्गे वर्तमानस्य संवरः ॥46॥

There is *saṁvara* for him who with devotion is engaged in equanimity, eulogization, salutation, counter-acting (of sinful actions), renunciation, and detachment of body.

This verse enumerates the six essential duties meant

mainly for sanits who aim at and make attempts for achieving *saṁvara.* The *āchārya* explains the contents of these items (essentials) in the following verses.

यत् सर्वद्रव्य-सन्दर्भे रागद्वेष-व्यपोहनम्।
आत्मतत्त्व-निविष्टस्य तत्सामायिकमुच्यते ॥47॥

The total liquidation of attachment and aversion in the context of all the substances is the essential of equanimity for one who is fully engaged with the principle of (his) soul.

By diverting one's conscious mind from the states of attachment with and aversion from all the objects of the world one gains the power of staying within one's own soul. This amounts to self-concentration which excludes everything that is extraneous to the soul. The gradual practice of this essential duty brings the novice nearer and nearer to his soul with the diminution of his concern for other things.

रत्नत्रयमयं शुद्धं चेतनं चेतनात्मकम्।
विविक्तं स्तुवतो नित्यं स्तवजैः स्तूयते स्तवः ॥48॥

By the knowers or creators of eulogies the eulogization of the pure, identical with consciousness, imbued with the three jewels (i.e. right faith, right knowledge and right conduct) and distinct soul is said to be the eulogization.

The second essential of eulogization consists in pronouncing eulogies of the pure soul and its pure attributes and pure modes. This keeps the novice always mindful of the pure ideal of his soul by being conscious of the pure liberated souls.

पवित्र-दर्शन-ज्ञान-चारित्र-मयमुत्तमम्।
आत्मानं वन्ध्यमानस्य वन्दनाकथि कोविदैः ॥49॥

By the learned, the (essential of) salutation is said to be the homage paid to the excellent soul imbued with the holy faith, knowledge and conduct for one, observing this (essential of) salutation.

The third essential of salutation consists in paying homage, respect and bowing one's head to the pure souls. This is another way of reminding oneself of the purity of souls that have actually attained final release from the world. This humility on the part of the novice is potent to give firmness to his steps on the right path.

कृतानां कर्मणां पूर्वं सर्वेषां पाकमीयुषाम् ।
आत्मीयत्त्वपरित्यागः प्रतिक्रमणमीर्यते ॥50॥

The renunciation of the relation of identity of oneself with all the *karmas* done in the past and maturing (at present) is said to be the (essential of) counter acting.

This fourth essential of counter acting is so called, because the novice is already under the attack of *karmas* and observing this essential, he is making to give them a counter attack as a rectification for his past *karmas,* both bound and maturing. This sort of detachment of *karmas* and their fruition is bound to grant him freedom and firmness to his steps on the path he has already taken.

आगाम्यागोनिमित्तानां भावानां प्रतिषेधनम् ।
प्रत्याख्यानं समादिष्टं विविक्तात्मविलोकिनः ॥51॥

The negation of manifestation which may become helping causes for future inflow of *karams,* is termed as the essential of renunuciation by those who (constantly) perceive the pure soul.

Now the novice applies his efforts to check the generation of such manifeststions of his soul which may lead to further inflow and bondage of *karmas.* This he would try by turning his consciousness exclusively to the ideal of pure soul, which in turn, would save him from indulging in such activities of his soul as may causes and elongate his entanglement into the world. This essential, by its very description, is very necessary for his progress on the path.

ज्ञात्वा योऽचेतनं कायं नश्वरं कर्म-निर्मितम्।
न तस्य वर्तते कार्ये कायोत्सर्गं करोति सः ॥52॥

Knowing the body as unconscious, mortal and produced by the *karmas* one who does not engage himself in activities (related with) the body, performs the (essential of) detachment from the body.

The last and the sixth essnetial consists in the complete loss of interest in body on the part of the novice. The body, as described in the verse, only goes to be an instrument for dragging the soul backwards, because it is a product of the *karmas,* and all sorts of relations with *karmas* are inimical to the spiritual good of the novice. *Karmas,* being material, are the antithetical to the soul. The body, being a direct outcome of *karmas,* is absolutely worth disassociation and detachment on the path leading to emancipation of the soul.

यः षडावश्यकं योगी स्वात्मतत्त्व-व्यवस्थितः।
अनालस्य करोत्येव संवृतिस्तस्य रेफसाम् ॥53॥

The yogī, well established in the principle of his soul, observes the hexad of the six essentials with no indolence, achieves *saṁvara* (the protection) from sinful actions for himself.

Now the *Āchārya* winds up the topic of the hexad of the essentials after describing them with the necessary prescriptions, prohibitions and cautions. It may appear that the entire course of discipline meant for a novice is covered under the concept of the six essentials. The novices are required to keep these duties and the connected observance constantly in the focus of their attention. With an honest, streneous and strict observance of the six essentials they can provide themselves, so to call, with a coat of arms for protection against all that is inimical to their souls.

मिथ्याज्ञानं परित्यज्य सम्यग्ज्ञानपरायणः ।
आत्मानात्मपरिज्ञायी विधत्ते रोधमेनसाम् ॥54॥

Completely keeping off the wrong knowledge and having attained expertise in right knowledge, one who well understands the distinction between the soul and the non-soul accomplishes the check against sinful activities.

So long as a *jīva* is under the influence of wrong knowledge, it must suffer from an incessant inflow of *karmas;* hence the right knowledge, the antithesis of wrong knowledge, must enable it to fight against the *karmas* and provide it a sure protection against them.

द्रव्यतो भोजकः कश्चिद्भावतोऽस्ति त्वभोजकः ।
भावतो भोजकस्त्वन्यो द्रव्यतोऽस्ति त्वभोजकः ॥55॥

A person who is an enjoyer externally i.e. with respect to external things may not be an enjoyer internally i.e. with respect to his internal manifestations. Conversely, one who is an enjoyer internally may not be enjoyer externally.

द्रव्यतो यो निवृत्तोऽस्ति स पूज्यो व्यवहारिभिः ।
भावतो यो निवृत्तोऽसौ पूज्यो मोक्षं यियासुभिः ॥56॥

One who has externally withdrawn himself from the worldliness is venerable by those who adopt a practical point of view. One who has withdrawn himself from worldliness internally is venerable by those desirous of liberation.

द्रव्यमात्रनिवृत्तस्य नास्ति निर्वृत्तिरेनसाम् ।
भावतोऽस्ति निवृत्तस्य तात्त्विकी संवृत्तिः पुनः ॥57॥

For one who has withdrawn himself (from worldliness) only externally there is no riddance for him from sins; again for one who has withdrawn (from worldliness) internally, there is the real *saṁvara* (protection from sins)for him.

विज्ञायेति निराकृत्य निवृत्तिं द्रव्यतस्त्रिधा।
भाव्यं भाव-निवृत्तेन समस्तैनोनिषिद्धये ॥58॥

Knowing thus and eliminating the external withdrawal in the three ways (of mind, speech and body), the practice for attaining internal one should be resorted to by one who has withdrawn internally with a view to check (the inflow of) all the sinful activities.

The *āchārya* explains the process of *saṁvara* in its two aspects: the internal and the external. The former refers to the manifeatation of the soul with respect to their causation and emergence. This internal aspect is held to be real, as it is directly related with the soul. The external one refers to the factors which depend on what is extraneous to the soul but may have a bearing on the process indirectly i.e. by an intervention of the internal ones. As such there is no perfect and necessary correspondence between the two. In other words one may be present even in the absence of the other. The situation is explained by illustrations of endurance (enjoying and not enjoying) and the withdrawal from worldliness on the part of a *jīva*. As a conclusion it is made very clear that the true *saṁvara* is achieved only in its internal aspect on which the seekers of liberation concentrate their efforts. But the external aspect of *saṁvara* may also be resorted to but only in a practical and concessional sense.

शरीरमात्मनो भिन्नं लिङ्गं येन तदात्मकम्।
न मुक्ति-कारणं लिङ्गं जायते तेन तत्त्वतः ॥59॥
यन्मुक्तिं गच्छता त्याज्यं न मुक्तिजयिते ततः।
अन्यथा कारणं कर्म तस्य केन निवर्तते ॥60॥

The body is different from (opposed to) the soul and

hence any bodily mark is identical with it (the body). Hence the bodily mark cannot constitute a cause of liberation in the true sense of the term.

Liberation cannot be achieved by what is worth giving up by one advancing on the path of liberation. Otherwise (i.e. by upholding that liberation goes with the bodily marks) by what can the *karmas* responsible for (the emergence of) such marks be warded off?

The bodily specialities emerge in the body of a living being on the operation of the body-making *karma (nāma karma)* conceived as having a number of subdivisions *(uttara prakrtiś)* to determine the type of the body (by *śarīra nāma karma*), the bony and muscle structure (by *saṁhanana nāma karma*), the limbs and minor limbs (by *aṅgopāṅga nāma karma*) etc. All these marks and parts of the body are caused by the material *karmas* and are in themselves material products. Hence these cannot be held to be the causes for bringing about liberation for the *jīva,* being completely opposed to the realization of the pure soul. If these bodily products are supposed to cause and help the attainment of the spiritual ideal, the position will suffer from a very serious and glaring contradiction. Then, it will also not be possible to get rid of the *karmas* in general and the body-making *karmas* in particular; while the total expulsion of the unconscious *karma* from the soul is a necessary prerequisite for mokṣa.

अचेतनं ततः सर्वं परित्याज्यं मुमुक्षुणा।
चेतनं सर्वदा सेव्यं स्वात्मस्थं संवरार्थिना ॥61॥

Therefore (for reasons explained above) the unconscious (the antithesis of the conscious) is to be totally renounced by one desirous of *mokṣa,* the final release of the soul from the world. The conscious soul established in itself is always to be resorted to or repeatedly pondered by one who is desirous of *saṁvara*–a sure protection for the soul.

This verse contains a sobre advice and instruction for those who aim at the attainment of *mokṣa* through *saṁvara*. Such a novice must make a discrimination and choice between the conscious and the unconscious, by resorting to the former and completely abstaining from the latter.

आत्म तत्त्वमपहस्तितरागं, ज्ञान-दर्शन-चरित्रमयं यः ।
मुक्तिमार्गमवगच्छति योगी, संवृणोति दुरितानि सः सद्यः ॥62॥

The yogī, who understands the way to liberation where the (pure) soul is the only essential entity, where attachment is dropped down completely and which (the way) is constituted by (right) knowledge, (right) faith and (right) conduct, very soon raises a (strong) defence against the *karmas*.

Here ends Chapter-5, Saṁvarādhikāra of Yogasāra-prābhṛta by Āchārya Amitagati.

Chapter 6

Nirjarādhikāra

पूर्वोपार्जित-कर्मैकदेशसंक्षय-लक्षणा ।
निर्जरा जायते द्वेधा पाकजापाकजात्वतः ॥1॥

Nirjarā – the process of the expulsion of *karmas* – is defined as the partial destruction (separation) of the *karmas* earned (accumulated) before (in past lives). It is of two kinds being born on the maturity or the immaturity (of *karmas*).

This chapter deals with the principle and practice of gradual separation and fall of the *karmas* from the soul. The channels of the inflow of *karmas* being plugged under the principle of *saṁvara,* it is becomes highly expedient to exaust the *karmas* already bound with the soul. *Karmas* on the expiry of their duration fall off in the natural course; but it is not sufficient to grant release to the soul from the grip of the *karmas.* Hence a way or a disciplinary course is necessarily required to deal with the already accumulated *karmas* for this gradual and piece-meal separation without allowing them their full span of time to mature and work. This is the other type of *nirjarā* most necessary and sufficient to grant *mokṣa* or complete freedom from *karmas* for a soul. The last state of this gradual expulsion of *karmas* from the soul is the attainment of *mokṣa* by the soul.

प्रक्षयः पाकजातायां पक्वस्यैव प्रजायते ।
निर्जरायामपक्वायां पक्वापक्वस्य कर्मणः ॥2॥

शुष्काशुष्का यथा वृक्षा दह्यन्ते दव-वह्निना।
पक्वापक्वास्तथा ध्यान-प्रक्रमेणाघ-संचयाः ॥3॥

Under the *nirjarā* of the matured karmas the destruction of only the mutured *karmas* takes place; but under the *nirjarā* of immatured *karmas*, the destruction of both the mature and immature (*karmas* takes place).

Just as the dry and the green trees are burnt by the forest-fire; so also the accumulations of *karmas*, matured or immatured (are burnt) by the procedure of meditation.

दूरीकृत-कषायस्य विशुद्धध्यान-लक्षणः।
विधत्ते प्रक्रमः साधोः कर्मणां निर्जरां पराम् ॥4॥

The procedure (programme) defined by the highly pure meditation achieves the *nirjarā* of a high degree for the saint who keeps the passions at a distance (from himself).

The most potent means to achieve *nirjarā* is the meditation of the pure soul; but it must be supported by a passionless state of the mind. Passions and pure meditation cannot go together. Actually speaking one disturbed by the passions cannot perform meditation of the type required on the path of liberation.

आत्मतत्त्वरतो योगी कृत-कल्मष-संवरः।
यो ध्याने वर्तते नित्यं कर्म निर्जीयतेऽमुना ॥5॥

A yogi, absorbed in the principle of soul, who has achieved *saṁvara* (protection) from *karmas*, and who always engages (himself) in meditation, by him the *karmas* are always dropped (from his soul).

संवरेण विना साधोर्नास्ति पातक-निर्जरा।
नूतनाम्भः प्रवेशे(शो)ऽस्ति सरसो रिक्तता कुतः ॥6॥

For a saint the *karma*-destroying *nirjarā* is not possible without achieving *saṁvara*. Whence is emptiness for a tank possible in the presence of the entry (inflow) of new water?

It is quite reasonable that for pumping out water completely from a tank, it is necessary that the channels for the incoming water are be plugged first. On the analogy of this illustration, the importance and priority assigned to *saṁvara* over *nirjarā* can be well understood.

रत्नत्रयमयं ध्यानमात्मरूप-प्ररूपकम् ।
अनन्यगत-चित्तस्य विधत्ते कर्म-संक्षयम् ॥7॥

Meditation which is all imbued with the three jewels (right faith, right knowledge and right conduct) and which presents the picture of the soul (to us) brings the destruction of *karmas* for one whose mind is engaged with the soul, leaving all else.

Complete concentration on the soul and its attributes with no diversion of mind to anything else except the soul is, what is basically essential for the expulsion of *karmas* from the soul. The ideal of the pure soul must always be kept in view to achieve the most needed liquidation of *karmas* from the soul on the path to liberation.

त्यक्तान्तरेतर-ग्रन्थो निर्व्यापारो जितेन्द्रियः ।
लोकाचार-पराचीनो मलं क्षालयतेऽखिलम् ॥8॥

One who has left all possessions (internal or external), who does not engage (himself) in any activity, who has conquered (his) senses and who has lost all interest in the worldly conduct of life washes off the filth of the *karmas* in its entirety.

As the novice is required to turn inward to his soul, so he is required not to turn outward to varied possessions, activities, sense pleasures and the conduct of the worldly cult and rites. So, equipped internally and externally, he will be able to destroy the *karmas* completely.

शुभाशुभ-विशुद्धेषु भावेषु प्रथमद्वयम्।
यो विहायान्तिमं धत्ते क्षीयते तस्य कल्मषम् ॥9॥

For him who, relinguishing the dyad of the first two from amongst the good, bad and pure manifestations (of the soul) resorts to the last. The *karmas* are destrayed.

Here in the *āchārya* mentions the theory of the three types of the spiritand manifestations. The good and the bad manifestations result from the operation of the meritorious and demeritorious *karmas* repectively, hence both of them have a material origin. The pure manifestations do not require anything else other than the soul for their emergence, they are solely determined by the soul itself. They naturally flow from the pure nature of the soul and hence are ethically desirable on the path of spiritual progress being potent to break the bondage by *karmas*.

बाह्यमाभ्यन्तरं द्वेधा प्रत्येकं कुर्वता तपः।
नैनो निर्जीर्यते शुद्धमात्मतत्त्वमजानता ॥10॥

By one not knowing the principle of pure soul and practising each type of penance out of the two i.e. the external and the internal, the *karmas* are not expelled (from his soul).

कर्म निर्जीर्यते पूतं विदधानेन संयमम्।
आत्मतत्त्व-निविष्टेन जिनागम-निवेदितम् ॥11॥

By one who is well established in the principle of soul and observing the pure restraint prescribed in the scripture of *Jina*, *karmas* are liquidated (from one's soul).

Penance (*tapas*) and restraint (*saṁyama*) come very close to each other or are mutually complementary to each other in the process of lifting the soul to ethically higher stages of spiritual evolution. Hence a resort to the observance of restraints which mainly consists of the control of desire for worldly things and objects of sense-pleasure.

अन्याचार-परावृत्तः स्वतत्त्व-चरणादृतः।
सम्पूर्ण-संयमो योगी विधुनोति रजः स्वयम् ॥12॥

One who has retired from conduct related with what is other then the soul, and entertains respect for the conduct related with the principle of one's soul is an observer of the complete restraint brushes off the dust of *karmas* himself (not requiring any other help).

हित्वा लोकोत्तराचारं लोकाचारमुपैति यः।
संयमो हीयते तस्य निर्जरायां निबन्धनम् ॥13॥

For him who having relinquished conduct related with what is beyond worldliness resorts to the conduct related with worldliness which is (also) an obstructive condition in the process of *nirjarā*, the restraint suffers deminution.

चारित्रं विदधानोऽपि पवित्रं यदि तत्त्वतः।
श्रद्धत्ते नार्हतं वाक्यं न शुद्धिं श्रयते तदा ॥14॥

If one, who, in the real sense, does not cherish the holy faith in the Word of Arhat (*Jina*) does not approach (spiritual) purity, though observing holy conduct (the rules of holy conduct),

विचित्रे चरणाचारे वर्तमानोऽपि संयतः।
जिनागममजानानः सदृशो गतचक्षुषः ॥15॥

One with restraint, in spite of being engaged in the various types of observance of conduct but not knowing the scripture of *Jina*, is like one who has lost (his) eyes.

साधूनामागमश्चक्षुर्भूतानां चक्षुरिन्द्रियम्।
देवानामवधिश्चक्षुर्निर्वृत्ताः सर्व-चक्षुषः ॥16॥

Āgama, (the holy Word of *Jina*) is the eye for the (homeless) saints, the ocular (sense) is the eye for the *jīvas* (with body), clairvoyance is the eye for the celetial beings (and) the liberated ones have (the entire substance of) their very souls as eyes..

The *āchārya* has pointed to the main instruments for perception and knowledge for different classes of *jīvas* in a very beautiful and attractive way. The truth and value of these instruments can be upheld only in a practical way. But coming to the liberated souls this instrumentality disappears completely but it has also been described in the same poetic way. Then, the entire expansion of the substance of soul is potent in effect the process of direct perception and knowledge, with his unlimited and infinite other powers.

प्रदर्शितमनुष्ठानमागमेन तपस्विनः।
निर्जरा-कारणं सर्वं ज्ञाततत्त्वस्य जायते ॥17॥

The (entire) code of conduct as described well by the Āgama (the holy Word of Jina) constitutes the cause of *nirjarā* for the saint with penance, and who has known the reality in its essence.

अज्ञानी बध्यते यत्र सेव्यमानेऽक्षगोचरे।
तत्रैव मुच्यते ज्ञानी पश्यताश्चर्यमीदृशम् ॥18॥

Whereas one, with wrong knowledge, suffers bondage (of *karmas*) on induliging in (objects) perceptible with the senses, the other, with right knowledge, is favoured with freedom (from *karmas*). (Just) see such an amazement.

शुभाशुभ'विकल्पेन कर्मायाति शुभाशुभम्।
भुज्यमानेऽखिले द्रव्ये निर्विकल्पस्य निर्जरा ॥19॥

Meritorious and demeritorious *karmas* enter a soul with good or bad fluctuations of mind. For one, bereft of such fluctuations (tainted with attachment and aversion) (only) *nirjarā* takes place inspite of (one's) indulgence in the (other) substances in their totality.

The pure soul is central to the entire ethical philosophy of Jainism. It is characterised by right faith, right knowledge and right conduct. The way to realize it also lies through and with these three jewels. Among these, it is right faith that imparts rightiousness to knowledge and conduct. It has been taught us by Lord *Jina* whose holy Word becomes a sure guide for us on the path of liberation. With this background every item and topic of the ethical philosophy of Jainism is viewed and valued with reference to the pure soul and its pure attributes. Divorced from such a reference, every item, whether it is restraint or penance, loses its importance or rather leads on the wrong path, resulting in the whirlings of the world. The main cause of our deviation from the right path is the association of delusion, attachment and aversion with the functions of the attributes of the soul. These very enemies of the soul turn the attributes of the soul into what has been named as wrong faith, wrong knowledge and wrong conduct which maintain the continuance of the worldly existence. So it has been advised that, if one chooses to advance on the right path, one must keep off these enemies of the soul, otherwise all his efforts are bound to end not only in utter uselessness but also turn seriously harmful.

अहमस्मि न कस्याऽपि न ममान्यो बहिस्ततः ।
इति निष्किंचनो योगी धुनीते निखिलं रजः ॥20॥

Neither I belong to anyone else and no one extraneous to me is mine. Thus, being bereft from the sense of belongingness, the yogi shrugs off the entire dust of *karmas*.

मुक्त्वा विविक्तमात्मानं मुक्त्यै येऽन्यमुपासते ।
ते भजन्ति हिमं मूढा विमुच्याग्निं हिमच्छिदे ॥21॥

Those foolish ones who learning the chiselled (pure) soul resort to the 'other' for the sake of liberation, resort, (as if) to snow leaving the other (the right means) for getting riddance from cold.

योऽन्यत्र वीक्षते देवं देहस्थे परमात्मनि।
सोऽन्ने सिद्धे गृहे शङ्के भिक्षां भ्रमति मूढधीः ॥22॥

One who perceives the divine *(Arhat)* elsewhere in spite of His being in (his) body, (is) foolish-minded and wanders for alms, I think, (elsewhere) in spite of the house with well-cooked food being in reach.

कषायोदयतो जीवो बध्यते कर्मरज्जुभिः।
शान्त-क्षीणकषायस्य त्रुट्यन्ति रभसेन ताः ॥23॥

A *jīva* is bound with the strings of *karmas* on account of the operation of passions. But for one whose passions are subsided or destroyed, they get soon (immediately) broken.

सर्वत्र प्राप्यते पापैः प्रमादनिलयीकृतः।
प्रमाद-दोष-निर्मुक्तः सर्वत्रापि हि मुच्यते ॥24॥

One who has housed indolence earns sin (and *karmas*) everywhere. One who is free from the blemish of indolence achieves riddance (from *karmas*) even everywhere.

स्वतीर्थममलं हित्वा शुद्धयेऽन्यद् भजन्ति ये।
ते मन्ये मलिनाः स्नान्ति सरः संत्यज्य पल्वले ॥25॥

Those who make efforts for the purity of the soul elsewhere leaving the clean holy place (base) of their souls, I believe, they bathe in the (dirty) pond leaving the lake (of pure water).

स्वात्मानमिच्छुभिर्ज्ञातुं सहनीयाः परीषहाः।
नश्यत्यसहमानस्य स्वात्मज्ञानं परीषहात् ॥26॥

The occasions of trouble and tribulation are to be borne by those desirous of knowing their (own) souls. The knowledge of their souls gets destroyed on account of (such) occasions in case of those who fail to bear them.

The term *'parīṣaha'* means what is to be endured by the saints. There are occasions of bodily and mental unrest in the lives of the saints. They have been counted as twenty-two in number, some of them being related with the body and others are of mental nature. Some of them are caused by external factors and others arise in the mind and are not very closely connected with the external factors. In the same chain the possibility of the joint occasions depending on the external and the mental factors cannot be denied. Basically all these occasions assume a mental form and only then they can be termed as *parīṣahas.* The concern of a saint in not only limited to understand the origination and variety of these occasions, but has to go beyond them to the conquest over them to obtain a state of tranquility for himself. So the true discipline consists in overcoming them successfully, and hence it is better known by the term *'parīṣaha jaya'* meaning the conquest over these occasions. If the course of fighting against these occasions is ignored, the conquest over them will become certainly impossible and thus there may be a loss of right knowledge for him.

अनुबन्धः सुखे दुःखे न कार्यो निर्जरार्थिभिः।
आर्तं तदनुबन्धेन जायते भूरिकर्मदम् ॥27॥

No agreement (with the *parīṣahas*) is to be made by those, desirous of *nirjarā,* during moments of rest and trouble. Such an agreement results in helpless and painful thinking (an undesirable type of meditation) full of the mud (of *karmas*).

A saint always aims at the expulsion of *karmas* from his soul, hence he should not surrender in favour of these *parīṣahas* to save himself from the pain and unrest these are likely to cause to him. This surrender would bring to him a bondage of a huge amount of *karmas* in place of granting him freedom from the existing *karmas*.

आत्मावभबोधतो नूनमात्मा शुद्ध्यति नान्यतः।
अन्यतः शुद्धिमिच्छन्तो विपरीतदृशोऽखिलाः ॥28॥

Verily, by the wisdom (right understanding) of the (pure) soul the soul is purified, not by any other means. They who expect the purity of the soul from anything (other than the pure soul) are all with a perverted vision.

स्पृश्यते शोध्यते नात्मा मलिनेनामलेन वा।
परद्रव्य-बहिर्भूतः परद्रव्येण सर्वथा ॥29॥

The soul, extraneous to all other substances, is absolutely not touched or purified by other substances, whether filthy or pure.

स्वरूपमात्मनो भाव्यं परद्रव्य-जिहासया।
न जहाति परद्रव्यमात्मरूपाभिभावकः ॥30॥

The practice to realize the identity of the soul along with a desire to renounce (its association with) other substances is worthwhile. (Only) he who does not respect (such a practice for) the identity of the (pure) soul does not renounce the 'other' substance.

विज्ञातव्यं परद्रव्यमात्मद्रव्य-जिघृक्षया।
अविज्ञातपरद्रव्यो नात्मद्रव्यं जिघृक्षति ॥31॥

All the substances (other than the soul) are worth knowing by one with a desire to realize the substance of the soul. One, by whom the other substances are not known, cannot desire (to realize) the substance of the soul.

स्वतत्त्व-रक्तये नित्यं परद्रव्य-विरक्तये।
स्वभावो जगतो भाव्यः समस्तमलशुद्धये ॥32॥

The nature of the world always is worth our repeated concentration and practice for creating interest in our own (spiritual) identily and for creating disinterest in the other substances; and (finally) for achieving purity (of the soul) from the entire filth (resulting from its association with the 'other' including the *karmas*) the nature of the world is worth (our) concentration.

The knowledge of the soul or self is the most potent instrument with one to realize the true identity of one's soul with the total exclusion of what is other than the soul. This 'other' always stands as an impediment on the way to realization of the self; nay, it causes deviations from the path by leading one to lose sight of the true path. Hence to keep off this 'other' is highly desirable throughout the entire journey started in search of the true self. But this precaution and measure for the safe conduct of the journey is possible, if one has sufficient knowledge the soul and its 'other' to select the one and to reject the other. Only with such a discrimination between the two, one will develop interest in and inclination to the soul and disinterest in and abstention from everything that is antithetical with the soul. So this knowledge must proceed on the mutually opposing duality between the two. The foregoing verses lay emphasis on this discriminatory knowledge of the two – the soul and the non-soul.

यत्पञ्चाभ्यन्तरैः पापैः सेव्यमानः प्रबध्यते।
न तु पञ्चबहिर्भूतैराश्चर्यं किमतः परम् ॥33॥

One indulging in the internal five sins gets bound (with the *karmas*) and not by the (participation in) external (practical) five sins. What more amazing instance (than this) can be there?

The list of five vows as prescribed in Jaina Ethics is aimed at fighting the five sins so enumerated there. The five sins are violence, untruthfulness, theft, sexual impurity and possession. The antithesis of these are non-violence, truthfulness, non-theft, absence of sex and non-possession, all distinguished in their two dimensions, the great and the small. The former are observed by the sanits, while the latter are meant for the house-holders. In both the cases their internal observance and the resulting purity is what is reckoned to be most desirable by reducing their external observance to only a secondary status.

ज्ञानस्य ज्ञानमज्ञानमज्ञानस्य प्रयच्छति।
आराधना कृता यस्माद् विद्यमानं प्रदीयते ॥34॥

Efforts made to attain (right) knowledge, result in the gain of (right) knowledge; and those made to attain wrong knowledge, result in the gain of wrong knowledge, for (only) that can be given which is under possession.

न ज्ञान-ज्ञानिनोर्भेदो विद्यते सर्वथा यतः।
ज्ञाने ज्ञाते ततो ज्ञानी ज्ञातो भवति तत्त्वतः ॥35॥

Because there is no absolute distinction between knowledge and the owner of knowledge, therefore in the real sense, the owner of knowledge becomes the possesser of knowledge on knowledge being attained by him.

ज्ञानं स्वात्मनि सर्वेण प्रत्यक्षमनुभूयते।
ज्ञानानुभवहीनस्य नार्थज्ञानं प्रसिद्ध्यति ॥36॥

All directly experience knowledge in their souls. For one bereft of the experience of knowledge the knowledge of objects is not well proved.

प्रतीयते परोक्षेण ज्ञानेन विषयो यदि।
सोऽनेन परकीयेण तदा किं न प्रतीयते ॥37॥

If objects are experienced by the indirect (depending on senses) knowledge, why then is the object i.e. the soul (itself) not experienced by the indirect knowledge?

येनार्थो ज्ञायते तेन ज्ञानी न ज्ञायते कथम्।
उद्योतो दृश्यते येन दीपस्तेन तरां न किम् ॥38॥

How is the onwer of knowledge not known by a knowledge with which the object is known? How can a lamp be not perceived by a perception with which its light is perceived?

विदन्ति दुर्धियो वेद्यं वेदकं न विदन्ति किम्।
द्योत्यं पश्यन्ति न द्योतमाश्चर्यं वत कीदृशम् ॥39॥

Why do the persons with vitiated intellect know the knowable but not the knower? What type of amazment it is that they see the objects enlightened by light but not the light (itself).

Knowledge and the soul are very closely connected; nay, they are indisguishably identical with each other. Those who fail to realize this truth are suffering from a vitiation of their capacity for understanding. This thesis is supported by an example of the lamp which performs a double function of enlightening itself and the objects covered under its light. We are not to posit any other power in the soul to know itself besides the power of knowing the objects. In common parlance we are habituated to effect knowing in terms of its subject and object. So, regarding the knowledge of the soul, we appear to divide the soul into two parts representing the subject and the object of the process of knowning. But as we go deep into the problem, we well experience the double nature of the soul, enlightening itself and the objects simultaneously. We may hold that the knowledge of objects obtained by a soul is simultaneously translated into the knowledge of the soul with its knowledge of the objects. Such a knowledge is a very powerful factor, supported and enriched by austerity to cause a very heavy expulsion of *karmas* from the soul.

ज्ञेय-लक्ष्येण विज्ञाय स्वरूपं परमात्मनः।
व्यावृत्त्य लक्ष्यतः शुद्धं ध्यायतो हानिरंहसाम् ॥40॥

Having known the identity of the soul with a reference of the knowable and then diverting it from the knowable, the destruction of *karmas* takes place for meditating on the (pure) soul.

चट्टुकेन यथा भोज्यं गृहीत्वा स विमुच्यते।
गोचरेण तथान्मानं विज्ञाय स विमुच्यते ॥41॥

Just as after taking food (articles) with the help of a spoon; it (the spoon) is left (there); so also after knowning the soul with the help of the perception of the sense objects, the sense perception is dropped.

उपलब्धे यथाहारे दोषहीने सुखासिकः।
आत्मतत्त्वे तथा क्षिप्रमित्यहोज्ञानिनां रतिः ॥42॥

Just as one finds satisfaction on getting (and consuming) food free from all defects, so those with right knowledge centre their interest (and liking) immediately in the principle of the (pure) soul.

परद्रव्यं यथा सद्भिर्ज्ञात्वा दुःख-विभीरुभिः।
दुःखदं त्यज्यते दूरमात्मतत्त्वरतैस्तथा ॥43॥

Just as by the good persons who specially fear the (association of) other things causing distress; in the same way those who have centred their interest in the principle of the soul leave the trouble-bearing other substances at a distance.

ज्ञाने विशोधिते ज्ञानमज्ञानेऽज्ञानमूर्जितम्।
शुद्धं स्वर्णमिव स्वर्णे लोहे लोहमिवाश्नुते ॥44॥

In purified knowledge, knowledge (itself) gains in quality (but) in (wrong) knowledge (wrong) knowledge itself gets intesified, as in gold pure gold (is obtained) and in iron (only) iron (is obtained).

प्रतिबिम्बं यथादर्शे दृश्यते परसङ्गतः।
चेतने निर्मले मोहस्तथा कल्मषसङ्गतः ॥45॥

Just as an image is seen in a mirror on acount of its association with the other (object), so also delusion is seen in pure consciousness on account of its association with *karmas*.

धर्मेण वासितो जीवो धर्मे पापे न वर्तते।
पापेन वासितो नूनं पापे धर्मे न सर्वदा ॥46॥
ज्ञानेन वासितो ज्ञाने नाऽज्ञानेऽसौ कदाचन।
यतस्ततो मतिः कार्या ज्ञाने शुद्धिं विधित्सुभिः ॥47॥

A *jīva* effected by meritorious actions engages (itself) in such actions, not in sinful ones. Certainly, one effected by sinful actions engages (oneself) in such actions, not in meritorious ones.

Because one effected by (right) knowledge engages oneself in (right) knowledge, never in wrong knowledge; therefore intellect is to be applied to (right) knowledge by those desirous of achieving purity (of their souls).

ज्ञानी निर्मलतां प्राप्तो नाज्ञानं प्रतिपद्यते।
मलिनत्वं कुतो याति काञ्चनं हि विशोधितम् ॥48॥

Having attained (spiritual) purity, one with (right) knowledge does not resort to wrong knowledge. Whence does purified gold turn to be impure? (It never becomes impure).

अध्येतव्यं स्तिमितमनसा ध्येयमाराधनीयं,
पृच्छ्यं श्रव्यं भवति विदुषाऽभ्यस्यमावर्जनीयम् ।
वेद्य गद्यं किमपि तदिह प्रार्थनीयं विनेयं,
दृश्यं स्पृश्यं प्रभवति यतः सर्वदात्मस्थिरत्वम् ॥49॥

In the world a thing always becomes worth study, worth meditating, worth resorting to, worth questioning, worth hearing, worth practising, worth prohibiting, worth touching, for a learned person with concentration of mind, for it augments the stability of soul (for him).

इत्थं योगी व्यपगतपरद्रव्य-संगमप्रसंगो
नीत्वा कामं चपल-करण-ग्राममन्तर्मुखत्वम् ।
ध्यात्वात्मानं विशदचरण-ज्ञान-दृष्टिस्वभावं
नित्यज्योतिः पदमनुपमं याति निर्जीर्णकर्मा ॥50॥

Thus the yogi, for whom the context of the association of other substances is exhausted and who has subjected the *karmas* to the process of *nirjarā*, attains the unparalled and ever enlightened status, having turned the group of the unstable senses sufficiently inward, and having meditated on the soul whose nature is vivid (faultless) conduct, knowledge and faith.

Here ends Chapter-6, Nirjarādhikāra of Yogasāra-prābhṛta by Āchārya Amitagati.

Chapter-7

Mokṣādhikāra

अभावे बन्धहेतूनां निर्जरायां च भास्वरः।
समस्तकर्म-विश्लेषो मोक्षो वाच्योऽपुनर्भवः ॥1॥

In the absence of the causes of bondage (of *karma*) and the process of the expulsion (of *karmas-nirjarā*) being in action, the dissociation of all the *karmas* (from the soul) is said to be (the principle of) the effulgent *mokṣa* or liberation, not followed by further birth.

The *mokṣa* or liberation is the last and seventh principle of Jaina philosophy. It is the culmination of the process for the salvation of the *jīva* suffering in the whirlpool of *saṁsāra*. It is attained by a *jīva* because it has been able to achieve *saṁsāra*—the process of the check of the inflow of *karmas* on one hand, and on the other, it has been able to continue the process of *nirjarā* for the expulsion of the *karmas* already accumulated by the *jīva*. As a necessary consequence, its association of the *karmas* must come to an end. This is the state of *mokṣa* or liberation, after which, in the absence of causes for the further entry into the world, there is no further birth in the *saṁsāra*. Then the *jīva* has to suffer no limitation and distortion of its pure powers; it then shines and will continue to shine in full effulgence of its powers infinitely in time. It has achieved the final goal and has nothing to achieve further.

उदेति केवलं जीवे मोह-विघ्नावृति-क्षये।
भानु-बिम्बमिवाकाशे भास्वरं तिमिरात्यये ॥2॥

On the destruction of the repetitions of the obstruction of delusion, omniscience emerges, as on the removal of darkness the brilliant disc of the sun (is seen) in the sky.

न दोषमलिने तत्र प्रादुर्भवति केवलम्।
आदर्शे न मलग्रस्ते किंचित् रूपं प्रकाशते ॥3॥

There (in the soul) defiled by the filth of the *karmas* omniscience does not emerge as in a mirror soiled by dirt no visible object is reflected.

न मोहप्रभृतिच्छेदः शुद्धात्मध्यानतो विना।
कुलिशेन विना येन भूधरो भिद्यते न हि ॥4॥

Without the meditation of pure soul the destruction of delusion etc, omniscience does not arise (in a soul), as without the *vajra*–the weapon of the lord of the celetial beings-certainly a mountain cannot be broken.

विभिन्ने सति दुर्भेदकर्मग्रन्थि-महीधरे।
तीक्ष्णेन ध्यानवज्रेण भूरि-संक्लेश-कारिणि ॥5॥
आनन्दो जायतेऽत्यन्तं तात्त्विकोऽस्य महात्मनः।
औषधेनेव सव्याधेर्व्याधेरभिभवे कृते ॥6॥

On the destruction of the mountain of the knots or complexes of *karmas* which are very difficult to break and which cause great affliction, there appears real happiness to this great soul in abundance, just as for a ailing person (there appears great rest) on the removal of the disease by (the use of) medicine.

Karmas obstruct the functions of the pure soul. Full knowledge or omniscience remains unmanifest in a soul on account of the operation of the knowledge-obscuring *karma*.

So also bliss does not manifest in a soul on account of the operation of the deluding *karma.* This underlying attribute of the soul i.e. the pure blissful nature also emerges in the soul on the destruction of the obstructing *karma.* In the mundane existence it was vitiated and hence it took the form of pain and pleasure. In the absence of the obstruction of these *karmas* omniscience and bliss manifest in the pure soul simultaneously.

साक्षादतीन्द्रियानर्थान् दृष्टा केवलचक्षुषा।
प्रकृष्ट-पुण्य-सामर्थ्यात् प्रातिहार्यसमन्वितः ॥7॥
अवन्ध्य-देशनः श्रीमान् यथाभव्य-नियोगतः।
महात्मा केवली कश्चिद् देशनायां प्रवर्तते ॥8॥

Having perceived directly (even) the extra-sensory objects with the eye of omniscience (*Kevala jināna*) and being accompanied by the (eight) material symbols (related with the status of the omniscient Lord) on account of the extremely high merit (attained by him), some great soul with omniscience and full spiritual prosperity proceeds to disseminate his preaching, which never fails to bring about its full fruitions, on account of the coincidence of the *jīvas* having capacity for liberation (with the preaching programme of the Tīrthaṅkara Kevalī).

All the souls that are able to destroy the obstructions generated by the *karmas* in their progress towards liberation are not expected to hold the *samavasaraṇa*—the grand meeting for propagating the truth revealed to them by the attainment of omniscience. Out of these perfect souls only a few arc with the *karma*-adjunct of *Tīrāthaṅkara*-nāma-prakṛti, the operation of which is responsible for holding the *samavasaraṇa.* As the *Tīrthaṅkaras* have already destroyed the deluding *karma* such a divine programme cannot be expected to be actually willed by them; nor are they on the same ground, at all worried about its success. They are so destined for preaching the truth and for being surrounded by pompous preparations by the operation of the *karma* already mentioned and named above. The presence of the liberable *jīvas* in the audience is only an accident and may be held to be auxiliary condition for the auspicious occasion. Such souls are born on this earth for the revival of truth, and which are counted as only twenty four in number for a particular aeon of time. The aeons have been repeated in the past and will be repeated in future, being separated from each other by very long intervals of time.

विभावसोरिवोष्णत्वं चरिष्णोरिव चापलम् ।
शशाङ्कस्येव शीतत्वं स्वरूपं ज्ञानमात्मनः ॥9॥

Knowledge holds (a relation of) identity with the soul, as heat with the sun, as movement with air and as pleasant cool with the moon.

Under the relation of identity the relata cannot be separated from each other; but we can talk about them in an analytic way introducing a distinction between them. The examples cited in the verse make the situation understandable.

चैतन्यमात्मनो रूपं तच्च ज्ञानमयं विदुः ।
प्रतिबन्धक-सामर्थ्यान्न स्वकार्ये प्रवर्तते ॥10॥

Consciousness is the identity of the soul, it is said to be (all) imbued with knowledge; (but) it is not engaged in performing its (pure) function because of the force of the obstruction (of *karmas*).

If consciousness and knowledge are very closely intrinsic to the soul, then why are they not able to perform their pure functions always? The answer to this question is given in the verse. The soul has been in association with *karmas* from beginningless times, and these *karmas*, by nature, create difficulties for the functions of the soul. So the soul continues to be so affected by the *karmas*, until and unless it is able to break this association finally and completely.

ज्ञानी ज्ञेये भवत्यज्ञो नासति प्रतिबन्धके।
प्रतिबन्धं विना वह्निर्न दाह्येऽदाहकः कदा ॥11॥

In the absence of the obstruction a knower does not become bereft of knowledge about the knowable. When does fire, in the absence of obstruction, become unable to burn objects fit to be burnt?

प्रतिबन्धो न देशादि-विप्रकर्षोऽस्य युज्यते।
तथानुभव-सिद्धत्वात् सप्तहेतेरिव स्फुटम् ॥12॥

The great separation by space etc. (time also) is not applicable as an obstruction in case of this (omniscience), because it is so certified by experience as (it is) clear in case of the sun.

Basically the objects of knowledge and knowlege are bound with a relationship of knowability and knowership. Knowledge must know objects and objects must be known by knowledge. If there are no obstructions between them, our own experience proves the above mentioned relationship. Conversely, we can say that no knowledge can refuse to know an object, and no object can refuse to be known by knowledge. The example given in the verse is only partial just to give us an idea of the situation.

सामान्यवद् विशेषाणां स्वभावो ज्ञेयभावतः।
ज्ञायते स च वा साक्षाद् विना विज्ञायते कथम् ॥13॥
सर्वज्ञः सर्वदर्शी च ततो ज्ञानस्वभावतः।
नाऽस्य ज्ञानस्वभावत्वमन्यथा घटते स्फुटम् ॥14॥

The nature of the particulars becomes known on account of their knowability like that of the universal. This nature is known directly. How can these be (so) known without direct knowledge?

Therefore the omniscient lord is the knower and the perceiver of all (the objects) on account of (his) knowing-nature. It is clear that (this) knowing-nature of the soul does not find consistency in any other way.

If omniscience is not imbued with the capacity for knowing and perceiving the entirety of the contents of the universe, it will not be able to know all the universals and the particulars with which the contents of the universe are identical. Hence the omnicient being is held to be imbued with the capacity of knowing and perceiving all the contents existent in the universe. This process can be consistent only when it is effected in a direct way i.e. directly by the knowing soul without any intervention from outside. Thus omniscience is established on the ground of the intrisic power of the soul for knowing and the capacity of knowability on the part of the objects of the universe including the souls. Thus the soul comes out to be a self-knowing entity on the basis of this mutual position. This position may not be taken to be suffering from mutual dependence, because such a situation must be resorted to in case of a beginningless and endless continuance of the universe.

वेद्यायुर्नाम-गोत्राणि यौगपद्येन केवली।
शुक्लध्यानकुठारेण छित्त्वा गच्छति निर्वृतिम् ॥15॥

A *kevalī* (as explained above) attains liberation (the final release from the mundane existence) by destroying the feeling (*vedanīya*), the age-determining (*āyur*), the body making (*nāma*) and the status-determining (*gotra*) karmas simultaneously with the hammer of the purest meditation (*śukla dhyana*).

In the stage of *kaivalya* or *arhathood* only the four destructive types of *karmas* are destroyed by a soul. These are the knowledge-obscuring, conation-obscuring, deluding and obstructing *karmas*. They stand as great impediments in the way of attaining omniscience by a soul. After destroying them and attaining omniscience the soul continues to exist in the world with four non-destructive types of *karmas* in the presence of which omniscience can flourish without any difficulty. But still the final aim i.e. the complete and final release from the mundane existence is not achieved. Hence the destruction of the remaining four *karmas*, though of the non-destructive type, still remains to be achieved. For this, the soul has to undergo and perform specially the highest type of meditation named as the *śukla dhyana* which alone is potent to destroy all the remaining four *karmas* simultaneously. Then the perfect soul flies to the top of the universe and takes only one instant of time to reach it, as the Jaina philosophy holds traditionally and logically. From this home of the liberated ones no return is possible in the absence of causes which can lead to such a fall.

कर्मैव भिद्यते नास्य शुक्लध्यान-नियोगतः ।
नासौ विधीयते कस्य नेदं वचनमञ्चितम् ॥16॥
कर्मव्यपगमे (मो) राग-द्वेषाद्यनुपपत्तितः ।
आत्मनः(ना) संगं(सह) रागाद्याः न नित्यत्वेन संगताः ॥17॥

It is not fair to say that on account of the association of pure meditation *karmas* are not destroyed for this soul and the liberation is not attained by anyone. The reason is that on the destruction of *karmas*, attachment and aversion are not generated (in the soul), and (secondly) attachment etc. are not the permanent accompaniments of the soul.

In the present context a question and doubt is raised that *karmas* are destroyed by the pure meditation and the final release from mundanity is granted to none on that account. In answering the question a reference to the basic theory of the soul and its bondage by the *karmas* is made. Though the soul and the *karmas* have been found to exist together in the mundane existence, but this togetherness between the two is not permanent, it is only accidental. It means it can be brought to an end by a proper disciplinary course. *Karmas* are the causes of generating attachment, delusion and aversion in a soul, hence in the absence of *karmas* these will not originate in the soul to make it again liable to bondage by *karmas*. In this way the chain of *karmas* and passions gets broken, and the soul is left free both from *karmas* and passions. It is why, as the *āchārya* says, it is not consistent to raise such a question.

न निर्वृतः सुखीभूतः पुनरायाति संसृतिम् ।
सुखदं हि पदं हित्वा दुःखदं कः प्रपद्यते ॥18॥

The liberated soul, having attained spiritual bliss does not return to mundanity. Certainly, who will like to attain a state full of restlessness after leaving one of (spiritual) bliss?

शरीरं न गृह्णाति भूयः कर्मव्यपायतः ।
कारणस्यात्यये कार्यं न कुत्रापि प्ररोहति ॥19॥

A liberated soul does not become again embodied on account of the destruction of *karmas*. On the destruction of the cause the (concerned) effect does not grow up anywhere.

It is well-known dictum of Jaina philosophy that a soul after attaining liberation does not return to and fall into any form of mundane existence. On the total destruction of *karmas*–the causes that could drag it back to the world and its various embodiments–its fall from the highest status of liberation must become impossible. The soul has now reached as if, its own home and is now all full with its intrinsic and pure attributes which will naturally disallow its association with all that is the other for the pure soul. Practical understanding as exemplified above also supports the truth of the non-return of the pure soul.

न ज्ञानं प्राकृतो धर्मो मन्तव्यो मान्य-बुद्धिभिः।
अचेतनस्य न ज्ञानं कदाचन विलोक्यते ॥20॥

Knowledge should not be held to be the property born of (unconscious) *prakṛiti* by those whose understanding is worth honouring. Knowledge has never been seen a property of an unconscious entity.

Here, a reference seems to have been to the *Sāṅkhya* philosophy which starts with the dualism of *Puruṣa,* with immutable consciousness and *Prakṛti,* basically unconscious. Knowledge is supposed to originate from *Prakṛti* by the mere presence of *Puruṣa.* The objection against this position is that *Prakṛti* which is unconscious by its very nature can, in no case, be held to give rise to knowledge which is by its very nature, conscious. The position can be extended to materialism also, which holds that matter, uncounscious by its very nature, gives rise to knowledge independently of any other conscious entity unlike the *Sāṅkhya.* The Jaina philosophy holds that the soul is, by its very nature, conscious and matter, by its very nature, unconscious. One cannot be converted into the other; nor are the properties of one transformed into those of the other.

दुरितानीव न ज्ञानं निर्वृतस्यापि गच्छति।
काञ्चनस्य मले नष्टे काञ्चनत्वं न नश्यति ॥21॥
न ज्ञानादि-गुणाभावे जीवस्यास्ति व्यवस्थितिः।
लक्षणापगमे लक्ष्यं न कुत्राप्यवतिष्ठते ॥22॥

Knowledge does not go away (from the soul) as *karmas* go away for the liberated soul. On the removal of filth of gold, the quality of its being gold is not destroyed.

The *jīva* cannot be established in the absence of (its) attributes like knowledge etc. On the destruction of the differentia (of an entity) the differentiated (entity) is no where found to be existent.

What is extraneous to an entity can be destroyed or separated from it without the least danger of extinction of the entity itself. Under this rule *karmas* can be destroyed and separated from the soul, but not knowledge, which is the differentia of the soul. Moreover, in the absence of knowledge etc. which are the very defferentia of the soul, the existence of the soul cannot be consistently established. The same will be the situation if knowledge etc. are held accidental to the soul.

विविधं बहुधा बन्धं बुध्यमानो न मुच्यते।
कर्म-बद्धो विनोपायं गुप्ति-बद्ध इव ध्रुवम् ॥23॥
विभेदं लक्षणैर्बुद्ध्वा स द्विधा जीवकर्मणोः।
मुक्तकर्मात्मतत्त्वस्थो मुच्यते सदुपायवान् ॥24॥

It is certain that a *jīva* bound with *karmas* does not get riddance from them without resorting to ways (necessary for it), though it may know the bondage with its variety in many a way like one imprisoned in a jail.

The *jīva*, having shaken off the *karmas* and establishing (itself) in the principle of soul, achieves freedom from bondage, if he is equipped with ways (and means required for it) after knowing the difference of their being two, as the *jīva* and the *karmas*, by means of their differentiating qualities.

Mere knowledge of bondage with its varieties is not sufficient to achieve freedom from bondage, unless this knowledge is supplemented by a course of discipline necessary and potent for taking the *jīva* to a successful end. It must entertain not only knowledge about the duality of the soul and *karmas* but should also cherish such a faith. Equipped with these requirements of right faith and right knowledge it must undergo a course of discipline covered under the term right conduct, if it is at all desirous to attain the full fruits of his preparations and attempts. Thus the way to liberation is constituted by the three jewels-right faith, right knowledge and right conduct-in Jaina philosophy.

एको जीवो द्विधा प्रोक्तः शुद्धाशुद्ध-व्यपेक्षया।
स्वर्णमिव लोकेन व्यवहारमुपेयुषा ॥25॥
संसारी कर्मणा युक्तो मुक्तस्तेन विवर्जितः।
अशुद्धस्तत्र संसारी मुक्तः शुद्धोऽपुनर्भवः ॥26॥

The *jīva* is one, it has been described as of two kinds with reference to pure and impure points of view by those resorting to the practical point of view, like gold (as pure gold and impure gold) talked over in the popular parlance.

The mundane *jīva* is with *karma*, the liberated *jīva* is bereft of *karma.* There the mundane *jiva* is impure and the liberated one is pure and is not liable to further births.

भवं वदन्ति संयोगं यतोऽत्रात्म-तदन्ययोः।
वियोगं तु भवाभावमापुनर्भविकं ततः ॥27॥

As (they) hold mundanity (as) the association of the soul with its 'other', dissociation (between the two) (is called) the absence of mundanity, therefore (the pure liberated *jīva*) is beyond rebirth.

निरस्तापर-संयोगः स्व-स्वभाव-व्यवस्थितः।
सर्वोत्सुक्यविनिर्मुक्तः स्तिमितोदधि-सन्निभः ॥28॥
एकान्त-क्षीण-संक्लेशो निष्ठितार्थो निरञ्जनः।
निराबाधः सदानन्दो मुक्तावात्मावतिष्ठते ॥29॥

In the state of liberation the soul continues as dissociated from the 'other', established in its pure nature, bereft of (all) enthusiasm, stable like the (deep) ocean, with complete destruction of distress, with accomplishment of (his final) aim, free from (all) blemishes, with no obstruction (against its natural and pure functions), and always blissful.

These verses enumerate some of the divine gains and gifts that result from the destruction of the totality of *karmas* and thus qualify the existence and continuance of the soul for all times to come.

ध्यानस्येदं फलं मुख्यमैकान्तिकमनुत्तरम्।
आत्मगम्यं परं ब्रह्म ब्रह्मविद्भिरुदाहृतम् ॥30॥
अतोऽत्रैव महान् यत्नस्तत्त्वतः प्रतिपत्तये।
प्रेक्षावता सदा कार्यो मुक्त्वा वादादिवासनाम् ॥31॥

The realization of the pure soul by the self is the main, absolute and unparalled result of this meditation, so say those who know the Brahma (the pure soul).

Leaving aside the long imbibed passion and habit for debate (and discussion) etc., the great effort should really and always be made here for the realization (of the Brahma) by those with comprehensive perceptive power.

ऊचिरे ध्यान-मार्गज्ञा ध्यानोद्धूत-रजश्चयाः।
भावि-योगि-हितायेदं ध्वान्त-दीपसमं वचः ॥32॥
वादानां प्रतिवादानां भाषितारो विनिश्चितम्।
नेवं गन्छन्ति तत्त्वान्तं गतेरिव विलम्बिनः ॥33॥

Those who know the way of meditation and who have shrugged off the heaps of dust (of *karmas*) have pronounced this word (preaching) which removes the ignorance as a lamp removes darkness, for the benefit of the future yogis.

It is certain that the participants in a debates in favour of and against some contentions do not get at the norm of a principle in this way, as one with the habit of being late (in start) does not reach the end of (his) journey.

The *āchārya* now wants to discourage useless debates and discussions conducted with an aim of gaining superiority and pedantry. Such debates lead only to huge wastage of time and intellectual energy, and there is no positive gain in the form of enlightenment in the field of knowledge and conduct of life. At the same time it should not be forgotten that mutual discussions, seminars and symposia are great sources of expanding the field of knowledge and diving deep into the ocean of knowledge. A close scrutiny must be made about these ways as to see whether they assume the form the *āchārya* has advised to refrain from or they are of the second type really helping us on the way of attaining pure knowledge and the ways of right and moral conduct.

विभक्तचेतन-ध्यानमत्रोपायं विदुर्जिनाः।
गतावस्तप्रमादस्य सन्मार्ग-गमनं यथा ॥34॥
योज्यमानो यथा मन्त्रो विषं घोरं निषूदते।
तथात्मापि विधानेन कर्मानेकभवार्जितम् ॥35॥
चिन्त्यं चिन्तामणिर्दत्ते कल्पितं कल्पपादपः।
अविचिन्त्यमसंकल्प्यं विविक्तात्मानुचिन्तितः ॥36॥

In this context Lord Jinas have pronounced the meditation of the conscious soul chiselled of the 'other' as the way (to realize the soul), just as to follow the right way is a means in the journey for one who has given up laziness.

Just as the use of a text (*mantra*) destroys the intense poison, in the same way the soul, too, destroys *karmas* assimilated during many past lives by the discipline (of the meditation of the pure soul).

The wish-fulfilling ruby grants the gift of the thought–of (articles), the wish-fulfilling tree grants the gift of the (article) wanted; but thinking about the chiselled soul, grants the gift of both the articles thought-of and wanted.

जन्म-मृत्यु-जरा-रोगा हन्यन्ते येन दुर्जयाः।
मनोभू-हनने तस्य नायासः कोऽपि विद्यते ॥37॥

For the meditation of the pure soul, by which the birth, death, old age and diseases difficult to conquer, are (easily) destroyed, there is no exertion for it in destroying the (instinct and passion of) sexuality.

मुक्त्वा वाद-प्रवादाद्यमध्यात्मं चिन्त्यताम् ततः।
नाविधूते तमःस्तोमे ज्ञेये ज्ञानं प्रवर्तते ॥38॥

Therefore after leaving (the way of) debate and discussion, engage (your self) in thinking about the pure soul. Without removing the expansion of darkness, knowledge cannot flouerish in the knowable.

In the region of pure spirituality holding debates and discussions create difficulties in the way of self-realization, hence such ways have been compared with darkness which obstructs our perception of the objects.

उपेयस्य यतः प्राप्ति र्जायते सदुपायतः।
सदुपाये ततः प्राज्ञैर्विधातव्यो महादरः ॥39॥

On account of the (application of) right ways the gain of that for which ways are applied is made actual. Therefore the wise persons should pay (attach) great respect (importance) to the right ways.

नाध्यात्म-चिन्तनादन्यः सदुपायस्तु विद्यते।
दुरापः सः परं जीवैर्मोहव्यालकदर्थितैः ॥40॥

There is no right way other than the meditation of the pure soul (for realizing oneself); but that is very difficult to adopt on the part of the *jīvas* made restless by the serpent of delusion.

उत्साहो निश्चयो धैर्यं सन्तोषस्तत्त्वदर्शनम्।
जनपदात्ययः षोढा सामग्रीयं बहिर्भवा ॥41॥

Enthusiasm, determination, perseverence, contentment, perception of the principles and avoidance of the contact with people are the six external accessories (of the spiritual meditation).

Though meditation is an internal mental process, yet it is assisted by some factors which are external to it. These very factors have been enumerated in this verse as six in number. The importance of these six factors can be very well realised by one who adopts this way of meditation to realize his pure soul.

आगमेनानुमानेन ध्यानाभ्यास-रसेन च।
त्रेधा विशोधयन् बुद्धिं ध्यानमाप्नोति पावनम् ॥42॥

Purifying one's intellect in the three ways i.e. by the tradition of scriptures, by syllogistic arguementation and the taste (experience) resulting form the practice of meditation one attains the holy meditation.

The tradition of scriptures is a highly esteemed source of learning and knowing the principles of existence. This knowledge can be further strengthened by making use of logical methods in their study. Alongwith these two equipments a constant practice of meditation specially that of the pure soul is very necessary. Such a practice is bound to yeild special experience of self-realization, which, in turn, will increase our interest and efforts to advance in the direction pointing to meditation. With the intensification of these factors one will surely reach the stage of self-realization.

आत्मध्यानरतिर्ज्ञेयं विद्वत्तायाः परं फलम्।
अशेष शास्त्र-शास्तृत्वं संसारोऽभाषि धीधनैः ॥43॥

The interest in the meditation of the soul should be known to be the best result of (our) learming. The capacity to preach (the contents of) all the scriptures has been called mundanity by those possessed of the wealth of intellect.

Again it is emphasized that the ability to comment on the contents of all the varied works of learning is not sufficient and potent for achieving the aim of self-realization. It must be supplemented by and should lead to the meditation of the soul. Such a superfluous learning is not required in its variety and magnitude, if one resorts to the way of meditaion of the soul. It is, in no way, useful and advisable to confine oneself to the aquisition of knowledge and the ways of its explanation and expansion in the absence of the spiritual meditation, which alone is competent to bring about the most desired fruit of self-realization.

संसारः पुत्र-दारादिः पुंसां संमूढचेतसाम् ।
संसारो विदुषां शास्त्रमध्यात्मरहितात्मनाम् ॥44॥

For the people with a foolish mind the son, wife etc. constitute mundanity—the whirl of wanderings in the world. For the learned persons with no interest and efforts to attain pure spiritual nature, the scripture (works of learning) itself constitutes mundanity.

ज्ञानबीजं परं प्राप्य मनुष्यं कर्मभूमिषु ।
न सद्ध्यानकृषेरन्तः प्रवर्तन्तेऽल्पमेधसः ॥45॥

Those with poor intellect do not engage themselves in the agriculture (growth and development) of right meditation (even) having attained the human form in the work-regions, and the best seed of knowledge.

Herein a reference is made to the two types of geographical regions mentioned in Jaina literature on the subject. They are the work region *(karma-bhūmi)* and the enjoyment region *(bhoga-bhūmi.)* In the latter the means of life and its pleasures are supplied by nature, the people of this region are not required to sweat themselves for living cosy and comfortable lives. As such they are not even mindful about achieving the spiritual rest and peace for themselves, so engrossed in pleasures they are. In the former i.e. the work-region the people get chances for turning their lives in a direction they choose for themselves. So the option to advance on the path of righteousness including the spiritual meditation is open to them. Hence *āchārya* states that the gain of the human form is like the gain of seeds of knowledge, which the human beings must sow in the fields of work-region to get the harvest of the meditation of the soul. On account of the operation of deluding *karma* they are rendered poor of intellect and thus are disenabled to start the programme for self-realization.

बडिशाभिषवच्छेदो दारुणो भोगशर्मणि।
सक्तास्त्यजन्ति सद्ध्यानं धिगहो! मोहतामस् ॥46॥

In the (course) of pleasure born of (worldly) enjoyments there is extremely unbearable pain like that caused (to a fish) by the cut (wound) of the fish-hook fitted with a piece of meat. (But unfortunately) those engrossed (in pleasure) abandon the (way of) right meditation. Oh, damn the darkness (ignorance) caused by delusion!.

आत्मतत्त्वमजानाना विपर्यास-परायणाः।
हिताहित-विवेकान्धाः खिद्यन्ते साम्प्रतेक्षणाः ॥47॥

Those who do not know the principle of soul, who are expert in the opposite (of the principle of non-soul) , who are blind to discrimination between the beneficial and the non-beneficial and who percieve the (pleasures of) present (alone), suffer restlessness.

आधि-व्याधि-जरा-जाति-मृत्यु-शोकाद्युपद्रवम्।
पश्यन्तोऽपि भवं भीमं नोद्विजन्तेऽत्र मोहिनः ॥48॥

Here the persons under delusion do not apprehend the fearful worldly existence inspite of (clearly) seeing (it) with mental tribulence, bodily (unhealth) disease, old age, birth, death, grief and (so many) other troubles.

अकृत्यं दुर्धियः कृत्यं कृत्यं चाकृत्यमञ्जसा।
अशर्म शर्म मन्यन्ते कच्छू-कण्डूयका इव ॥49॥

Certainly the persons with wrong understanding think that what ought not to be done as worth doing, what ought to be done as worth not doing, and what is not beneficial as beneficial (also vice versa) like those, suffering from itch who take rubbing the spot as pleasant (till blood oozes from it).

Such is the perversion of intellect under the operation of the deluding *karma* that one loses one's capacity to evaluate things in their right perspective; nay, one goes just to the opposite side and suffers very seriously on account of one's wrong judgement. It is a very unfortunate state where the very capacity which initiates the course of our knowing and practice gets vitiated and even perverted.

क्षाराम्भस्त्यागतः क्षेत्रे मधुरोऽमृत-योगतः।
पुरोहति यथा बीजं ध्यानं तत्त्वश्रुतेस्तथा ॥50॥

Just as a seed sprouts in the field by keeping off the saltish water and by supplying sweet water (for irrigation); in the same way meditation (of the soul) grows by hearing the (dissertations of the) principles.

क्षारारम्भः सदृशी त्याज्या सर्वदा भोगशेमुषी।
मधुराम्भोनिभा ग्राह्या यत्नात्तत्त्वश्रुतिर्बुधैः ॥51॥

By the wise persons the intellect which is inclined to enjoyments (of the world) is like the choice for saltish water, and should always be discarded; while hearing of the (dissertations of) the principles (of the soul etc.) which is like a choice for sweet water, should (always) be resorted to with (necessary) carefulness (by them).

बोधरोधः शमापायः श्रद्धाभङ्गोऽभिमानकृत्।
कुतर्को मानसो व्याधिर्ध्यानशत्रुरनेकधा ॥52॥
कुतर्केऽभिनिवेशोऽतो न युक्तो मुक्ति-काङ्क्षिणाम्।
आत्मतत्त्वे पुनर्युक्तः सिद्धि-सौध-प्रवेशके ॥53॥

Obstruction against wisdom, the cessation of tranquility (of mind), the breach of faith, and the misuse of reasoning which is a mental disease causing augmentation of pride, are the various enemies of meditation.

Therefore, for those desirous of achieving liberation, it is not consistent to waste (their mental energies) in the misapplication of reasoning; but again it is proper to apply (them) to the principle of the soul, which allows entry into the palace of success.

विविक्तमिति चेतनं परम-शुद्ध-बुद्धाशयाः
विचिन्त्य सतताहता भवमपास्य दुःखास्पदम्।
निरन्तमपुनर्भवं सुखमतीन्द्रियं स्वात्मजं
समेत्य हतकल्मषं निरुपमं सदैवासते ॥54॥

Those with highly pure and enlightened inner-selves and cherishing respect (for the way of meditation), thinking the conscious soul free from all the 'other', discarding mundanity as an abode of distress, find a permanent lodgement in the state of liberation which knows no end and return (to mundanity), after attaining extra-sensuous, and soul-generated bliss on the attainment of the (total) destruction of *karmas*.

This is the concluding verse of the chapter. It summarizes the main steps and stages of the path to liberation. The yogi must be conscious of the basic and pure nature of the soul, should meditate on it and should be desirous of and respectful to the way of spiritual meditation. His attitude towards the world must be repulsive realizing it not only a source of distress and restlessness but also as all full of them. The fruits of his strenous efforts to realize his pure soul are the total destruction of the *karmas* and the conequent gain of intrinsic and natural bliss. The continuance of this stage is without an end, but certainly with a beginning; hence the danger of a fall to the varying conditions of life in the whirling world is finally got rid of. This is a stage to which no match or transcendence can be concieved. It is earned by the yogi as his permanent abode with no diminution of his pure and self-determined attainments.

Here ends Chapter-7, Mokṣādhikāra of Yogasāra-prābhṛta by Āchārya Amitagati.

Chapter 8

Chāritrādhikāra

विमुच्य विविधारम्भं पारतन्त्र्यकरं गृहम्।
मुक्तिं यियासता धार्यं जिनलिङ्गं पटीयसा ॥1॥

Having abandoned the house which is full of varied activities and causes of enslavement (as against freedom of the soul) the recognition-mark of Lord *Jina*) is worth being borne by one with (spiritual) knowledge and desire to attain liberation.

सोपयोगमनारम्भं लुञ्चित-श्मश्रुमस्तकम्।
निरस्त-तनु-संस्कारं सदा संगविवर्जितम् ॥2॥
निराकृत-परापेक्षं निर्विकारमयाचनम्।
जातरूपधरं लिङ्गं जैनं निर्वृतिकारणम् ॥3॥

The recognition-mark of a Jaina saint consists in being with conation and knowledge (in activity), in plucking the hair of the beard and the head (with hands), in leaving (all) beautification of the body, in abandoning all possesions (internal and external), in brushing aside dependence on others, in being with no blemishes, in not begging (anything), and having the appearance or features of a newly-born baby. These (taken collectively) become the marks of a Jaina (monk) and the causes of the final freedom.

नाहं भवामि कस्याऽपि न किंचन ममापरम्।
इत्यंकिंचनतोपेतं निष्कषायं जितेन्द्रियम् ॥4॥

नमस्कृत्य गुरुं भक्त्या जिनमुद्रा-विभूषितः।
जायते श्रमणोऽसङ्गो विधाय व्रत-संग्रहम् ॥5॥

Having bowed with devotion to the preceptor who cherishes a feeling of non-belongingness (*akiñcana*) like one who thinks as neither I belong to anyone else, nor does anyone else belong to me, who is with no passion and who has conquered one's senses, the *śramaṇa* or the saint, embelished with the posture of the *Jina*, becomes possessionless, having promised to observe the (code of) vows.

These verses mainly deal with the qualifications of the preceptor (*guru*) whom a śramaṇa would approach for initiation. He would first bow to the preceptor so qualified, then place himself in the posture of a *Jina* and then he would accept and observe all the vows prescribed for a saint. Then alone the *śramaṇa* or the saint is said to be possessionless.

महाव्रत-समित्यक्षरोधाः स्युः पञ्च चैकशः।
परमावश्यकं षोढा, लोचोऽस्नानमचेलता ॥6॥
अदन्तधावनं भूमिशयनं स्थितिभोजनम्।
एकभक्तं च सन्त्येते पाल्या मूलगुणा यतेः ॥7॥

Great vows, carefulness, control of senses each of these with their five kinds, six highly essential duties, uprooting of hair, not bathing, no use of cloth, not brushing teeth, sleeping on (bare) ground, partaking of food in the standing posture, and taking food once (only a day), are the primarily qualifying rules worth observance for a saint.

The five great vows are fomulated to fight against the five types of sinful activities, namely violence, untruthfulness, theft, vitiated actions like sex indulgence, and possesions. Consequently the vows have been named as non-violence, truthfulness, non-theft, perfect chastity and non-possession.

The five types of carefulness related to the activities of

movement, speech, taking of food, placing and lifting up things and excretion of the filth of the body. These activities are to be conducted with due carefulness so that they may not lead us to origination and augmentation of sins.

The third item points to the conquest of the pleasures of the five senses of touch, taste, smell, sight and hearing. These senses are a great source of allurment and attraction for pleasures of the fields with which they are concerned. Hence the control of the five senses is considered very necessary to check one from going astray under their sway.

The six essential duties have already been dealt and explained in detail by the *Āchārya* in verses nos. 46, 47, 48, 49, 50, 51 and 52 of the chapter on saṁvara. The remaining seven primary and qualifying conditions or rules are self-explained and need not much of comments.

These twenty eight basic rules have been in practice and uniformly discussed in the Jaina practical philosophy. One who develops a spirit and inclination to adopt the life-style of a homeless seeker of one's true self and approaches a preceptor for initiation in the order of saints, must observe these primary rules and qualities to qualify oneself to advance on the path of liberation. This is the start of the course of discipline required for attaining sainthood or the status of a *śramaṇa.*

निष्प्रमादतया पाल्या योगिनां हितमिच्छता।
सप्रमादः पुनस्तेषु छेदोपस्थापको यतिः ॥8॥

These (primary rules) are worth observance without (any) indolence by the yogīs desirous of (their real) beneficence. On being with indolence in their observance the saint becomes '*chhedopasthāpaka*', which means that he has commited the breach and is required to re-establish himself (in the lost status).

The observance of the primary rules is essential for a

śramaṇa without a slight omission due to lack of necessary precaution; still such occasion of breach may arise in respect of one or the other rule. Such an undesirable incident does not lead to expulsion of the *śramaṇa* from the order of the saints, but can be redressed by undergoing a course of atonement under the guidance of the preceptor. The code of conduct does not allow the formation of any casuistic laws to meet the situation; but admits of rectification.

प्रव्रज्यादायकः सूरिः संयतानां निगीर्यते।
निर्यापकाः पुनः शेषाश्छेदोपस्थापका मताः ॥9॥

The saint who initiates the would-be saints (to the order) is said to be the initiator-saint, the remaining (saints) who help the '*chhedopasthāpaka*'-saints (in re-establishing himself in the lost status) are called the '*niryāpaka*' (observing the course of discipline in general) saints.

प्रकृष्टं कुर्वतः साधोश्चारित्रं कायचेष्टया।
यदिच्छेदस्तदा कार्या क्रियालोचन-पूर्विका ॥10॥
आश्रित्य व्यवहारज्ञं सूरिमालोच्य भक्तितः।
दत्तस्तेन विधातव्यश्छेदश्छेदवता सदा ॥11॥

If the breach occurs for a saint, observing high conduct, (only) by bodily activity, he should follow the way with self-censure.

Having approached a preceptor expert in the practice and having censured (his fault) with devotion (before him) the necessary rectification prescribed by him should always be undergone by the defaulting saint.

If the breach of the rules is only external i.e. due to the bodily activity, the process of rectification is simple and can be done by the defaulting saint himself. If the breach of the rules is internal by way of affecting his spiritual modifications, then the process of rectification must be conducted in the presence and guidance of a capable preceptor by following all the instructions from him (the preceptor).

भूत्वा निराकृतश्छेदश्चारित्राचरणोद्यतः।
मुञ्चमानो निबन्धानि यतिर्विहरतां सदा ॥12॥

Having completed the process for rectification and being engaged in the practical observance of the conduct-rules, the saint may always go on (his) tours, avoiding all the obstacles (that come in his way).

It is necessary for a saint to go on tours in his own interest for avoiding attachment for a particular place and people and also for propagating the religious ways among the people. But while taking up the programme of touring he will not ignore the faultless observance of rules and practice, both internal and external.

शुद्ध-रत्नत्रयो योगी यत्नं मूलगुणेषु च।
विधत्ते सर्वदा पूर्णं श्रामण्यं तस्य जायते ॥13॥

A yogī with the pure three jewels (right faith, right knowledge and right conduct) gains complete sainthood (the status of a *śramaṇa*), if he also endeavours for the observance of the primary rules (of conduct).

उपधौ वसतौ सङ्घे विहारे भोजने जने।
प्रतिबन्धं न बध्नाति निर्ममत्वमधिष्ठितः ॥14॥

A yogī, established in detachment, does not entangle (himself) in the obstructions caused by possession, living place, the organization, the tour, the food and the people.

अशने शयने स्थाने गमे चङ्क्रमणे ग्रहे।
प्रमादचारिणो हिंसा साधोः सान्ततिकीरिता ॥15॥

For one indulging with indolence in activities like taking food, sleeping in place (for short stay), movement (from place to place), movement of limbs of the body, and placing and lifting articles, continued violence has been described.

गुणायेदं सयत्नस्य दोषायेदं प्रमादिनः ।
सुखाय ज्वरहीनस्य दुःखाय ज्वरिणो घृतम् ॥16॥

These (activities) are potent for upgrading one with necessary endeavours (in the direction of spiritual discipline), but they are potent to downgrade one who is with indolence; just as clarified butter leads one, free from fever, to the pleasure (of good health) and one, suffering from it (fever), to the restlessness (of bad health).

ज्ञानवत्यपि चारित्रं मलिनं परपीडके ।
कज्जलं मलिनं दीपे स प्रकाशेऽपि तापके ॥17॥

For one with knowledge, (but) causing violence to others conduct becomes filthy, as in a lamp with light and (but also) heat the carbon (emitted by it) is dirty (black).

भवाभिनन्दिनः केचित् सन्ति संज्ञावशीकृताः ।
कुर्वन्तोऽपि परं धर्मं लोक-पङ्क्ति-कृतादराः ॥18॥

There are some saints who are enslaved by the instincts of food, fear, coition and possession and who appreciate the practices of the people (masses) and encourage them. They are approving all that is worldly (in nature), inspite of practising high religious conduct.

मूढा लोभपराः क्रूरा भीरवोऽसूयकाः शठाः ।
भवाभिनन्दिनः सन्ति निष्फलारम्भकारिणः ॥19॥

The saints who approve of all that is worldly, are foolish (with wrong faith), obsessed by greed, cruel, cowardly, envious and stupid; they perform (spiritually) useless activites.

आराधनाय लोकानां मलिनेनान्तरात्मना ।
क्रियते या क्रिया बालैर्लोकपङ्क्तिरसौ मता ॥20॥

The actions done by the internally unclean and ignorant persons to allure (and attract) the common masses, constitute the traditional practice of the masses technically named as *'lokapañkti'*.

धर्माय क्रियमाणा सा कल्याणाङ्गं मनीषिणाम्।
तन्निमित्तः पुनर्धर्मः पापाय हतचेतसाम् ॥21॥

The follow-up of the *'lokapañkti'* for the sake of righteousness becomes an organ of beneficence for the wise persons. The religious practice, to add further, resulting from it, becomes a (source of) sin for those whose (true) conscience is destroyed.

मुक्तिमार्गपरं चेतः कर्मशुद्धि-निबन्धनम्।
मुक्तिरासन्नभव्येन न कदाचित् पुनः परम् ॥22॥

The conscience advancing on the path of liberation is the cause of purity (of the soul) from the (filth of) *karmas.* But liberation is attained only by one whose adgecency for liberation is there, never by any other.

कल्मषक्षयतो मुक्तिर्भोगसङ्गम(वि)वर्जिनाम्।
भवाभिनन्दिनामस्यां विद्वेषो मुग्ध चेतसाम् ॥23॥

On account of the destruction of *karmas* liberation is (granted), to those who renounce the association of the (sense) pleasures. (But) the *'bhavānandi'* saints (as described above) with a deluded conscience entertain an aversion (for liberation).

नास्ति येषामयं तत्र भवबीज-वियोगतः।
तेऽपि धन्या महात्मानः कल्याण-फल-भागिनः ॥24॥

Where there is no aversion (for liberation) on account of the separation (destruction) of the very seed of worldly existence i.e. the wrong faith, such great souls, too, are praiseworthy and they are (also) enjoyers of the fruits (of their attempt) in the form of beneficence.

In the foregoing seven verses the *āchārya* develops a topic of such saints who may be externally following the discipline prescribed but internally are not following the path truthfully and honestly. The true aim of the sainly life is lost sight of by them because of the up-rise of the delusive *karma.* They fail to realize that they have adopted this particular life-style to attain the final release from the world by fighting against the *karmas.* They are compelled to go astray by the various insticts, and thus they develop in themselves such traits of character and behaviour as would lead them farther and farther from their true aim. So much so they do not only feel interested in worldly activities but actually indulge in them so as to attract the people towards them, and as a consequence earn respect from them. Such saints have been named as the *'bhavābhinandis'* for their approval and praise for worldly activities, functions and organizations which are collectively termed as *'lokapañkti'* meaning the ways adopted to attract people towards themselves. These saints resorting to the popular *'lokapañkti'* fail to achieve any spiritual attainment for themselves, nor are they able to lead their followers on the right path. Still a distinction among them is located by the *āchārya.* If these activities are performed by them with a view to propagating the grandeur of religion, they may bring some good (*śubha*), but not spiritual purity (*śuddhi*) for themselves and their followers. If their conscience behind these activities is vitiated or drawn away from the true aim, these activities will earn only sin for themselves and their followers. Briefly speaking, the saints, to follow the right path leading to the final eradication of the *karmas,* must turn their back to what is worldly and keep the true ideal always in view turning their face in its direction.

संज्ञानादिरुपायो यो निर्वृतेर्वर्णितो जिनैः।
मलिनीकरणे तस्य प्रवर्तन्ते मलीमसाः ॥25॥

Persons (householders as well as saints) with an unclean conscience engage themselves in defiling the way of right knowledge etc. which has been described as the way of final release by the *Jinas.*

आराधने यथा तस्य फलमुक्तमनुत्तरम्।
मलिनीकरणे तस्य तथानर्थो बहुव्यथः ॥26॥

Just as the result of practising the way (of right knowledge etc.) is said to be unparalled, in the same way the result of defiling it is (most) undesired and full of many kinds of distress.

तुङ्गारोहणतः पातो यथा तृप्तिर्विषान्नतः।
यथानर्थोऽवबोधादि-मलिनीकरणे तथा ॥27॥

As the fall from the high stair-case is undesired and as the satisfaction from consuming poisonous food is undesired, so is the defilement of knowledge etc. undesired.

Right faith, right knowledge and right conduct have been described as leading to total expulsion of *karmas* from the soul. But there are some persons in the organization of house-holders as well as from that of saints who, because of their polluted conscience, defile the way in more than one way. There is a serious warning and advice for them from the *āchārya.* Such persons will certainly meet very seriously painful and undesired results for their sinful activities. They must avoid such activities very thoughtfully and carefully.

अयत्नचारिणो हिंसा मृते जीवेऽमृतेऽपि वा।
प्रयत्नचारिणो बन्धः समितस्य वधेऽपि नो ॥28॥

For the one acting with indolence, there occurs violence, whether the *jīva* (object of violence) is killed or not killed. For one acting carefully and observing the vows of carefulness, there is no bondage (of *karmas*) inspite of the death (of the *jīva*–the victim of killing).

The conditions that lead to violence are viewed in two ways—the internal and the external. The intention and negligence of precautions constitute the internal conditions, and the rest including the actual occurence of destruction of life are the external ones. The bondage of *karmas* and moral accountability for an action is determined by the internal conditions; it is only a coincidence that the two may occur simultaneously. The measure of bondage and accountability solely depend on the internal conditions. This truth of the theory of non-violence has not only been mentioned but also emphasized at more than one place in the Jaina works. The secret of the theory lies in the metaphysical fact that the manifestations of the *jiva* and the fine matter of *karma* are very closely connected with each other. The external events are connected with the *karmas* only through the occurence of spiritual changes. This disturbs the apparent correspondence between bondage of *karmas* and the external events. The presence or the absence of indolence relates to the internal changes in the *jīva*. Hence where indolence is present with an action bondage of *karma* must occur, and where external actions are not accompanied by the internal component, no liability for bondage can be conceived there. This is why in many instances of external violence the agent is not held responsible for them.

पादमुत्क्षिपतः साधोरीर्या-समितिभागिनः।
यद्यपि म्रियते सूक्ष्मः शरीरी पाद-योगतः ॥29॥
तथाऽपि तस्य तत्रोक्तो बन्धः सूक्ष्मोऽपि नागमे।
प्रमाद-त्यागिनो यद्वत्निर्मूर्च्छस्य परिग्रहः ॥30॥

For the saint observing (the vow of) carefulness in movement (*iryāsamiti*), while moving his feet subtle organisms are destroyed by the contact of his feet (with the organisms), still even slight bondage has not attributed (to him) in the scriptures (of the Jainas), as no (sin of) possession (has been attributed) to one who has renounced (all) indolence and (hence) has become free from infatuation.

The secret of non-violence and the consequent non-bondage of *karmas* has been illustrated by an example of a saint moving with avoidence of all chances of indolence. For strengthening the truth of the fact another example is made use of where one not attached with possession internally is held to suffer from no sin (due to external possession). Both the examples lay emphasis on the internal conditions determined by the pollution of the soul.

प्रमादी त्यजति ग्रन्थं बाह्यं मुक्त्वापि नान्तरम्।
हित्वाऽपि कञ्चुकं सर्पो गरलं न हि मुञ्चते ॥31॥

A saint with indolence gives up external possession without renouncing the internal one, as a snake does not leave poison even after giving up (its) film-like extra-skin (casting).

अन्तःशुद्धिं विना बाह्या न साश्वासकरी मता।
धवलोऽपि बको बाह्ये हन्ति मीनाननेकशः ॥32॥

Without the internal purity the external one is not held to be promising (any thing), as even the externally white heron kills the fish in may ways.

An ordained saint may observe all the rules and the routines prescribed for the conduct of his life, all this amounts only to the external conditions. Unless he turns himself inward and is alert about the internal conditions constantly going on within himself, the external and apparent side of his conduct is not helpful to enable him to advance on the path. The examples given above are proposed to give an easy understanding of the situation.

योगी षट्स्वपि कायेषु सप्रमादः प्रबध्यते।
सरोजमिव तोयेषु निष्प्रमादो न लिप्यते ॥33॥

A yogī, so long as he deals with the six kinds of organisms with indolence, suffers bondage (of *karmas*). If he is (there) without indolence, he does not come in contact (with *karmas*) like a lotus in water.

An organism is an embodiment vitalised by the presence of a soul. Such organisms have been conceived as of six kinds in Jaina philosophy. There is life in organisms developing from earth, water, fire, air and vegetables, collectively named as the immovable (*sthāvara*) *jīvas*. The other category of *jīvas* consists of organisms having two, three, four or five senses, collectively named as the movable (*trasa*) *jīvas*, so termed for their capacity of experiencing fear. Everyone of us has to deal with these six types of organisms, so also the yogi has to deal with them. But the yogi has to conduct his behaviour with them without indolence so as to grant them safety and feedom from pain in all possible ways. This attitude on the part of the yogī secures for him safety against incurring sin and consquent bondage of *karmas*.

साधुर्यतोऽङ्घ्रिघातेऽपि कर्मभिर्बध्यते न वा।
उपधिभ्यो ध्रुवो बन्धस्त्याज्यास्तैः सर्वथा ततः ॥34॥

A saint may get bound with *karmas* or may not; but from possessions, bondage becomes certain (necessary). Hence possessions must be given up by them (the saints) in all (possible) ways.

एकत्राप्यपरित्यक्ते चित्तशुद्धिर्न विद्यते।
चित्तशुद्धिं विना साधोः कुतस्त्या कर्म-विच्युतिः ॥35॥

The purity of conscience is not there if possession is not given up even in respect of one (article). Whence can liquidation of *karmas* be possible for the saint without the purity of conscience?

'सूत्रोक्त'मिति गृह्णान् श्चेलखण्डमिति स्फुटम्।
निरालम्बो निरारम्भः संयतो जायते कदा ॥36॥

If a saint owns (even) a piece of cloth under the pretension that such possession is clearly prescribed in the scripture (sūtra), when can he become independent (of possession), (also) without indulgence in activities and (hence) an observer of restraint?

Occurence of violence and sin has been seen in its two aspects, the internal and the external. The internal aspect leads to bondage without fail, but external aspect results in bondage, not indepently but through the internal one. The correspondence between the two is not certain and uniform. In case of possession (*parigraha*) the *āchārya* holds very firmly that the acceptance of the external possession necessarily leads to the infatuation of conscience. No one, in general is able to accept any external possession without being affected by it internally. Hence stress has been laid on the renunciation of external possession. External possession is not permissible for a saint under any condition or plea, without risking his purity and tranquility of conscience. So much so, he cannot be said to deserve sainthood even in the presence of a slight external possession.

अलाबुभाजनं वस्त्रं गृह्णतोऽन्यदपि ध्रुवम्।
प्राणारम्भो यतेश्चेतोव्याक्षेपो वार्यते कथम् ॥37॥

How can the violent action and the (consequent) contamination of mind be warded off for a saint really handling the gourd (for water), cloth (for covering the body) and other (such) articles?

स्थापनं चालनं रक्षां क्षालनं शोषणं यतेः।
कुर्वतो वस्त्रपात्रादेर्व्याक्षेपो न निवर्तते ॥38॥
आरम्भोऽसंयमो मूर्च्छा कथं तत्र निषिध्यते।
परद्रव्य-रतस्यास्ति स्वात्मसिद्धिः कुतस्तनी ॥39॥

For a saint engaged in placing, moving, saving, washing and drying of cloth, utensils etc. mental infatuation is not (cannot be) got rid of.

How can the engagement in activities, absence of restraint and infatuation (due to possessions) be denied there for a saint attached with the other substance (articles) and whence is the realization of the soul possible (for him)?

If one aims at the realization of his (pure) soul, one must not be attached with and engaged in anything other than his soul. If one ignores and defies this basic necessity for adopting a life-style required of the saint and engages oneself in the care for conducting activities related with the 'other' of one's soul under any plea, is really violating the path of spiritual liberation. Such an indulgence leads one to non-restraint and infatuation caused by the attachment with all these things. Hence to renounce all relationship with the 'other' of the soul comes out to be a very strict rule for a saint, if he at all desires to achieve self-realization.

न यत्र विद्यते च्छेदः कुर्वतो ग्रह-मोक्षणे।
द्रव्यं क्षेत्रं परिज्ञाय साधुस्तत्र प्रवर्तताम् ॥40॥

A saint, after judging well (the whole situation) in respect of substance, place (also time and mode of existence) may engage himself only there where no damage is done (to his pure routine of life) while accepting and relinquishing the 'other' (of his soul).

Herein the *āchārya* initiates an ethical concept like casuistry but with all honesty of aim and practice. Casuistry mostly consists in finding out ways to go against the prescribed rules to meet a difficult and odd situation. Owing to some weakness and pressure of circumstances, a saint is obliged to deviate from the unblemished path and practice. How should we justify such a devitation on the part of a saint? The first consideration is that the saint should eusure that no serious damage is caused to his way of life by it. Thus he is allowed to take up such activities as have been prohibited for him in the general course of discipline. Secondly he is to make an assessment of the situation with reference to the objects along with their potency and present actuality under the frame of time and place (ie. circumstances). Again he is to judge well that this type of indulgence in what is other than the soul will bring him a result which is in agreement with the purity of his conduct. Such occasions are not very rare in the practical observance of the rules of conduct. The acceptance of the gourd (*kandalu*) and the brush of peacock feathers is justified; nay, it has been considered essential for the conduct of life of restraint and non-voilence. We can very well understand that this allowance is made with an honest purpose, and is finally an advantageous step in the interest of the soul.

संयमो हन्यते येन प्रार्थ्यते यदसंयतैः।
येन सम्पद्यते मूर्च्छा तन्न ग्राह्यं हितोद्यतैः ॥41॥

What damages the (life of) restraint, what is needed by persons with no restraint and what brings about infatuation (a siezer of unconsciousness) should not be accepted by saints attempting for their (spiritual) beneficence.

मोक्षाभिलाषिणां येषामस्ति कायेऽपि निस्पृहा।
न वस्त्वकिंचनाः किञ्चित् ते गृह्णन्ति कदाचन ॥42॥

They (the saints), with no sense of belongingness for anything, who entertain a (strong) desire for liberation and who are completely disinterested in their bodies, never accept anything (other than their souls).

यत्र लोकद्वयापेक्षा जिनधर्मे न विद्यते।
तत्र लिङ्गं कथं स्त्रीणां सव्यपेक्षमुदाहृतम् ॥43॥

Whereas in the religion of *Jina* there is no dependence (and consideration) for the two worlds (i.e. this world and the world beyond it), how then the sexmark of women been described as a consideration (though negatively)?

A very important question of the capacity and moral right of women for the practice for and the attainment of liberation has been raised. This very question has been disturbing the unity among the followers of Jainism for a long time and has resulted in an actual split in the Jaina order. The basic position is that Jainism does not consider any thing other than the soul on the path of liberation. Then, how can we be bothered about women with their bodily sex-mark as an obstruction on the path of liberation.

नामुना जन्मना स्त्रीणां सिद्धिर्निश्चयतो यतः।
अनुरूपं ततस्तासां लिङ्गं लिङ्गविदो विदुः ॥44॥

Because the spiritual (realization) is not really possible for women from the present birth (the faminine condition), so their sex-mark is in agreement (with their incapacity for liberation). (So) say those, who know the implication of the mark of sex.

प्रमादमय-मूर्तीनां प्रमादोऽतो यतः सदा।
प्रमदास्तास्ततः प्रोक्ताः प्रमाद-बहुलत्वतः ॥45॥

विषादः प्रमदो मूर्च्छा जुगुप्सा मत्सरो भयम्।
चित्ते चित्रायते माया ततस्तासां न निर्वृतिः ॥46॥

As in women, who are (as if) the images all full of indolence, indolence is always found, so they have been described as *pramadā* meaning having indolence, on account of the abundance of this indolence (in them).

Sorrow, indolence, infatuation disgust, envy, fear and deceit are pictured in their minds. Therefore liberation is not possible (for them).

Pramāda, generally described by the terms indolence, carelessness, laziness, lack of interest and activity, has got a big family of psychoses. This family consists of fifteen members according to Jaina philosophy. These members have been enumerated as anger, pride, deceit and greed the four kinds of passion, the vitiated narratives of four kinds i.e. relating to woman, government, food and thieves, attachment, sleep and five objects of sense-pleasure. These fifteen kinds of indolence (*pramāda*) overpower the minds of women and thus they make them basically unfit and incapable to advance on the path. Along with these obstacles a good number of pychoses–the spiritually unhealthy hinderances—augment their incapacity for liberation.

न दोषेण विना नार्यो यतः सन्ति कदाचन।
गात्रं च संवृतं तासां संवृतिर्विहिता ततः ॥47॥

Because women are not found without blesmishes (as enumerated above) and their body (the various parts of their body) is not covered i.e. is exposed (naturally), therefore the covering (of the body) is prescribed for them.

शैथिल्यमार्तवं चेतश्चलनं श्रा(स्रा)वणं तथा।
तासां सूक्ष्म-मनुष्याणामुत्पादोऽपि बहुस्तनौ ॥48॥

कक्षा-श्रोणि-स्तनाद्येषु देह-देशेषु जायते।
उत्पत्तिः सूक्ष्म-जीवानां यतो, नो संयमस्ततः ॥49॥

Passivity (of body), monthly course, unfixed mentality, flow of (dirty) blood, generation of subtle human organisms under their heavy bossoms, and also the generation of subtle *jīvas* in the parts of their bodies like armpits, vulva, bossoms (always) takes place. So the (necessary) restraint is not possible in women.

शशाङ्कामलसम्यक्त्वाः समाचार-परायणाः।
सचेलास्ताः स्थिता लिङ्गे तपस्यन्ति विशुद्धये ॥50॥

The women, with right faith as bright as moon; well-practised in the observance of (spiritual) discipline, with cloth, and with the adoption of (such) marks of sainthood in their female form perform penances for (attaining spiritual) purity.

The *āchārya* strongly confirms the view that liberation is not possible for women from their present frame of body. They must be reborn as male human beings to qualify themselves for the attainment of liberation. It may be noted that all male human beings are also not so qualified, as only a few of them get liberation after undergoing the course of necessary discipline; but women are disenabled to achieve this high aim for their distinct bodily structure. The bodily structure of women is not directly responsible for their failure, as is held to be so easily and commonly by the people. Really speaking, some spiritual and psychological incapacities and disqualifications accompany the bodily structure of women, and these constitute the actual difficulties. The women can very well fight against such difficulties in their present form of the body by adopting a course of spiritual discipline which just grants them freedom from the female form in their lives to follow in future. The obstacles enumerated in the above verses are mostly related with the bodily structure, but they equally reflect their psychological and spiritual aspects which actually become the causes of their incapacity for liberation.

शान्तस्तपःक्षमोऽकुत्सो वर्णेष्वेकतमस्त्रिषु ।
कल्याणाङ्गो नरो योग्यो लिङ्गस्य ग्रहणे मतः ॥51॥

A male human being with a meritorious (handsome and attractive) body, who is peaceful (by natures) who is capable of performing penance, who is free from blesmishes and who belongs to one of the first three varṇas out of the four classes of *varṇas* (i.e. *Brāhmaṇs*, *Kṣatrīya*, *Vaiṣya* and *Śūdra*) is said be qualified for adopting the way of nudity.

कुल-जाति-वयो-देह-कृत्य-बुद्धि-क्रुधादयः ।
नरस्य कुत्सिता व्यङ्गास्तदन्ये लिङ्गयोग्यता ॥52॥

The order (continuity) of family from the father's side (*kula*), the same from the mother's side (*jāti*), the age, the body, mental inclination for what is worth doing, anger etc. when vitiated, become opposite factors (for adopting the way of nudity); and others (when not so vitiated) constitute qualifications (for adopting the same way).

येन रत्नत्रयं साधोर्नाश्यते मुक्तिकारणम् ।
स व्यङ्गो भण्यते नान्यस्तत्त्वतः सिद्धिसाधने ॥53॥

That is called a vitiated factor by which the trio of the three jewels (i.e. right faith, right knowledge and right conduct) of a saint, which is (really) the cause of liberation, is destroyed (distorted); no other factor is really so obstructive to the effort for spintual realization.

यो व्याहारिको व्यङ्गो मतो रत्नत्रय-ग्रहे ।
न सोऽपि जायतेऽव्यङ्गः साधु(धोः) सल्लेखना-कृतौ ॥54॥

What has been considered to be a vitiated factor in practically adopting the trio of the three jewels, does not become a helping factor for the saint engaged in the observance of the vow of religious death.

The *āchārya* now distinguishes between the two kinds of factors that help or hinder the process started for spiritual realization. The helping factors are called simply factors (*aṅgas*) and those causing hinderances are called vitiated factors (*vyáñgas*). The saint makes a start with the aim of attaining right faith, right knowledge and right conduct, as they alone constitute the way to liberation. For this, he utilizes the helping factors and avoids the hindering ones. All these factors are mostly external, but have a bearing on and reflect the psychological and spiritual sides of his life. In this way the importance of the *aṅgas* for their help and of the *vyaṅgas* for their hinderance is recognized, but the purity of the soul is always kept at the centre. The *sallekhanā* or the vow of religious death is prescribed for both the saints and the house holders, certainly with a difference of quality of its observance. Both of them entertain a desire to observe it throughout their lives. The aim behind this vow is to save the religious merit earned by him and carry it to the next life. The position of *aṅgas* and *vyañgas* for the selection of the former and the rejection of the latter, continues to remain the same, at the time of accepting and adopting this vow of religious death.

यस्येह लौकिकी नास्ति नापेक्षा पारलौकिकी।
युक्ताहारविहारोऽसौ श्रमणः सममानसः ॥55॥

The *śramana* or saint for whom there is no concern and dependence relating to this world or the world beyond it, is with the equanimity of mind, being attentive of his food and tours in the proper (prescribed) way.

कषाय-विकथा-निद्रा-प्रेमाक्षार्थ-पराङ्मुखः।
जीविते मरणे तुल्याः शत्रौ मित्रे सुखाऽसुखे ॥56॥

आत्मनोऽन्वेषणा येषां भिक्षा येषामणेषणा।
संयता सन्त्यनाहारास्ते सर्वत्र समाशयाः ॥57॥

The saints, with equanimity of mind in all the circumstances and with restraint, who have turned their back to passions, vitiated narratives, sleep, love and the objects of senses, who remain equipoised free from attachment and aversion in the states of living and dying, with enemies and friends, and in pleasant and painful conditions, who are busy in realizing the soul and for whom begging is to desire nothing, are said to be not indulging in the partaking of food (are without food).

यः स्वशक्तिमनाच्छाद्य सदा तपसि वर्तते।
साधुः केवलदेहोऽसौ निष्प्रतीकार-विग्रहः ॥58॥

The saint who, without concealing his strength, engages himself in performing penances and who does not attempt to remedy his body (against diseases, calamities etc.) is said to be having possession of the body alone, (and nothing else).

एका सनोदरा भुक्तिर्मांसमध्वादिवर्जिता।
यथालब्धेन भैक्षेण नीरसा परवेश्मनि ॥59॥

For a saint (as described above) the discipline regarding the (rule of) consumation of food consist in one posture (i.e. the standing one), quantity (of food) less than what is required (by hunger), free from meat, wine etc. with no taste and as presented at other's house on begging (while visiting the house for the food).

This verse mentions some practices of the saints visiting the houses of the householders for taking food to maintain their observance of the discipline required of them. They take food only once a day in a standing posture and the quantity of food is always less than one required for satisfying the hunger; that is, they always remain underfed. They do not exercise their choice for food and accept it as presented by the house-holders at their houses. They are not at all interested in the taste of the articles of food. Their food must not contain anything unclean like meat, wine, honey and such articles prohibited for them. They do not allow even a slight breach of the rules regarding this item (of accepting food) of their conduct.

पक्वेऽपक्वे सदा मांसे पच्यमाने च सम्भवः ।
तज्जातीनां निगोदानां कथ्यते जिनपुङ्गवैः ॥60॥
मांसं पक्वमपक्वं वा स्पृश्यते येन भक्ष्यते ।
अनेकाः कोटयस्तेन हन्यन्ते किल जन्मिनाम् ॥61॥

It has been preached by the great *Jinas* that, in cooked, uncooked and being cooked meat there is a germination of very subtle (one sensed) organism (called the *'nigota' jīvas*) of the same kind (whose meat is subjected to any process.)

By one who touches or consumes meat, cooked or raw, many crores of the germinating lives are certainly destroyed.

Meat as an article of food is totally condemned, not only for a saint, but also for the house-holder. Meat is obtained only by killing the organisms of various kinds; and in itself is a place of germination of very fine and subtle *jīvas*. While consuming meat all these lives are destroyed in an immeasurable abundance. Thus a meat-eater incurs huge amounts of sins for the elongation of his entanglement in this whirling world of distress and pain. Even touching and handling meat is equally a great source of evil, and hence its touch is equally disallowed and condemned.

बहुजीव-प्रघातोत्थं बहुजीवोद्भवास्पदम् ।
असंयम-विभीतेन त्रेधा मध्वपि वर्ज्यते ॥62॥

कन्दो मूलं फलं पत्रं नवनीतमगृध्नुभिः।
अनेषणीयमग्राह्यमन्नमन्यदपि त्रिधा ॥63॥

By one who fears non-restraint renounces (eating of) honey which is obtained on the destruction of many lives (like the bees) and which is a place of germination for many lives, is also abandoned mentally, vocally and by the body.

Bulb, root, fruit, leaf, butter and other eatables are not worth consuming and accepting by the saints (as well the house-holders) in the (above) three ways.

As some reasons are advanced for the condemnation of meat as an article of food, so also honey has not been considered as a desirable article of food for the saints as well as the house holders. The reason given in favour of this rule and practice is that honey is obtained by crushing the bee-hive along with so many little bees and the eggs secured in the bee-hive by the bees. But now some ways have been found out to obtain honey without destroying the eggs, the little ones and the bees at all. It also does not make honey an eatable article, for in honey itself the germination of a subtle and fine life goes on naturally. Then the *āchārya* attempts to enumerate some classes of vegetables which too are not fit for consumption by the saints and the house holders, the reason behind them being that they are the germination-spots for subtle and fine living organisms. Violence and destruction of lives existing in huge numbers cannot be avoided, if we include them in the list of articles for human consumption. Butter is also included in the list of such articles unfit for human consumption for the same reason as given in case of other articles of food, though it is not produced in the manner meat and honey are produced, nor does it find a place among its products fit for consumation.

पिण्डः पाणिगतोऽन्यस्मै दातुं योग्यो न युज्यते।
दीयते चेन्न भोक्तव्यं भुङ्क्ते चेद् दोषभाग् यतिः ॥64॥

The morsel of food placed in the hand (of a saint) is not fit to be given to any other (person) (by the saint). If it is given so, the saint should not take food (thereafter). If he takes (food) (even then), the saint commits blemish (for himself).

The saint must partake food as offered by the householder keeping off all the blemishes as prescribed for him in the scriptures. He must not meddle with it or spare it for use by others. This rule should be observed very strictly by him or he will incur sin for himself.

बालो वृद्धस्तपोग्लानस्तीव्रव्याधि-निपीडितः ।
तथा चरतु चारित्रं मूलच्छेदो यथास्ति नो ॥65॥

If the saint happens to be a boy, and old man with disinterest for penances and suffering from a serious disease, he should so observe (the rules of) conduct as no damage to his basic (or root) conduct is done.

There are some concessions in the observance of the rules of conduct prescribed for a saint, if he happens to be disenabled to observe them strictly on account of some inability like maturity of age, the structure of his body, disinterest in austerities and some very painful diseases. But he can go down in the scale of conduct only to an extent where his basic conduct required to maintain sainthood for himself is not disturbed. If he overlooks this limitation of concessions, he is fallen and will be required to reinstate himself after undergoing the necessary procedure prescribed for it.

आहारमुपधिं शय्यां देशं कालं बलं श्रमम् ।
वर्तते यदि विज्ञाय 'स्वल्पलेपो' यतिस्तदा ॥66॥

The saint who engages himself in the observance of conduct after assessing food, accessories, sleep, place, time, strength (of body) and hard work (required of him) becomes liable to little (or light) bondage.

Along with securing his basic conduct the saint may have a consideration in respect of the items mentioned in this verse, just to provide some concession and ease in the observance of the rules of conduct; but by that he is not held exempt from incurring sin; but, because of his inner inclination and respect for pure conduct, he suffers light bondage of *karmas*.

संयमो हीयते येन येन लोको विराध्यते।
ज्ञायते येन संक्लेशस्तन्न कृत्यं तपस्विभिः ॥67॥

The saints with penaces are not to perform such actions by which (the quality of) the rule of restraint falls down, an obstruction is caused to the people, and a feeling of distress is caused.

एकाग्रमनसः साधोः पदार्थेषु विनिश्चयः।
यस्मादागमतस्तस्मात् तस्मिन्नाद्रियतां तराम् ॥68॥

As firm determination about the objects (of the world) is achieved by the tradition of scriptures, known as *Āgama*, therefore a saint, with a pointed concentration of mind, should specially entertain respect for (the *Āgama).*

परलोकविद्यौ शास्त्रं प्रमाणं प्रायशः परम्।
यतोऽत्रासन्नभव्यानामादरः परमस्ततः ॥69॥

Most generally, in dealing with the science (contents and conditions) of the other world (out of reach for the persons with feeble powers for perception and understanding) the tradition of the scriptures is the highly esteemed source of knowledge. Therefore, the saints, very closely on the verge of liberation, should hold highest respect (for the scriptures).

उपदेशं विनाऽन्यङ्गी पटीयानर्थकामयोः।
धर्मे तु न विना शास्त्रादिति तत्रादरो हितः ॥70॥

The *jīva* becomes expert in the fields of wealth and pleasures without any preaching (instruction and training); but in the realm of religion (it does not become expert) without (a study of) scripture; hence respect of scriptures is (spiritually) beneficial.

अर्थकामाविधानेन तदभावः परं नृणाम्।
धर्माविधानतोऽनर्थस्तदभावश्च जायते ॥71॥

By not making effort in the field of wealth and pleasure their deprivation is there for the people. By not making effort in the realm of religion (there is) not only the deprivation of religiousness but also the engrossment in the irreligious results (there).

तस्माद्धर्मार्थिभिः शश्वच्छास्त्रे यत्नो विधीयते।
मोहान्धकारिते लोके शास्त्रं लोक-प्रकाशकम् ॥72॥

Therefore, those, desirous of religiousness always make efforts for (studying) scripture. Scripture is the revealer of the reality (the contents of the cosmos) in the universe (all) wrapped in the (dense) darkness of delusion.

मायामयौषधं शास्त्रं शास्त्रं पुण्य-निबन्धनम्।
चक्षुः सर्वगतं शास्त्रं शास्त्रं सर्वार्थसाधकम् ॥73॥

The (study of) scripture is the medicine for the disease of deceit, the (study of) scripture is the cause of (earning) merit, the (study of) scripture is the all-perceiving eye, and the (study of) scripture is the instrument of accomplishment of all the objectives.

न भक्तिर्यस्य तत्रास्ति तस्य धर्मक्रियाखिला।
अन्धलोकक्रियातुल्या कर्मदोषादसत्फला ॥74॥

The entirety of the relegious activities is like the actions of the blind persons, and it is the producer of the evil fruits on account of the blemish of *karmas* for those, who do not entertain devotion for scripture (or *Āgama*).

यथोदकेन वस्त्रस्य मलिनस्य विशोधनम्।
रागादि-दोष-दुष्टस्य शास्त्रेण मनसस्तथा ॥75॥

Just the cleamsing of dirty cloth is done by water; so also the purification of mind, made filthy by blemishes like attachment etc., is done by the (study) of scripture.

आगमे शास्वती बुद्धिर्मुक्तिस्त्री-संफली यतः।
ततः सा यत्नतः कार्या भव्येन भवभीरुणा ॥76॥

The intellect continuously engaged in the study of *Āgama* or scripture is a mediator (good friend) for wooing the damsel of *'mukti'* or liberation; therefore, it is worth achieving with effort by a liberable *jīva* afraid of the worldly existence.

कान्तारे पतितो दुर्गे गर्ताद्यपरिहारतः।
यथाऽन्धो नाश्नुते मार्गमिष्टस्थान-प्रवेशकम् ॥77॥
पतितो भवकान्तारे कुमार्गापरिहारतः।
तथा नाप्नोत्यशास्त्रज्ञो मार्गं मुक्ति-प्रवेशकम् ॥78॥

Just as a blind person being lost in a dense forest, finds it difficult to move about and does not get the (right) way leading to the entry of the desired destination, on account of the failure to avoid the pits (obstacles) etc.; in the same way the *jīva,* with no knowledge of scriptures and being fallen in the forest of wordly existence, does not get the (right) way leading to the entry into liberation, on account of his failure to avoid the vitiated paths (of the world).

The foregoing eleven verses of this chapter deal with the importance of the study of scriptures by a novice on the path leading to the final emancipation or complete freedom from the *karmas*. The collection of scriptures is called *Āgama* meaning the Holy Word or tradition that has come to us right from the omniscient Lord through a series of *āchāryas* and saints. The authenticity of the scriptures lies in the fact that omniscient Lord percieves all the contents of the universe directly. This is why the *Āgama* is kept in a very high esteem and is said to be the very eye for the saints. It is the most believable and dependable source of knowledge. Specially in case of things which are separated from us by long distances, by long intervals of time (past and future both) and by the subtlity of the existents, *Āgama* is the only source of our knowledge. Hence a close and constant study of *Āgama* is a emphasized and advised by the *āchāryas* for everyone with all possible resources and efforts. The way of release from the shackles of *karmas* is enlightened and revealed for us by the study of the scripture, which on the one hand adds to the purity and stability of faith and, on the other hand, provides firmness and perseverence in the observance of the rules of conduct. This ensures heavy expulsion of *karmas* from the soul, bringing the *yogi* closer to the final aim of his life. Without necessary knowledge of the right path and the obstacles that generally befall us on the path, it is very difficult to follow the way and bring the wordly existence to an end. Moreover, unfortunately there is a general tendency among the *jīvas* to engage themselves in the wordly activities and get allured by the resulting pleasures. Hence special and willful efforts are required on our part to divert it in the direction of the good of the soul; then alone we can fight against these allurements successfully. The *āchārya* views this world as very extensive and dense forest wherein the *jīvas* have lost the right way and are vainly wandering here and there facing so many painful situations, being drifted away from the goal. Under such circumstances the knowledge of the scriptures is the only resort to render us necessary help and guidance for a firm follow-up of the way.

यतः समेऽप्यनुष्ठाने फलभेदोऽभिसन्धितः।
स ततः परमस्तत्र ज्ञेयो नीरं कृषाविव ॥79॥
बहुधा भिद्यते सोऽपि रागद्वेषादिभेदतः।
नाना फलोपभोक्तॄणां नृणां बुद्ध्यादिभेदतः ॥80॥

Because, inspite of putting in an equal amount of action (labour), the difference of fruition (is seen) on account of the psychoses (behind action); therefore that (the difference of psychoses) carries very great importance like water in farming.

That (the difference of psychoses), too, is distinguished on account of the difference of attachment, aversion etc. and also because of understanding etc. on the part of the persons enjoying a variety of fruition.

बुद्धिर्ज्ञानमसंमोहस्त्रिविधः प्रक्रमः स्मृतः।
सर्वकर्माणि भिद्यन्ते तद्भेदाच्च शरीरिणाम् ॥81॥

The (course of) action is said to be supported by three factors—the intellect, the comprehension, and the absence of delusion. On account of the difference of these all the actions (and their fruition) of the *jīvas* are (mutually) distinguished.

बुद्धिमक्षाश्रयां तत्र ज्ञानमागमपूर्वकम्।
तदेव सदनुष्ठानमसम्मोहं विदो विदुः ॥82॥

The learned ones described intellect as dependent on senses, knowledge as preceded (supported) by *Āgama* (scriptures) and the absence of delusion as only that (the union of these two) course of meritorious actions.

It is an admitted fact that preconditions of an action also lead to a distinction in the effect thereof. It is true of the mechanical world as well as the human one. In the human world, specially in the ethical context, these preconditions have been grouped under three heads : the intellect, the comprehension and the absence of delusion in the carriage of our efforts. The first i.e. the intellect consists of our perceptions with the senses. The second i.e. the comprehension is specially designed to include the help derived from the study of scriptures, which alone can equip us with the rich treasure of experiences of the past saints and sages. When these two conditions are at our disposal, the third precondition of the absence of delusion about the course of action, automatically follows; but it has been counted separately for its great importance on the path of liberation. Now the saint is ready to make a start and to follow the action to its very end in view. When the course of action is supplemented by the preconditions, it, itself gets diverted in the right direction. Then there remains no room to doubt the efficacy of the varying modifications and their fruition (the results) on the path. This provides a confirmation to our belief and conduct.

चारित्रदर्शनज्ञानतत्स्वीकारो यथाक्रमम् ।
तत्रोदाहरणं ज्ञेयं बुद्ध्यादीनां प्रसिद्धये ॥83॥

The acceptance with the order (as prescribed) of conduct, faith and knowledge is there; there the use of illustration should be known as pinpointing (the relative and distinct prominence of) intellect etc.

The order of the trio of the three jewels of the path of liberation is the right faith, right knowledge and then right conduct. Right conduct is re-inforced by the first constituent, then alone it can bring about the desired result. It blooms in full in the absence of delusion.

बुद्धिपूर्वाणि कर्माणि समस्तानि तनूभृताम् ।
संसारफलदायीनी विपाके विरसस्वतः ॥84॥

All the actions of the *jivas* are preceded by intellect (as described above) result in *saṁsāra*–the whirling world, because of their fruition as vitiated experience (not granting the blissful experience of pure soul).

तान्येव ज्ञानपूर्वाणि जायन्ते मुक्तिहेतवे।
अनुबन्धः फलत्वेन श्रुतशक्तिनिवेशितः ॥85॥

The very actions when supported by knowledge (of scriptures) become causes for (attaining) liberation, because (their), (causal) agreement, being invested with the power of scriptural knowledge in respect of their fruition.

सन्त्यसंमोहहेतूनि कर्माण्यत्यन्तशुद्धितः।
निर्वाणशर्मदायीनि भवातीताध्वगामिनाम् ॥86॥

The actions of those who follow the way leading to the extinction of worldly life are causes (of the state) of delusionlessness on account of being extremely pure, and (hence) are the grantors of the bliss of liberation.

Our sense perceptions and the intellect lead to such actions as promise the gift of the *saṁsāra* only. It is so fixed by nature, hence the first pre-condition is not at all potent for advancement on the spiritual path. It must be supplemented by the second pre-comdition of scriptural knowledge. Then the two taken together enable one to follow the path, as they are also potent to wipe out delusion. Really speaking, the importance of scriptural knowledge is very high. On the one hand it changes the direction of the sense perception and intellectual knowledge soulwards, on the other hand it helps the process of eradication of delusion, which is also an equally important condition for achieving the aim of perfect tranquility of the soul.

भावेषु कर्मजातेषु मनो येषां निरुद्यमम्।
भवभोग-विरक्तास्ते भवातीताध्वगामिनः ॥87॥

Those, whose mind has become effortless about manifestations generated by the *karmas* and those who are averted from the enjoyments of the world are the followers of the way leading beyond the worldly existence.

एक एव सदा तेषां पन्थाः सम्यक्त्वचारिणाम् ।
व्यक्तीनामिव सामान्यं दशाभेदेऽपि जायते ॥88॥

For them whose conduct is supported by right faith the way is always only one as the universal of the individuals remains (one) inspite of the differences of conditions.

निर्वाणसंज्ञितं तत्त्वं संसारातीतलक्षणम् ।
एकमेवावबोद्धव्यं शब्दभेदेऽपि तत्त्वतः ॥89॥

The principle named *nirvāṇa* or liberation, whose differentia is being beyond worldly existence, should, in essence, be known as one inspite of the difference of words (to describe it).

विमुक्तो निर्वृतः सिद्धः परंब्रह्माभवः शिवः ।
अन्वर्थः शब्दभेदेऽपि भेदस्तस्य न विद्यते ॥90॥

Completely free, completely detached (retired), finally accomplished, highly progressed, without further births and all blissful—all these terms carry the same meaning inspite of the difference of words; there exists no difference in respect of it (the reality implied by them).

Some characteristics of the path of final emancipation of the *jīva* are described here. It is emphatically upheld that this path in reality is one and one alone though described by a variety of terms and definitions. Persons who have lost interest in the worldly allurements and activities are the true followers of the path. It leads to the end of the chain of worldly existence and grants the *jīvas* an unforseen status described by means of several terms in the above verse. Just as the way, followed by such *jīvas* whose liberation is very close in time, is one, so also the status finally attained by them is the same. The only difference that continues throughout is that of the individuality of the *jīvas* in respect of their substantive basis which they can never lose. In the liberated state there is nothing like the grand soul in which the individual liberated souls may be allowed to merge. All the characteristics associated with the state of liberation are individually granted to all such *jīvas*.

तल्लक्षणाविसंवादा निराबाधमकल्मषम् ।
कार्यकारणतातीतं जन्ममृत्युवियोगतः ॥91॥

Its recognition-marks, free from all doubt and discussion, are that there is no obstruction (in the way of their continuance), there is no association of *karmas* (with them), and they have gone beyond the (relation of causality in terms of) cause and effect, because there is (now) no birth and death (for them).

ज्ञाते निर्वाण-तत्त्वेऽस्मिन्नसंमोहेन तत्त्वतः ।
मुमुक्षाणां न तद्युक्तौ विवाद उपपद्यते ॥92॥
सर्वज्ञेन यतो दृष्टो मार्गो मुक्ति-प्रवेशकः ।
प्राञ्जलोऽयं ततो भेदः कदाचिन्नात्र विद्यते ॥93॥

This principle of *nirvāṇa* or liberation being really known in the absence of delusion, there is no debate about the use of arguments (to establish it) for those desirous of attaining liberation.

Because, the way, which grants entry into (the state of) liberation, has been seen by the omniscient (lord), hence this way being evident, as pure and free from blemishes never suffers from differences of existence and opinions.

विचित्रादेशनास्तत्र भव्यचित्तानुरोधतः ।
कुर्वन्ति सूरयो वैद्या यथाव्याध्यनुरोधतः ॥94॥

There the *āchāryas* conduct the preaching in various forms on account of the need (request) of the liberable minds (disciples), as do the the masters of medicines (for their patients) on account of the pressure of the disease.

In the process of preaching about the course for the attainment of liberation, the *āchāryas* take into account the capacity and requirement of the disciples placed in varying conditions of life. Hence the way and style and also the contents of teaching may undergo some changes. This opposes the absolute form of their preaching which is variable only under the pressure of situation to some extent. In essence, the way and its preaching is always the same with respect to the ideal in view.

कारणं निर्वृतेरेतच्चारित्रं व्यवहारतः।
विविक्तचेतनध्यानं जायते परमार्थतः ॥95॥

From the practical point of view the cause of (this) release is the conduct (observance of conduct rules). From the real point of view it (the cause) is the meditation on the (pure) consciousness free from all 'other'.

यो व्यवहारिकः पन्थाः सभेदद्वय-संगतः।
अनुकूलो भवेदेको निर्वृतेः संसृतेः परः। ॥96॥

The practical path goes with its two kinds. One is suitable for release (of the soul from *karmas*); and the other, for (the prolongation of) the whirlings of the world.

निर्वृतेरनुकूलोऽध्वा चारित्रं जिनभाषितम्।
संसृतेरनुकूलोऽध्वा चारित्रं पर-भाषितम् ॥97॥

The way suitable for the release of the soul is the conduct (course of discipline) as preached by Lord Jina. The way suitable for the *saṁsāra* is (transmigration of the *jīva*) is the conduct preached by other (inefficent) persons.

Lord Jina is the only personage to reveal to us the right path for the emancipation of the soul by virtue of his omniscience. This very revelation is carried further by the great seers and *āchāryas* selflessly without delusion and doubt for the beneficence of the followers of the true path. Other preachers lacking omniscience are unable to understand the way themselves and to preach the same to others.

चारित्रं चरतः साधोः कषायेन्द्रिय-निर्जयः।
स्वाध्यायोऽतस्ततो ध्यानं ततो निर्वाणसङ्गमः ॥98॥

Following the conduct (as prescribed by Lod Jīna) the victory over passion and sense takes place for a saint. Then follows the study of the soul, which, in turn, is followed by meditation. Then finally, there is the realization of the state of *nirvāna.*

For the attainment of final release from *karmas* the observance of conduct rules is the first and most primary requirement. One who is well-pratised in the necessary discipline meant for the purpose, is alone able to achieve control over one's passions and sense-pleasures. Then the novice moves to achieve the second requirement in the form of a clear understanding about the soul by self-study. So equipped, he advances to the third requirement of the path which is meditation. Meditation is actually the culmination of the process of self-study and consists in the lasting fixation of the ideal of pure soul in the mind of the saint. The result of the process and practice of meditation just places the soul in a state of perfect release i.e. the *nirvāṇa* where all 'other' of the soul is completely wiped out.

इदं चरित्रं विधिना विधीयते, ततः शुभध्यान-विरोधि-रोधकम्।
विविक्तमात्मानमनन्तमीशते, न साधवो ध्यातुमृतेऽमुना यतः ॥99॥

One becomes competent to meditate on the infinite (with

limitless power) and the distinctive (chiselled of all the 'other') soul which obstructs the meditation opposed to the auspicious ones, only when one observes this conduct (as preached by *Jina*) with the details (of its observance), as the saints, without this conduct, are not able to meditate (on the pure soul).

The attainment of liberation is directly connected with meditation, there is no interuption between the two. This meditation is a mode or form of deep knowledge. When it attains a state of fixation, knowledge itself takes the form of meditation. In general this meditation has been seen in its four aspects : two of them lead to worldly existence directly, the third is a help on the way to liberation, and the last, as already mentioned, leads to the final release of the soul from the *karmas*. The Sanskrit terms used for these four types of meditation are the *ārta*, the *raudra*, the *dharmya* and the śukla. The first type of meditation is full of anguish and helplessness. The second type is full of fury and aggression. By their very nature it is evident that these two types of meditations cannot help us on the path of liberation, they are bound to drag us into the worldly conditions of pain and restlessness. They may be better called the passionate obsessions of the mind. That is why they have been described as opposed to meritorious and righteous meditations. The third type of medition is desirable, as it paves the passage of and leads to the entry into the fourth type of meditation which alone can be held to the meditation in the true sense of the term. Rising higher and higher in the scale of spiritual realization and passing through various stages under this pure meditation named as *śukla dhyāna* (the pure and white meditation) the saints find themselves firmly placed in the highest position attainable. There is no height of spiritual evolution to be achieved by them hereafter. They have reached their original home which remained lost to them so far.

रागद्वेष-प्रपञ्च-भ्रम-मद-मदन-क्रोध-लोभ-व्यपेतो
यश्चारित्रं पवित्रं चरति चतुरधीर्लोकयात्रानपेक्षः।
स ध्यात्वात्म-स्वभावं विगलितकलिलं नित्यमध्यात्मगम्यं
त्यक्त्वा कर्मारिचक्रं परमसुखमयं सिद्धिसद्म प्रयाति ॥100॥

The saint, who is bereft of the network of attachment, aversion, confusion, pride, sex, anger, and greed, who has practical intellect and who has lost all interest in the carriage of worldliness, practices the sacred conduct, and attains the abode of the liberated ones which is all full of bliss of high order, having meditated on the nature of the (pure) soul itself from which all the *karmas* have been liquidated, which is permanent and can be realized by souls (directed soulward), after freeing (itself) from the siege of the enemies of *karmas.*

This is the last verse of the chapter on conduct and summarizes the various contents described therein. It gives a list of such characteristics, which are bound to take the novice to a fall and which therefore must be disdained and discarded by him who is a true seeker of self-realization. With full disinterest in what is wordly, he must keep the ideal of the pure soul always in view. He must follow the discipline and the rules of conduct as prescribed by the great seers of truth. He must centre his entire attention and effort to attain the purity of the soul, and must renounce all his concern with the *karmas* and the worldly activities which have been contaminating the purity from beginningless times. He must respect the process of meditation which alone can save him from the cobweb of worldliness. Thus he is able to move towards the highest aim of his existence, the complete breach of *karmas* and the gain of purest powers of the soul to last infinitely with him hereafter.

There is a concept of the abode of such liberated souls under the names *siddhaślā, siddhakśetra*, situated at the top of the cosmos (loka) as conceived in the Jaina tradition. After destroying the *karma* shackles completely and leaving the last vestige of the embodiment here, the soul immediately flies to the top of the cosmost (*loka*) to reside there for ever with full effulgence of its powers. It does not fly further to enter the realm of the acosmos (*aloka*) for the absence of the medium of motion (*dharma dravya*) there, as (this) is also conceived in the cosmology of the Jainas. An infinite number of the liberated souls is accommoted in the limited space of the *siddha-kśetra*, because all the souls being pure offer no resistance to any other soul or anything else (of the nature of non-soul) existing there. All such liberated souls are perfect and self-absorbed; they have attained the status of Godhood and they are the gods of the Jaina philosophy.

Here ends Chapter-8, Chāritrādhikāra of Yogasāra-prābhṛta by Āchārya Amitagati.

Chapter 9

Chūlikādhikāra

दृष्टिज्ञानस्वभावस्तु सदानन्दोऽस्ति निर्वृतः।
न चैतन्य-स्वभावस्य नाशो नाश-प्रसङ्गतः ॥1॥

The soul that has attained liberation always continues with bliss and its nature of conation and knowledge. Its nature as consciousness its not destroyed (in liberation), because then there will be the destruction (of the soul itself).

Consciousness is the very essence and nature of the soul. It manifests in two forms—conation and knowledge. Bliss is the necessary accompaniment of pure consciousness. There is a relation of identity between the soul and its attribute of consciousness covering conation and knowledge, and also bliss. Hence the presence of these attributes with the soul is necessary in liberation. These attributes can never meet their extinction in liberation. If they are supposed to be destroyed there, the destruction of the soul itself will be a necessary and unavoidable result.

सर्वथा ज्ञायते तस्य न चैतन्यं निरर्थकम्।
स्वभावत्वेऽस्वभावत्वे विचारानुपपत्तितः ॥2॥

For the soul consciousness cannot be held to be absolutely defunct (without conation and knowledge), as thinking cannot proceed on the acceptance of a defunct consciousness as the nature of the soul or as (consciousness) not the nature of the soul.

Some thinkers uphold the view that in liberation consciousness continues with the soul, but there it has no function and becomes superfluous and totally passive. They think such is the nature of the soul in liberation. We must note that there is no entity in nature which has no function to perform. In the absence of the function the entity itself will be wiped out of existence. If a defunct consciousness is admitted as the nature of the soul, it is all superflous to the soul and is as good as non-existent in the soul. If (such a) consciousness is not the nature of the soul, then how it can be related with the soul at all. Therefore, both the alternatives contended in this context are in themselves meaningless and deserve no consideration. Consiousness must continue to manifest in its two main forms of conation and knowledge, certainly in its full purity and freedom from any kind of contamination in liberation.

निरर्थक-स्वभावत्वे ज्ञानभावानुषङ्गतः।
न ज्ञानं प्रकृतेर्धमश्चेतनत्वानुषङ्गतः ॥3॥
प्रकृतेश्चेतनत्वे स्यादात्मत्वं दुर्निवारणाम्।
ज्ञानात्मकत्वे चैतन्ये नैरर्थक्यं न युज्यते ॥4॥

If the nature of the soul is consciousness without any function (totally passive), then knowledge will not be possible for the soul; and also knowledge cannot be held to be the nature of *Prakṛti* (the basic primal unconscious entity) for then consciousness must be admitted (as a nature) of *Prakṛti.*

If consciousness is admitted of Prakṛti, then for it the acceptance of being of the nature of a soul will become difficult to avoid. If consciousness is of the nature of knowledge, then assigning no function to consciouness is not consistent.

The dualism of *puruṣa* (soul) and prakṛti (the unconscious

primal entity) is under consideration. A special attention is drawn to that consciouness which is supposed to exist in liberation completely passively without a function assigned to it. In such a situation the possibility of knowledge, a form of consciousness, will be totally denied of the soul. If *prakṛti* is resorted for the generation of knowledge or is held responsible for the emergence of knowledge, then the difficulty will arise from the basic fact that consciousness is not a characteristic of the unconsious *prakṛti* which as such can never give birth to consciousness. Then under the pressure of logic and the connected situation, if *prakṛti* is held to be conscious, *prakṛti* itself will become the soul, disturbing the basic distinction upheld between the puruṣa and *prakṛti*. If consciousness itself is of the nature of knowledge which has a distinct function for itself, then the contention that consciousness in liberation is without function and completely passive becomes untenable even as an hypothesis. The conclusion that follows from the above discussion is that the relation of identity between the soul and consciousness is a fact and consciousness in liberation also has got a distinct function, as it manifests, as usual, in the form of conation and knowledge without any contamination whatsoever.

नाभावो मुक्तयवस्थायामात्मनो घटते ततः ।
विद्यमानस्य भावस्य नाभावो युज्यते यतः ॥5॥

(Moreover) because the non-existence of an existent entity is in no way consistent, hence in the state of liberation the non-existence of the soul is not admissible.

The state of liberation is only a change of form for the soul under the general law stated in the above verse, the soul can never lose it existence in any form it happens to assume like other entities. The question of the annihilations of the soul in liberation does not at all arise.

यथा चन्द्रे स्थिता कान्तिर्निर्मले निर्मला सदा।
प्रकृतिर्विकृतिस्तस्य मेघादिजनितावृतिः ॥6॥
तथात्मनि स्थिता ज्ञप्तिर्विशदे विशदा सदा।
प्रकृतिर्विकृतिस्तस्य कर्माष्टककृतावृतिः ॥7॥
जीमूतापगमे चन्द्रे यथा स्फुटति चन्द्रिका।
दुरितापगमे शुद्धा तथैव ज्ञप्तिरात्मनि ॥8॥

Just as the clear brilliance (of the clear moon) always remains bright (naturally) but the distorted state of the moon is caused by the covering of the clouds etc.

In the same way pure (vivid) knowledge is always found in the pure soul (naturally); but its distortion (also limitation) is caused by the covering of the eight (kinds of) *karmas.*

Just as on the disappearance of the clouds from (in front of) the moon, the moon-light spreads clearly, in the same way, on the disappearance of *karmas* the pure knowledge shines in the soul.

The examples given above explain the truth of the universal law that all the entities in the world including the principle of soul undergo a series of changes of form, and, in this variation, they are never destroyed tracelessely. The substance behind these entities continues permanantly, while their modes go on changing on account of external causes. This copresence of permanance and change is the very nature of reality which, in other words, endures through change.

धुनाति क्षणतो योगी कर्मावरणमात्मनि।
मेघस्तोममिवादित्ये पवमानो महाबलः ॥9॥

A yogī fluffs off the cover of *karmas* (existing with) in the soul within no time like a very strong blast of wind (which blows off) the expanse of clouds in (from) the sun.

विविक्तात्म-परिज्ञानं योगात् संजायते यतः।
स योगो योगिभिर्गीतो योगनिर्धूत-पातकैः ॥10॥

The 'yoga', which gives birth to the comprehension of the discriminated (pure) soul, has been described as (a real) 'yoga' by the yogīs who have washed off the sins (*karmas*) by means the 'yoga'.

The 'yoga' is the way that leads to the gain of the pure soul through the comprehension of the soul shorn off all that is other than the soul. Such a rare comprehension of the pure soul is possible only on the destruction of the barring *karmas*. Thus the yoga performs a double function of destroying the *karmas* and realizing the pure soul.

निरस्त-मन्मथातङ्कं योगजं सुखमुत्तमम्।
शमात्मकं स्थिरं स्वस्थं जन्म-मृत्यु-जरापहम् ॥11॥

The excellent bliss generated by yoga is free from the terror of sexuality, is identical with tranquility, is stable, resides in the soul itself and grants riddance from birth, death and old age.

The 'yoga', along with the destruction of *karmas* and the gain of the recognition of the pure soul, also grants the gift of the unforseen bliss to the yogī, which possesses the characteristics as described in the above verse. These characteristics mark a clear release of the soul from the turmoils of the worldly existence.

सर्वं परवशं दुःखं सर्वमात्मवशं सुखम्।
वदन्तीति समासेन लक्षणं सुख-दुःखयोः ॥12॥

All that is dependent on the 'other' (than the soul) is distress, all that is dependent on soul is bliss. Thus in brief they pronounce the difference of bliss and distress.

A general definition of bliss and distress is given in this verse. To be dependent on the 'other' is itself a form of distress and to be free from this dependence and hence to be self-determined is a form of bliss. A quantitative concommitance between the dependence on the 'other' and the dependence on the soul itself may provide us a clue for judging the quality of steps we take on the path.

ततः पुण्यभवा भोगा दुःखं परवशत्वतः।
सुखं योगभवं ज्ञानं स्वरूपं स्ववशत्वतः ॥13॥

Therefore, the enjoyments generated by the meritorious *karmas* are (the forms of) distress on account of their dependence on the other; and the knowledge (of the pure soul) all imbued with 'yoga' is bliss and it is the identity of the self on account of its dependence on the self (soul itself.)

On the basis of the general definition of bliss and distress, a distinction is drawn between the knowledge of the soul on one hand and the pleasures of the world on the other. This distinction is potent to divert the interest and attention of any individual from the worldly pleasures and direct them to the way of the beneficence of the soul.

ध्यानं विनिर्मलज्ञानं पुंसां सम्पद्यते स्थिरम्।
हेमं क्षीणमलं किं न कल्याणत्वं प्रपद्यते ॥14॥

The stable and thoroughly purified knowledge called *dhyāna* or meditation accomplished for the people. Does gold, being cleaned of the dross, not attain the pure form of gold?.

Basically meditation is a mode and form of knowledge, it is not distinct from knowledge. By undergoing an ethical course of discipline in respect of conduct and knowledge, knowledge itself gains in firmness and stability gradually. This process marks the drift of knowledge towards meditation. When it attains a satisfactory level, the knowledge itself is transformed into meditation. Higher and higher stages of the progress of medition lead the seekers of the principle of pure soul nearer and nearer to their aim, finally to place them in the highest status of spirituality. Thus 'yoga' justifies its title by enabling a yogī to gain his lost status of purity or by uniting and identifying him with his Godhood.

गन्धर्वनगराकारं विनश्वरमवास्तवम् ।
स्थावरं वास्तवं भोगं बुध्यन्ते मुग्धबुद्धयः ॥15॥

Persons with deluded intellect understand the (worldly) enjoyments which are unreal and subject to destruction like a city made of clouds in the sky to be stable and real.

चित्तभ्रमकरस्तीव्ररागद्वेषादिवेदनः ।
संसारोऽयं महाव्याधिर्नानाजन्मादि-विक्रियः ॥16॥
अनादिरात्मनोऽमुख्यो भूरिकर्मनिदानकः ।
यथानुभवसिद्धात्मा सर्वप्राणभृतामयम् ॥17॥

This world (*saṁsāra*) is the creator of confusion of mind, is full of anguish of attachment, aversion etc. is vitiated by imṇumerable births (deaths and old age) etc, (and hence) is a very serious disease (for the soul).

This world (*saṁsara*) is without beginning, is with no significance, is a cause of bondage of many *karmas*, and is so established in accordance with (individual) experience for all the *jivas* having vitalities.

The worldly existence is totally opposed to the divine and pure state of the yogis and the liberated *jīvas* on account of the characteristics of the former as described in the above two verses. The worldly existence implies all these conditions and qnalities and is almost identical with them. They are by their very nature anti-spiritual and prolong the worldly existence indefinitely. This worldly existence keeps the vision of the *jīvas* confined to the mode and worldly form in which they happen to exist. The vision of the ideal of the pure soul is not at all allowed to them. This is why the saints and sages make strenuous efforts to end the worldly existence, and they preach and recommend the same to those who have turned their faces soulward.

सर्वजन्मविकाराणामभावे तस्य तत्त्वतः ।
न मुक्तो जायतेऽमुक्तोऽमुख्योऽज्ञानमयस्तथा ॥18॥

Really speaking on the liquidation of all the vitiations of the worldly existence for him (*jīva*), the liberated soul never becomes unliberated, unimportant and imbued with nescience.

When the beginningless chain of the worldly lives of a *jīva* comes to an end on account of the observance of the necessary discipline prescribed for such a release from the *karmas*, the possibility of a fall into the world is also finally destroyed for it. It will continue there in its pure state for all times to come. Thus the state of liberation has a beginning, but no end. The *jiva* is placed there as if in itself, free from all conditions and associations not relevant to its existence. Because it has achieved omniscience by completely destroying the obstructive *karmas*, the danger of losing this capacity for knowing the universe in all its capacities and manifestations, is also evaded forever.

यथेहामयमुक्तस्य नामयः स्वस्थता परम् ।
तथा पातकमुक्तस्य न भवः स्वस्थता परम् ॥19॥

Just as there is no disease for one free from disease but (there is) perfect health (for the one), so also there is no worldly existence for one free from sins (*karmas*) but (there is perfect stability in the self (or soul).

शुद्धज्ञाने मनो नित्यं कार्येऽन्यत्र विचेष्टिते ।
यस्य तस्याग्रहाभावान् न भोगा भयहेतवः ॥20॥

For one whose mind is always engaged in pure knowledge and not in any vitiated activity, the pleasures of the world are not the cause of fear (of bondage) because of the absence of their grip.

The grandeur of pure knowledge is such that it secures safety for a yogī against the allurements and delusions caused by the objects of the world. He becomes completely disinterested in and unattentive of them. The pleasures of the world are no more potent to attract and vitiate his mind and thus engulf him in the world.

मायाम्भो मन्यतेऽसत्यं तत्त्वतो यो महामनाः ।
अनुद्विग्नो निराशङ्कस्तन्मध्ये स न गच्छति ॥21॥
मायातोयोपमा भोगा दृश्यन्ते येन वस्तुतः ।
स भुञ्जानोऽपि निःसङ्गः प्रयाति परमं पदम् ॥22॥

One who, with a big mind, thinks, the mirage (the pleasure of the world) as really false, does not delve in it (the mirage) being not disturbed and not terrified (by it).

He, by whom, the pleasures of the world are really seen as a mirage, gets the highest (ethical) status being dissociated with them inspite of (apparently) enjoying them.

भोगांस्तत्त्वधिया पश्यन् नाभ्येति भवसागरम् ।
मायाम्भो जानतासत्यं गम्यते तेन नाध्वना ॥23॥

A yogi seeing (understanding) the pleasure of the world with a real vision does not enter the ocean of the world. By one knowing the mirage to be false the way (leading to that spot) is not followed.

The pleasures of the world are very much comparable with the spot of thc mirage. During hot summers, the deer, with a parched-up throat, run long distances to reach the spot of the mirage which reflects the rays of the sun in such a way as to give an impression of a pond of water. On reaching the spot where there is no water, they face a fatal disappointment. In essence, the same is the position of the objects of the worldly pleasures. Being deluded and almost blinded by them the *jivas* run after them and waste long years in sense-indulgence, finally to get no satisfaction but a intenser thirst for them. Such is the nature of the worldly pleasures. Hence a yogī with a clear vision to realize their reality and relevance for himself renounces them completely. This very right vision and knowledge keeps him quite unaffected by and free from their charm. Apparently he may be seen to be attached with and entangled in them, but in reality, on account of the gain of pure and right knowledge, his detachment from them does not suffer at all. The external picture of his behaviour fails to give us a real and true form of his soul behind. Therefore this external picture which suggests a bondage of *karmas* with his soul, comes out to be falsified. His internal self is quite different from his external behaviour.

स तिष्ठति भयोद्विग्नो यथा तत्रैव शङ्कितः।
तथा निर्वृतिमार्गेऽपि भोगमायाविमोहितः ॥24॥

As he continues there (in the world) highly disturbed by fear and also uncertain everywhere, so he continues to be deluded by the illusions of the worldy pleasures even on the path of redemption (of the soul).

धर्मतोऽपि भवो भोगो दत्ते दुःख-परम्पराम्।
चन्दनादपि सम्पन्नः पावकः प्लोषते न किम् ॥25॥

The (worldly) enjoyments resulting from even the observance of the auspicious conduct produce a (long) chain of unrest (uneasiness). Does the fire obtained by burning sandal wood not burn (the objects that come in contact with it)?

The fruition of *karmas* in the form of pleasure and pain is obtained by the observance of the meriterious and the demeritorious kinds of conduct. The latter are disliked and faced unwillingly, while the former generally keeps the *jīvas* attached and entangled with them. For this difference between the two, the former also does not deserve our inclination to and selection for them. They are like gold chains as against the iron chains to keep the soul imprisoned in the world. The pain of imprisonment is equally present in both the cases. Hence for a yogi who is trying to get unmitigated pure bliss the former course of conduct is equally condemnable.

विपत्सखी यथा लक्ष्मीर्नानन्दाय विपश्चिताम् ।
न कल्मषसखो भोगस्तथा भवति शर्मणे ॥26॥

As for the learned (wise) persons, wealth being an accomplice of adversity, is not a means of happiness; so also the enjoyments, being friendly with *karmas* are not (potent) for granting beneficence (to the soul).

भोग-संसार-निर्वेदो जायते पारमार्थिकः ।
सम्यग्ज्ञान-प्रदीपेन तन्नैर्गुण्यावलोकने ॥27॥

With the torch of right knowledge, the spiritually valuable detachment from the pleasures and the world, is generated for detecting their quality of being worthless (irrelevant) (on the path of *nirvāṇa*).

It is only with the light of right knowledge that one becomes capable to evaluate the nature of the world (*saṁsāra*) and its pleasures as obstructive to one's spiritual progress on the path of final release. This knowledge leads on to a state of detachment for all that is of the nature of the non-soul. With this discriminatory knowledge one is well able to advance on the path of spiritual good.

निर्वाणे परमा भक्तिः पश्यतस्तद्गुणं परम् ।
चित्र-दुःखमहाबीजे नष्टे सति विपर्यये ॥28॥

ज्ञानवन्तः सदा बाह्यप्रत्याख्यान-विशारदाः।
ततस्तस्य परित्यागं कुर्वते परमार्थतः ॥29॥

On the destruction of the opposite (of the right knowledge) which is the highly fertile seed (the root cause) for the growth of various distresses, a very high type of devotion in *various* distresses, and a very high type of devotion in *nirvāna* is obtained on seeing its excellent merit.

Therefore the wise saints, who are expert in the renunciation of external objects, give up that (wrong knowledge) completely in the highly real (spiritual) sense.

Right knowledge is truly a great friend of a yogī on the path of redemption of his soul. It not only helps him to recognize the right path but also enables him to distinguish it from the wrong path. This most valuable light of right knowledge always helps him to take firm steps on the right path and secures for him safety against a fall or deviation from it. That is why the wrong knowledge—a knowledge vitiated and limited by the operation of *karmas*–is not at all welcome to the yogī, who distains and avoids it, thinking it as a sure and constant source of restlessness for him.

न ज्ञानी लिप्यते पापैर्भानुमानिव तामसैः।
विषयैर्विध्यते ज्ञानी न सन्नद्धः शरैरिव ॥30॥

One with right knowledge does not get painted (affected) by sins (*karmas*) as the sun, by dense darkness. One with right knowledge is not pierced (purturbed) by the pleasures of the world like a worrior (putting on a coat of arms) by the arrows.

The right knowledge provides the yogi, the warrior, against the world to save the spirit with a protective coat against all the dangers and devitions on the path to *nirvāṇa*. It is the grandeur of right knowledge that reveals the unreality and futility of the worldly existence and its pleasures. Hence the yogi is not at all deluded and allured by them.

अनुष्ठानास्पदं ज्ञानं ज्ञानं मोहतमोऽपहम् ।
पुरुषार्थकरं ज्ञानं ज्ञानं निर्वृति-साधनम् ॥31॥

(Right) knowledge is the base of all the practices (rites and rituals), knowledge is the destroyer of the darkness of delusion, knowledge impels (initiates) our efforts, and knowledge is the (main) instrument for (achieving) emancipation.

विकारा निर्विकारत्वं यत्र गच्छन्ति चिन्तिते ।
तत् तत्त्वं तत्त्वतश्चिन्त्यं चिन्तान्तर-निराशिभिः ॥32॥

That principle (spiritually real entity) about which the repeated thinking changes the distortions (of the soul) into a state of purity (freedom from the distortions), is really worth concentrating by those who are completely disappointed by the thinking about the 'other' of the soul.

Nothing other than the soul, rather the pure soul, is worth concentrating for the yogi advancing on the path of liberation. Such a concentration is bound to purify his soul from all the blemishes that may raise difficulties in his way.

विविक्तमान्तरं ज्योतिर्निराबाधमनामयम् ।
यदेतत् तत्परं तत्त्वं तस्यापरमुपद्रवः ॥33॥

What is the internal light which is chiselled of all the other (of the soul), which is without any obstruction and which is free from all vitiations is the highest (spiritual) reality. What is different from it is (all) a calamity.

न कुत्राऽप्याग्रहस्तत्त्वे विधातव्यो मुमुक्षुभिः ।
निर्वाणं साध्यते यस्मात् समस्ताग्रहवर्जितैः ॥34॥

An obstinate (one-sided and absolute) view about any principle (entity) is not to be upheld by those desirous of liberation, for *nirvāṇa*, the final release, is achieved (only) by those who have given up all forms of obstinacy (one sidedness and absolutism).

Non-absolution is the very soul of the Jaine philosophy. Every knowledge is to be seen and judged in its setting of substance, place, time and mode which effect a change in the real, and hence a change in the form of its comprehension. It is a universal truth that nothing can be held as true uniformly under all conditions. To know a thing truly it is necessary to take its setting also in view. Such an attitude and bent of mind is very necessary for conducting a correct process of judging and understanding. The yogīs and the saints must have a very soft and liberal mind as to accommodate other views about reality. They themselves are placed in a universe known by the Sanskrit term *'adhyātma'* meaning all centred in the beneficence of the soul. This embodies a spiritual point of view under the frame work of Jaina logic, and it recognizes the importance of and lays emphasis on the pure state of the soul. The *jīvas* that have so qualified themselves can well entertain interest in and a desisre for liberation.

कर्ताहं निर्वृतिः कृत्यं ज्ञानं हेतुः सुखं फलम्।
नैकोऽपि विद्यते तत्र विकल्पः कल्पनातिगे ॥35॥

I am the doer, emancipation is the object (to be achieved), (right) knowledge is the cause, and bliss is the fruit. Non of these differentiations are found in the state (of liberation) which is beyond these fluctuations (of mind).

In this verse the *āchārya* refers to the state of liberation or *mokṣa*, where the soul is freed from all the differentiations and fluctuations. The diffentiulions of the subject, the object, the instrument and the fruit all shrink into one unity of the pure soul. The liberated *jīvas* are completely absorbed in themselves, they are now pure souls and nothing else. They are fully effulgent with their own being. Such is the supreme consciousness and experience of the liberated souls.

आत्मव्यवस्थिता यान्ति नात्मत्वं कर्मवर्गणाः।
व्योमरूपत्वमायान्ति व्योमस्थाः किमु पुद्गलाः ॥36॥

The conglomerations of *karmas*, co-spatial with the soul, do not gain the nature of the soul. Do the particles of matter, lodged in space, gain the nature of space?.

स्थावराः कार्मणाः सन्ति विकारास्तेऽपि नात्मनः।
शश्वच्छुद्धस्वभावस्य सूर्यस्येव धनादिजाः ॥37॥

Even the inert (material) vitiations born of the *karmas* do not belong to the soul, which has a permanantly pure nature, like the obscurity of the sun, born of clouds etc.

रागादयः परिणामाः कल्मषोपाधिसम्भवाः।
जीवस्य स्फटिकस्येव पुष्पोपाधिभवा मताः ॥38॥

The manifestations of the *jīva* (like) attachment, aversion ect. are held to be born of the (external) obstruction of *karmas* like those of the (bright) quartz crystal gem born of the (external) intervention of the (varied colours of) flowers.

The conscious *jīvas* and the material *karmas* have been together occupying the same part of space from beginningless time; but by that affinity they have never been mutually transformed; nor have they ever developed and gained their natures mutually; basically so distinct they are. This is all due to the basic difference between their substances. The *jīvas* are by nature conscious and the *karmas*, being material, are by nature unconscious. We have already seen that this mutual irreducibility among the substances is very necessary for maintaining the cosmic order of the universe. For this very basic situation the manisfestations of one substance maintain their distinction from those of the other. On this very basis the perverted manifestations of like attachment and aversion are said not to pertain to *jīvas;* they are material in nature because of their birth from the material *karmas.* They represent only a sort of reflection of materiality in the *jīvas* on account of their association with them; substantially they do not at all belong to the *jīvas.* The illustrations mentioned in the above verses are meant to explain the situation in an easy manner.

परिणामाः कषायाद्या निमित्तीकृत्य चेतनाम् ।
मृत्पिण्डेनेव कुम्भाद्यो जन्यन्ते कर्मणाखिलाः ॥39॥

All the menifestations like passions etc. are generated by the *karmas* after making the consciousness (of the *jīvas*) an auxiliary cause (for them), as the pots etc. are produced from the lump of earth (with the auxiliary causation of the potter).

The passions and similar manifestations which we generally come across are material in nature, because they are born of *karmas* which are material. The only speciality about them is that they come into existence on account of the auxiliary (*nimitta*) causation of consciousness of the *jīvas.* Thereby they never gain the conscious nature of the soul. The position explained above resembles the theory of occasionalism to a great extent. Consciousness is only an occasion for their generation in the material substance of the *karmas.* They are basically the modes and forms of *karmic* matter, but they require the presence and auxiliary assistance of consciousness for their emergence. The potter makes earthen pots from the earth fit for their production. It is the substance of the earth that takes the various forms of the pots, but with the help of the potter who is external to and different from the earthen substance and its various products.

आत्मनो ये परीणामाः मलतः सन्ति कश्मलाः ।
सलिलस्येव कल्लोलास्ते कषाया निवेदिताः ॥40॥

Whatever are the manifestations (of the soul) polluted by the filth (of *karma*), they are said to be passions like the waves of (dirty) water.

The menifestations of the soul also get vitiated, in the same manner of auxiliary causation, by the *karmas* and are then named as various kinds of passion. It is not true that the *karmas* gain consciousness and pollute the conscious manifestations of the soul. The *karmas* are only an occasion for the pollution of the spiritual manifestations. Then follows the chain of passions like the waves in the pond of dirty water.

कालुष्याभावतोऽकर्म कालुष्यं कर्मतः पुनः।
एकनाशे द्वयोर्नाशः स्याद् बीजाङ्कुरयोरिव ॥41॥

In the absence of the pollution (by *karmas*) (a state of) freedom from *karmas* is achieved; (and) again the pollution is generated by the *karmas*. On the destruction of one (of them), the destruction of the other, follows as of (happens to) the seed and the sprout.

The pollution caused by *karmas* and the *karmas* themselves are so closely related with each other that one must be attended by the presence of the other; hence in the absence of the one (out of the pollution and the *karmas*) the other must disappear. The aforesaid pollution is the function of *karmas* which are the functionary behind the pollution.

यदास्ति कलुषा (त्मषा) भावो जीवस्य परिणामिनः।
परिणामास्तदा शुद्धाः स्वर्णस्येवोत्तरोत्तराः ॥42॥

When the freedom from the pollution or the *karmas* (themselves) is there for the *jīva* undergoing dynamism of manisfestations, then (these) manifestations become pure like the changes in gold following one after the other.

As the extraneous covering of the *karmas* with the soul gets thinned gradually, so also the pollution of the spiritual manifestations becomes weaker and weaker finally leading to the purity of these manifestations.

कल्मषाभावतो जीवो निर्विकारो विनिश्चलः।
निर्वात-निस्तरङ्गाब्धि-समानत्वं प्रपद्यते ॥43॥

The *jīva*, being free from (all) vitiations and being stable (in itself) on account of the absence of *karmas*, becomes comparable with the ocean without waves on account of the absence of wind.

अक्ष-ज्ञानार्थतो भिन्नं यदन्तरवभासते।
तद्रूपमात्मनो ज्ञातृज्ञातव्यमविपर्ययम् ॥44॥

What is experienced within (oneself) as distinct from the objects of the sensuous knowledge, is the (true) identity of the soul, un-perverted and worth knowing by the knower (the soul).

The sensuous perception of objects and the experience of the soul are very much different from each other. In the former the knowing capacity is directed outward to the objects of the sense–knowledge. When this capacity is directed inward, the result is the experience of one's inner self or the soul. The knowledge obtained with the help of the instrument of senses utterly fails to detect the existence of the soul. The way to comprehend and experience the soul is quite differenct from those of perceiving the external world. When one turns his attention inward, there results an overwhelming experience of one's soul to oneself. There the knower becomes the object of his own knowing; or rather, the distinction between the knower and the known vanishes. Such a knowledge is better re-named as experience–an experience of the soul by the soul itself.

यत्रासत्यखिलं ध्वान्तमुद्द्योतः सति चाखिलः।
अस्त्यपि ध्वान्तमुद्द्योतस्तज्ज्योतिः परमात्मनः ॥45॥

That is the light of the supreme soul, in the absence of which all is dark (with ignorance) and in the presence of which all is enlightened (with knowledge); and (also) in the presence of which darkness (of ignorance) is turned into brilliance of knowledge.

Omniscience belongs to the supreme souls that have attained liberation. It means that the liberated souls—the gods without body (the *Siddhas*) and the gods in body (the *Arhats*) are capable of comprehending all the substances, their attributes and their modes, as they exist in the present, as they have existed in the past and as they will happen to exist in future, simultaneously. Omniscience is the natural function of the pure souls with respect to the attribute of knowledge. The omniscient souls will continue to comprehend the entire system of reality, as would the brilliant sun brighten the objects with its bright light. Very often it is said that the objects of the world are reflected in the mirror of consciousness or this consciousness works like a mirror to reflect the objects of the world. This illustration should not be taken to imply the reflection theory of knowledge. No objects are literally reflected in knowledge, nor knowledge is a store of such reflections. Consciousness or knowledge is a knowing entity by nature, and the objects of the world possess the capacity of being known by knowledge. No knowledge can refuse to know the objects, and no objects can refuse to be known by knowledge. Such is the natural relation and setting between the knower and the knowables. On the very ground stands the all-covering and simultaneous comperhension of an omniscient *jīva*.

सर्वेभावाः स्वभावेन स्वस्वभावव्यवस्थिताः।
न शक्यन्तेऽन्यथा कर्तुं ते परेण कदाचन ॥46॥

All the existent entities exist well ordered in their individual identity by (their own) nature; they can never be turned otherwise by any other agency.

This verse contains the announcement of a universal law of nature. Considered substantially all entities are self-contained and self-sufficient, they do not need any other entity for their existence; nor do they extend any contribution to help the existence of other entities. This is the base for the Jaina theory of non-transformation among the various substances existent in the universe.

नान्यथा शक्यते कर्तुं मिलद्भिरिव निर्मलः।
आत्माकाशमिवामूर्तः परद्रव्यैरनश्वरः ॥47॥

The immortal pure soul is not possible to be turned otherwise by the other entities coming close to (and being co-spatial with) it like space.

The substance of space is also immortal, non-corporeal and un-contiminated. All the other substances find accommodation in its extension, and for that reason it becomes cospatial with them; but in no way it is transformed into them, or it does not lose its own existence into them. The same is the situation with souls. The existence of the substance of the soul is perfectly safe even though it is seen to exist co-spatially with them.

देहात्मनोः सदाभेदो भिन्नज्ञानोपलम्भतः।
इन्द्रियैर्ज्ञायते देहो नूनमात्मा स्वसंविदा ॥48॥

There is always a difference between the body and the soul, because of (their) perception by different types of cognitions. The body is known with the (instruments of) senses, and verily, the soul (is known) by self-experience.

The soul and the body have been accompanying each other from the infinitely extending past. This perhaps has been the cause of confusion between the two, as the body itself is the soul. But we have clearly seen and understood the difference between the ways of their perception as stated in the verse. On this very ground the difference between the conscious soul and the unconscious body is confirmed.

न कर्म हन्ति जीवस्य न जीवः कर्मणो गुणान्।
वध्य-घातकभावोऽस्ति नान्योऽन्यं जीवकर्मणोः ॥49॥

The *karma* does not destroy the attributes of the soul; nor does *jīva* destroy the attributes of the *karma*. There is no mutual relation of the destroyed and the destroyer between the *jīva* and the *karma*.

Substantially speaking the *jīva* and the *karma* are not mutually hostile, inimical and destructive to each other.

यदा प्रति परीणामं विद्यते न निमित्तता।
परस्परस्य विश्लेषस्तयोर्मोक्षस्तदा मतः ॥50॥

When the (possibility of) auxiliary causation for the manifestations of the one to the other is no more there, then follows the mutual separation of the two and it is the (state of) final freedom for the two. (soul and *karma*).

Between the souls and the *karmas*, mutually so different from each other, the main source of all trouble and turmoil is the fact of their auxiliary causation. By entering into the relationship of the auxiliary causation, the soul suffers a fall, and matter is transformed into *karmas*. Hence the breach of this relationship is very essential for the soul to achieve its freedom from *karmas*, leaving the *karmas* equally free.

येन येनैव भावेन युज्यते यन्त्रवाहकः।
तन्मयस्तत्र तत्रापि विश्वरूपो मणिर्यथा ॥51॥

The engineer-*jīva* (in charge of the machine of the embodied life) comes in association with whatsoever individual manifestation, it gets obsessed (identified) with such manifestations like the quartze crystal gem reflecting all the colours (which can be seen in all the different hues of the flowers or objects placed behind it).

तेनात्मभावनाभ्यासे स नियोज्यो विपश्चिता।
येनात्ममयतां याति निर्वृत्या परभावतः ॥52॥

Therefore the soul is to be engaged in the practice of achieving selfhood (purity of the soul) by the wise persons, so that it attains absorption in the (pure) soul turning away from the entity of the 'other'.

Under the metaphysical situation between the *jīva* and its 'other' (*karmas*) the ethical advice, as given by the *āchārya*, is to turn the soul inward and avoid all outward concerns.

युज्यते रजसा नात्मा भूयोऽपि विरजीकृतः।
पृथक्कृतं कुतः स्वर्णं पुनः किट्टेन युज्यते ॥53॥

After getting rid of the dust (of *karmas* the soul does not get associated with the dust (of the *karmas*). Does the gold, once seperated from the dross, again get impure with it?

The possibility of a return to the whirling world for a liberated soul is totally denied. The *karmas* kept the *jīvas* confined to and whirling in the mire of the world; the *karmas* being tracelessly liquidated from the soul, the cause of the worldly existence is totally eliminated leaving the soul in its pure state to continue endlessly in future.

दण्ड-चक्र-कुलालादि-सामग्री-सम्भवेऽपि नो।
सम्पद्यते यथाकुम्भो विनोपादानकारणम् ॥54॥
मनो-वचो-वपुःकर्म-सामग्री-सम्भवेऽपि नो।
सम्पद्यते तथा कर्म विनोपादानकारणम् ॥55॥

कालुष्यं कर्मणो ज्ञेयं सदोपादानकारणम्।
मृद्‌द्रव्यमिव कुम्भस्य जायमानस्य योगिभिः ॥56॥

Inspite of the auxiliaries like the stick, the disc (wheel) the potter etc. being available, the pitcher is not obtained without the material (substancial) cause (i.e. the lump of earth); so also inspite of the auxiliaries like the mind, the speech, the body, the *karma* (*karma* matter) etc. being available, the working (effective) *karma* is not obtained without the substantial cause (i.e. the passions etc. generated by the accumulated *karmas*).

The vitiation (passions etc.) should be known as the existent (real) substantial cause of the (effective *karma)* substance by the yogis like the substance (hump) of earth for the forthcoming pitcher.

A distinction between the material or substantial causes on the one hand and the auxiliary causes on the other is being drawn here. The former is the entity that is transformed from the cause to the effect; the latter are the auxiliaries that assist the process of transformation of the cause into the effect. These are the substantial (material) and the auxiliary causes of Jaina philosophy. As is evident the importance of the material or substantial cause is far greater than that of the auxiliary causes. A huge amount of the auxiliary causes is impotent to produce the effect in the absence of the material cause, though the material cause itself always stands in need of the proper auxiliary causes. Coming to the bondage of the soul by the *karmas* the situation needs a clarification. The cosmos is very much full of what we call the molecules (*vargaṇā*) of fine matter that possesses the capacity for transforming itself into the *karma*-matter which gets actually bound with the soul. But the capacity to be actually bound with the soul does not arise in the *karma*-matter unless the passionate states of the soul are not present there. These passionate states are themselves generated by the operative *karmas* in the soul. Hence these passionate states, for their importance and being generated by the *karmas*, are held to be the substantial cause of bondage in the present context of spiritual emancipation.

यथाकुम्भमयो जातु कुम्भकारो न जायते।
सहकारितया कुम्भं कुर्वाणोऽपि कथंचन ॥57॥
कषायादिमयो जीवो जायते न कदाचन।
कुर्वाणोऽपि कषायादीन् सहकारितया तथा ॥58॥

Just as a potter never becomes identied (one) with the pitcher, inspite of producing the pitcher by way of offering assistance, in the same way the *jīva* never becomes identified (one) with the passions etc. inspite of producing the passions etc. by way of offering assistance.

Dynamism of reality is the very back bone of existence; existence thrives through change. It is the unaviodable law of nature. Nothing can go beyond its substantial boundaries; nor can it shrink even a little leaving its boundaries untouched. All auxillaries related with an event or change remain to be auxiliaries alone, they are never transformed into the basic entity to which they are working as auxiliaries. The base for such existence and its continuance resides in the substances themselves in the form of intrinsic attributes or capacities. The attribute of *'dravyatva'* is responsible for the movement of a substance from one mode to another, and the attribute of *'agurulaghutva'* is responsible for confining a substance within the limits defined by the attributes and hence within the substance itself. Under such a situation the question of one substance transforming itself into any other substance or mutually borrowing their essential attributes does not arise. Then the question that liberation will become impossible, if the soul becomes substancially identified with the matter-born passions, is also out of place. The assistance offered by the auxiliaries is not potent to take a substance beyond the boundaries set by its attributes, the changes in reality or in a soul take place only within such boundaries. Thus the unity of change and permanence of a real is consistently maintained is Jaina philosophy.

यः कर्म मन्यते कर्माकर्म वाकर्म सर्वथा।
स सर्वकर्मणां कर्ता निराकर्ता च जायते ॥59॥

One who always holds *karma* as *karma* and the antithesis of *karma* as non-*karma*, becomes free from (all) doership (even) when indulged in all activities.

The accountability for action performed by one becomes proportionately weak and even reduced to zero with the realization of the true position of the *karma* and the non-*karma* by developing a right type of understanding, free from all attachment and aversion, about them. Then the actions become only apparent and ineffective for the doer by not touching his inner self.

विषयैर्विषयस्थोऽपि निरासङ्गो न लिप्यते।
कर्दमस्थो विशुद्धात्मा स्फटिकः कर्दमैरिव ॥60॥

(Apparently) placed in the midst of sense pleasures by the sense-objects one does not get painted (associated) with them, being (internally) unattached as the quartz crystal gem placed in mud (is not defiled) by the varities of mud.

देह चेतनयोर्भेदो दृश्यते येन तत्त्वतः।
न सङ्गो जायते तस्य विषयेषु कदाचन ॥61॥

For one by whom the distinction between the body and the conscious soul is perceived (or realized) in the real sense, the attachment (association) with the object of pleasure never occurs.

भावः शुभोऽशुभः शुद्धस्त्रेधा जीवस्य जायते।
यतः पुण्यस्य पापस्य निर्वृतेरस्ति कारणम् ॥62॥
ततः शुभाशुभौ हित्वा शुद्धं भावमधिष्ठितः।
निर्वृतो जायते योगी कर्मागमनिवर्तकः ॥63॥

The manifestations of the *jīva* take three forms; auspicious, inauspicious and pure, because these are the causes of merit, demerit and purity of the soul (respectively).

Therefore the yogi, by obstructing the influx of the *karmas,* becomes turned away (disinterested in and unattentive of the world) by establishing himself in the pure manisfestations after renouncing the auspicious and the inaupicious ones.

The theory of the three types of spiritual manifestations occupies a very important place in the realm of Jaina ethics. After the manner of auxiliary causation the auspicious and the inauspicious manifestations emerge in the *jīvas.* In general we find that the *jīvas* entertain an inclination to and attraction for the auspicious manifestation, as they lead to easy, comfortable and pleasant conditions of life. On the other hand the *jīvas* entertain a disinclination and disgust for the inauspicious menifestations as they lead to restlessness, discomfort, and unpleasant conditions of life. Both of these types of the *jīvas'* manifestations go to determine the conditions of their worldly existence. Only this much can be said about them that the former are the gold chains and the latter are the iron chains to keep them bound in the world. The third type or the pure manifestations are not so caused by the external factors like meritorious and demeritorious *karmas;* they emerge from the very nature of the pure *jīvas,* they are self-caused and self-determined. For the attainment of liberation it is the third type of pure manifestations that carry importance, value and relevance, as they gradually lead the *jīvas* to a state of perfect freedom from the *karmas*-a state which in the true sense, signifies *mokṣa* or liberation.

विनिवृत्या(वर्त्या)र्थतश्चित्तं विद्यायात्मनि निश्चलम् ।
न किंचिच्चिन्तयेद्योगी निरस्ताखिलकल्मषः ॥64॥

(Therefore) the yogi who has shaken off all the dirt of *karmas* should not think of any other thing (except his own soul) by turning away his mind from (other) objects and (thus) achieving (perfect) stability in his soul.

स्वार्थ-व्यावर्तिताक्षोऽपि विषयेषु दृढ-स्मृतिः ।
यदास्ति दुःस्थितो दीनो लोक-द्वय-विलोपकः ॥65॥

When one, inspite of turning away (his mind) from the objects of senses themselves, entertains an ineffable memory about the pleasures of the senses, then one becomes displaced (not placed within one's soul) and pitiable and (thus) vitiates (his) both the worlds i.e. the present and the future.

भोगं कश्चिदभुञ्जानो भोगार्थं कुरुते क्रियाम् ।
भोगमन्यस्तु भुञ्जानो भोगच्छेदाय शुद्धधीः ॥66॥

One, not enjoying the pleasures, conducts one's activities for the sake of pleasures; while the other, with a pure understanding, enjoying the pleasures (only externally) conducts his activities for cutting the (chain of) enjoyments.

स्वार्थ-व्यावर्तिताऽक्षोपि निरुद्धविषयस्मृतिः ।
सर्वदा सुस्थितो जीवः परत्रेह च जायते ॥67॥

The *jiva,* turning away (his mind) from the objects of the senses themselves and obstructing the (occurence of) memory of the pleasures (of the senses), always becomes well-established (in its soul) here (in this world) and in the world (to follow after death).

रागी भोगमभुञ्जानो बध्यते कर्मभिः स्फुटम्।
विरागः कर्मभिर्भोगं भुञ्जानोऽपि न बध्यते ॥68॥

One with attachment gets bound with the *karmas* despite not enjoying the pleasures. One bereft of attachment does not get bound with the *karmas* despite enjoying the pleasures. It is very clear.

A willful enjoyment of pleasures of the world leads to the bondage of the soul by the *karmas*. If one happens to be entangled in the network of pleasures of the world under certain pressing conditions of life but not with a will to enjoy them, one does not suffer from such bondage. The root cause of bondage is the presence of attachment, aversion and delusion in a soul, mere external behaviour is not sufficient for bringing about the bondage for the soul. The correspondence between the internal state of a soul and the external behaviour of a living being is not perfect, though we cannot dismiss the external behaviour completely from the scene. Under this failure of a correspondence between the 'internal' and the 'external', the above mentioned situations, looking odd apparently, come out to be true. This secret is made home to us by the *āchārya* with a definite purpose in view that the novices should attach more importance to their internal states, though the external behaviour also cannot be dropped completely.

विषयं पञ्चधा ज्ञानी बुध्यमानो न बध्यते।
त्रिलोकं केवली किं न जानानो बध्यतेऽन्यथा ॥69॥

One with (right) knowledge is not bound (with the *karmas*), though knowing the pleasures (of the world) in five ways (determined by the five senses). Otherwise, why would the omniscient lord not get bound, knowing the (contents of) the three worlds [i.e. the upper (*ūrdhva*), the middle (*madhya*) and the nether (*adho*) worlds (*lokas*)]?.

Comprehension or knowledge is the very essence of the soul. The soul must continue with this essential qualtitative entity in all its states of existence. Knowledge, as knowledge, never becomes contradictory to the nature of the soul, it can never be held to be a cause of its bondage by *karmas*. Hence merely by knowing the objects of pleasure a yogī can never suffer from any type of bondage by *karmas*. If this knowledge is contaminated by attachment etc., then also the attachment etc. are mainly responsible for the bondage. On this metaphysical ground the possibility of bondage is totally denied in case of the omniscient lord, inspite of his perfect knowledge, because of the total absence of attachment etc. in his pure mode of existence.

विमूढो नूनमक्षार्थ मगृह्णानोऽपि बध्यते ।
एकाक्षाद्या निबध्यन्ते विषयाग्रहिणो न किम् ॥70॥

Jīvas, suffering from delusion (and lack of descriminatory knowledge) are verily bound (with *karmas*), inspite of not indulging in the pleasures of the senses. Are the *jīvas* with one sense etc. not bound (with *karmas*) inspite of not indulging in the pleasures (of the senses)?

There are some *jīvas* not indulging in the enjoyment of pleasures because their span of knowledge is very poor and limited; but by that they do not become exempt from bondage of *karmas*. The span of knowledge is found least in the organisms with only one sense (of touch). Such organisms are possessed by some *jīvas* in the vegetable form of existence and by other *jīvas* in a very subtle form of existence. The *jīvas* rise higher in the scale of knowledge by the evolution of other senses from that of taste, smell, sight, hearing and lastly the sense of *manas* (mind). The increase in the span of knowledge does not grant any increase in or an exemption from bondage, because basically knowledge is no cause of bondage. The causality of bondage lies wholly in the emergence of passions and delusion from which even the lower organisms suffer very seriously. That is why no decrease in bondage or an exemption from it is described in case of the lower organisms. The variations of bondage with the advance of knowledge are said to result from the presence of passions and delutsion with knowledge. Ethically speaking, knowledge is made right or wrong by its association with passions and delusion, the former leading the *jīvas* towards *mokśa* or liberation and the other to a fall into the *saṁsāra*.

रागद्वेषनिवृत्तस्य प्रत्याख्यानादिकं वृथा।
रागद्वेषप्रवृत्तस्य प्रत्याख्यानादिकं वृथा ॥71॥

(The ethical measures like) renunciation etc. are of no avail for one who is turned away from attachment and aversion. (The ethical measures like) renunciation etc. are useless for one who is indulging in attachment and aversion.

One who has achieved freedom from attachment and aversion, does not need the help of ethical measures and discipline; which become superfluous to him. On the other hand one who is still a poor and helpless victim of the attachment and aversion, the adoption of ethical measures and discipline will not render any help to him in the presence of attachment and aversion; thus they have become unimportant and ineffective for him.

सर्वत्र यः सदोदास्ते न च द्वेष्टि न रज्यते।
प्रत्याख्यानादतिक्रान्तः स दोषाणामशेषतः ॥72॥

One who remains indifferent everywhere (in respect of everything), and who is neither averse to nor attached with them has gone beyond the (measure of) renunciation because of (there being) no remainder of impurites.

After attaining the purity of the soul, where the possibility of attachment and aversion is finished finally and where the souls rest in a state of complete indifference, there remains nothing to be abstained from or to be renounced for the soul, and thus the ethical measures and rules become unnecessary for it. The soul has then achieved its final aim and continues with the pure spiritual qualities.

रागिणः सर्वदा दोषाः सन्ति संसारहेतवः।
ज्ञानिनो वीतरागस्य न कदाचन ते पुनः ॥73॥

(All) the vices, that are the causes of wordly existence, are always present in the *jīvas* suffering form attachment; whereas they are never present in the *jīvas* with (right) knowledge and bereft from attachment (aversion, delusion etc.)

जीवस्यौदयिको भावः समस्तो बन्धकारणम्।
विमुक्तिकारणं भावो जायते पारिणामिकः ॥74॥

All operative manifestations of the *jīva* are the causes of bondage (of the soul); whereas the natural manifestations (of the *jīva*) are the causes of freedom (from *karmas*).

The *jīvas* pass through several types of spiritual manifestations. The worldly *jīvas* are always found associated with and contaminated by the *karmas*. The manifestations in case of such *jīvas* are determined by the operation of the *karmas* which never leave the *jīvas* free from their effect but sow the seeds for futher continuance of their worldly existence. Such is their nature, and hence with the operative manisfestations, the chain of *karmic* bondage can never come to an end. The natural manifestations of the *jīva* are in no way coloured by the operation of *karmas*; they are determined by the nature of the soul itself. Such manifestations lead to the complete freedom of the soul from the worldly existence.

विषयानुभवं बाह्यं स्वात्मानुभवमान्तरम्।
विज्ञाय प्रथमं हित्वा स्थेयमन्यत्र सर्वतः ॥75॥

The experience of the pleasures (of the world) is extraneous (to the soul), the experience of one's own soul is intrinsic to it. Knowing the situation, abandoning the first, one should establish his soul in the second with all the ways.

The way to liberation lies in the sole experience of one's soul. The enjoyment of and the engrossment in the pleasures of the world and the consequent experience are all opposed to the experience of the soul. Hence for a yogi the type of experience (i.e. that of the worldly pleasures) is condemnable, while the other (i.e. the experience of the soul) is worthy of our desire and action.

ज्ञानं वैषयिकं पुंसः सर्वं पौद्गलिकं मतम्।
विषयेभ्यः परावृत्तमात्मीयमपरं पुनः ॥76॥

For a man all knowledge associated with the objects of sense-pleasure is material (in nature); whereas that knowledge which is turned away from the objects of sense- pleasure is the other (non-material) spiritual one (in nature).

The objects of sense-pleasures are all material, hence knowledge vitiated by them is also material. To gain the soul, matter is to be totally abandoned. Therefore, knowledge which is born of the soul or pertains to the pure soul must be independent of the objects of sense-pleasures and the consequent experience.

गवां यथा विभेदेऽपि क्षीरभेदो न विद्यते।
पुंसां तथा विभेदेऽपि ज्ञानभेदो न विद्यते ॥77॥

Just as there is no difference in milk inspite of the difference among the cows (yeilding milk), so also there is no difference of knowledge inspite of the difference of persons (who possess this knowledge).

The cows may be mutually different in respect of their

colour, body, horns and appearance, but all these factors do not go to determine a difference in milk they give us. These factors are all extraneous to the quality of milk. Similarly persons may differ among themselves in respect of colour, body, height, senses and appearance, but these differing factors are extraneous to the knowledge attained by them and they do not go to mark any difference in knowledge. In the worldly state where external factors along with attachment and aversion contaminate knowledge, a difference of knowledge in percievable. Pure knowledge, free from all external associations, is self-determined and remains to be the same in respect of all the redeemed souls.

विज्ञाय दीपतो द्योत्यं यथा दीपो व्यपोह्यते।
विज्ञाय ज्ञानतो ज्ञेयं तथा ज्ञानं व्यपोह्यते ॥78॥
स्वरूपमात्मनः सूक्ष्ममपदेश(श्य)मव्ययम्।
तत्र ज्ञानं परं सर्वं वैकारिकमपोह्यते ॥79॥

As after perceiving the enlightened (thing) with the help of a lamp, the lamp is differentiated (from the enlightened thing); so also after knowing the knowables with the help of knowledge, knowledge is differentiated (from the knowables).

The identity of the soul is (very) fine, is inexpressible and it is not subject to decay. There, all knowledge that is the 'other' (different from the true realization of the soul) and (hence) vitiated, is differentiated (from the true one) and is also abandoned.

The purified soul is so fine that its description and communication (to others) is beyond the power of words. It is a state of self-comprehension and self-realization of the soul, wherein the distinction of the subject, the object and the process, all have disappered. As such no words are capable to give a form of expression to it. So long as the technology of the subject, object and the process is made use of, it is not the state of self-realization. This technology is adopted in case of lower forms of knowledge determined by the association of *karmas* with the soul, hence such knowledge is held to be very different from the trul knowledge, which alone yeilds self-realization. Knowledge other than the true one is, therefore, worth rejection by a true seeker of the pure soul.

स्कन्धच्छेदे पल्लवाः सन्ति भूयो
मूलच्छेदे शाखिनस्ते तथा नो।
देशच्छेदे सन्ति भूयो विकारा
मूलच्छेदे जन्मनस्ते तथा नो ॥80॥

On cutting the trunk of a tree the leaves again grow up in abundance, but on cutting the roots of tree the branches are not so (do not grow-up). (So) for a *jīva* many vitiations (blemishes) continue on the part-destruction (of the *karmas*), but they exist no more for the *jīva* on the destruction of the (very) roots (of the *karmas*).

Just by way of a warning it is suggested and advised to a yogī that he should never feel satisfied with a part-relief from the *karma* and stop his attemps to fight against them. Even a slight remainder of *karmas* is very likely, nay it is very sure to re-create the chain of obstacles for him. He should always concentrate upon and make efforts for the complete annihilation of *karmas* with no reconciliation with any accomplishment short of perfection. The possibility of any further bondage of *karmas* is totally negated when the purity of the soul is once attained, as a tree cannot grow up again when its roots are destroyed.

देशच्छेदे चरित्रं भवति भवततेः कुर्वतश्चित्ररूपं
मूलच्छेदे विविक्तं वियदिव विमलं ध्यायति स्वस्वरूपम्।

विज्ञायेत्थं विचिन्त्यं सदमितगतिभिस्तत्त्वमन्तस्थमग्र्यं
सम्प्राप्तासन्नमार्गा न परमिह पदप्राप्तये यान्ति मार्गम् ॥81॥

On the partial destruction of *karmas* (i.e. the meritorous and the demeritorious *karmas*) the varied practices of conduct become the causes of the chain of worldly auspecious and inauspecious existence for a *jīva;* (whereas) on the destruction of the *karmas* from their very root the soul meditates on its pure and completely chiselled identity like (that of) the sky. Thus after knowing the principle of the pure soul as real, internal, most prominent, and specially worth concentration for a saint, the *jīvas* which have found the closest (shortest) route in this world for achieving their aim, do not follow any other path.

The emergence of conduct takes two forms, partial and total, on account the relief from the *karmas* obstructing the faculty of conduct of a soul. A novice may also be successful in achieving partial relief from the *karmas* along with its partial and inefficient results. It means the remaining *karmas* and the blemishes resulting therefrom will still keep the soul entrapped in the network of *karmas*. The remaining demeritorious *karmas* will keep it confined to painful conditions. If the remaining *karmas* are of the meritorious type they will place the soul in pleasant conditions in the world. In both the cases the chains of bondage by *karmas* continue unbroken. Only when one is able to strike at the very root of the *karmas,* one will be blessed with the true knowledge of the soul. With this knowledge and the practice of meditation of the soul one will be able to see and follow the right and the shortest path leading finally to liberation—a state of complete freedom from the shackles of the *karmas* and also the achievement of the highest, most prominent, real and ever lasting status for the soul. The mention of the word *amitagati* in the verse is also suggestive of the name of writer of this work *Yogasāra* prābhṛta.

दृष्ट्वा बाह्यमनात्मनीनमखिलं मायोपमं नश्वरम्
ये संसार-महोदधिं बहुविधक्रोधादिनक्राकुलम् ।
तीर्त्वा यान्ति शिवास्पदं शममयं ध्यात्वात्मतत्त्वं स्थिरं
तेषां जन्म च जीवितं च सफलं स्वार्थैकनिष्ठात्मनाम् ॥82॥

Only for those with exclusive faith in the singular reality of their selves, (their) birth and life are fully awarded with fruits, who seeing this entire world as opposed to the soul, as delusive like false appearance and as mortal, and who meditating on the permanent principle (of the soul) identified with spiritual tranquility, attain the status of spiritual bliss after crossing the great (extensive) ocean of the *saṁsāra* which is all disturbed by the crocodiles of anger etc. of many kinds.

The saint must realize the entire paraphernalia of the worldly existence as opposed to the welfare of the soul. It is all unreal, apparent and fleeting; it is full of tribulence and turmoil all the time it continues. Contrary to it, the state of liberation is quite in agreement with the nature of the pure soul, it is all full of spiritual tranquility and bliss. The way to achieve this ideal of life lies through meditation on the pure soul and its pure attributes. One has to cross the ocean of *saṁsāra* to establish oneself in one's pure state of the soul, On achieving this ever unforeseen ideal of his soul the saint is able to get the full return and fruition of his efforts. Such souls are ever adorable and worshipable for us, as they always guide and inspire us to advance on the path they themselves have followed.

दृष्ट्वा सर्वं गगननगर-स्वप्न-मायोपमानं
निःसङ्गात्मामितगतिरिदं प्राभृतं योगसारम् ।

ब्रह्मप्राप्त्यै परममकृतं स्वेषु चात्म-प्रतिष्ठं
नित्यानन्दं गलित-कलिलं सूक्ष्ममत्यक्ष-लक्ष्यम् ॥83॥

Having realized all (other than the pure soul) as delusive like a city in the sky (made of clouds), like a dream and like a (false) appearance, *Āchārya Amitagati*, bereft of all associations (external to the pure soul), has composed (this) present of the *Yogasāra*, with the main aim of realizing the Brahma-the purified soul, which (the *Yogasāra*) has attained a prominent place for itself among the works on Yoga, which is highly esteemed and has not been attempted before, which is identified with ever-lasting bliss, which liquidates all sins (*karmas*), which is very fine, and which is comprehensible (only) by going beyond the senses (i.e. by an inner understanding).

The words '*Amitagati*' and '*Yogasāra*' are indicative of the names of the writer and his most valuable work. These may also be interpreted as one having an unlimited span of knowledge and the essence of the science of Yoga respectively. Really speaking, a continuous study of this holy work by *Āchārya Amitagati* will lead a *yogi* to complete destruction of *karmas*, and the consequent spiritual bliss and the realization of his pure soul.

योगसारमिदमेकमानसः प्राभृतं पठति योऽभिमानसः ।
स्वस्वरूप मुपलम्य सोऽञ्चितं सद्म याति भवदोष-वञ्चितम् ॥84॥

After realizing the (true) nature of one's own soul, one who, with a concentrated mind and with full attention, reads this present (offer) of the *Yogāsara*, attains the abode (of the perfect ones) which is worshipable (by all) and is free from (all) worldly blemishes.

This is the last and concluding verse of the *Yogasāra* by *Āchārya Amitagati*. It is potent to inspire the seekers of the true identity of the pure soul to read, practise and realize the essence of the science of Yoga and thus crown themselves with the highest success and the status of siddhahood.

Here ends Chapter-9, Chūlikādhikāra of Yogasāra-prābhṛta by Āchārya Amitagati.

●●●

भारतीय ज्ञानपीठ